Every Last One

Every Last One

A NOVEL

ANNA QUINDLEN

RANDOM HOUSE

NEW YORK

Published in the United States by Random House, an imprint of The Random House Publishing Group, a division of Random House, Inc., New York.

RANDOM HOUSE and colophon are registered trademarks of Random House, Inc.

Grateful acknowledgment is made to The Marvell Press for permission to reprint "Going" from *The Less Deceived* by Philip Larkin, copyright © 1955 by Philip Larkin. Reprinted by permission of The Marvell Press, England and Australia.

ISBN 978-1-4000-6574-5
eBook ISBN 978-0-679-60372-6

Printed in the United States of America on acid-free paper

www.atrandom.com

2 4 6 8 9 7 5 3 1

First Edition

Book design by Caroline Cunningham

For my children, who saved my life

There is an evening coming in
Across the fields, one never seen before,
That lights no lamps.

Silken it seems at a distance, yet
When it is drawn up over the knees and breast
It brings no comfort.

Where has the tree gone, that locked
Earth to the sky? What is under my hands,
That I cannot feel?

What loads my hands down?

—PHILIP LARKIN

Every Last One

This is my life: The alarm goes off at five-thirty with the murmuring of a public-radio announcer, telling me that there has been a coup in Chad, a tornado in Texas. My husband stirs briefly next to me, turns over, blinks, and falls back to sleep for another hour. My robe lies at the foot of the bed, printed cotton in the summer, tufted chenille for the cold. The coffeemaker comes on in the kitchen below as I leave the bathroom, go downstairs in bare feet, pause to put away a pair of boots left splayed in the downstairs back hallway and to lift the newspaper from the back step. The umber quarry tiles in the kitchen were a bad choice; they are always cold. I let the dog out of her kennel and put a cup of kibble in her bowl. I hate the early mornings, the suspended animation of the world outside, the veil of black and then the oppressive gray of the horizon along the hills outside the French doors. But it is the only time I can rest without sleeping, think without deciding, speak and hear my own voice. It is the only time I can be alone. Slightly less than an hour each weekday when no one makes demands.

Our bedroom is at the end of the hall, and sometimes as I pass I can hear the children breathing, each of them at rest as specific as they are awake. Alex inhales and exhales methodically, evenly, as though he were deep under the blanket of sleep even though he always kicks his covers askew, leaving one long leg, with its faint surgical scars, exposed to the night air. Across the room Max sputters, mutters, turns, and growls out a series of nonsense syllables. For more than a year, starting when he was eleven, Max had a problem with sleepwalking. I would find him washing his hands at the bathroom sink or down in the kitchen, blinking blindly into the open refrigerator. But he stopped after his first summer at sleepaway camp.

Ruby croons, one high strangled note with each exhale. When she was younger, I worried that she had asthma. She sleeps on her back most of the time, the covers tucked securely across her chest, her hair fanned out on the pillows. It should be easy for her to slip from beneath the blanket and make her bed, but she never bothers unless I hector her.

I sit downstairs with coffee and the paper, staring out the window as my mind whirrs. At six-thirty I hear the shower come on in the master bath. Glen is awake and getting ready for work. At six forty-five I pull the duvet off Ruby, who snatches it back and curls herself into it, larval, and says, "Ten more minutes." At seven I lean over, first Alex, then Max, and bury my nose into their necks, beginning to smell the slightly pungent scent of male beneath the sweetness of child. "Okay, okay," Alex says irritably. Max says nothing, just lurches from bed and begins to pull off an oversized T-shirt as he stumbles into the bathroom.

There is a line painted down the center of their room. Two years ago they came to me, at a loose end on a June afternoon, and demanded the right to choose their own colors. I was distracted, and I agreed. They did a neat job, measured carefully, put a tarp on the floor. Alex painted his side light blue, Max lime green. The other mothers say, "You won't believe what Jonathan"—or Andrew or Peter—"told me about the twins' room." Maybe if the boys had been my first children I would have thought it was insane, too, but Ruby broke me in. She has a tower of soda cans against one wall of her bedroom. It is either an environmental statement or just one of those things you do when you are fifteen. Now that she is seventeen she has outgrown it, almost forgotten it, but because I made the mistake of asking early on when she would take it down she never has.

I open Ruby's door, and although it doesn't make a sound—she has oiled the hinges, I think, probably with baby oil or bath oil or something else nonsensically inappropriate, so we will not hear it creak in the nighttime—she says, "I'm up." I stand there waiting, because if I take her word for it she will wrap herself in warmth again and fall into the long tunnel of sleep that only teenagers inhabit, halfway to coma or unconsciousness. "Mom, I'm up!" she shouts, and throws the bedclothes aside and begins to bundle her long wavy hair atop her head. "Can I get dressed in peace, please? For a change?" She makes it sound as though I constantly let a bleacher full of spectators gawk as she prepares to meet the day.

Only Glen emerges in the least bit cheerful, his suit jacket over one arm. He keeps his white coats at the office. They are professionally cleaned and pressed and smell lovely, like the cleanest of clean laundry. "Doctor Latham" is embroidered in blue script above his heart. From upstairs I can hear the clatter of the cereal into his bowl. He eats the same thing every morning, leaves for work at the same time. He wears either a blue or a yellow shirt, with either a striped tie or one with a small repeating pattern. Occasionally, a grateful patient gives him a tie as a gift, printed with tiny pairs of glasses, an eye chart, or even eyes themselves. He thanks these people sincerely but never wears them.

He is not tidy, but he knows where everything is: on which chair he left his briefcase, in what area of the kitchen counter he tossed his wallet. He does something with the corners of his mouth when things are not as they should be—when the dog is on the furniture, when the children and their friends make too much noise too late at night, when the red-wine glasses are in the white-wine glass rack. It has now pressed itself permanently into his expression, like the opposite of dimples.

"Please. Spare me," says my friend Nancy, her eyes rolling. "If that's the worst you can say about him, then you have absolutely no right to complain." Nancy says her husband, Bill, a tall gangly scarecrow of a guy, leaves a trail of clothing as he undresses, like fairy-tale breadcrumbs. He once asked her where the washing machine was. "I thought it was a miracle that he wanted to know," she says when she tells this story, and she does, often. "It turned out the repairman was at the door and Bill didn't know where to tell him to go."

Our washer is in the mudroom, off the kitchen. There is a chute from above that is designed to bring the dirty things downstairs. Over the years, our children have used the chute for backpacks, soccer balls, drumsticks. *Slam. Slam. Slam.* "It is a laundry chute," I cry. "Laundry. Laundry."

Laundry is my life, and meals, and school meetings and games and recitals. I choose a cardigan sweater and put it on the chest at the foot of the bed. It is late April, nominally spring, but the weather is as wild as an adolescent mood, sun into clouds into showers into storms into sun again.

"You smell," I hear Alex say to Max from the hallway. Max refuses to reply. "You smell like shit," Alex says. "Language!" I cry.

"I didn't say a word!" Ruby shouts from behind the door of her room. Hangers slide along the rack in her closet, with a sound like one of those tribal musical instruments. Three thumps—shoes, I imagine. Her room always looks as though it has been ransacked. Her father averts his head from the closed door, as though he is imagining what lies within. Her brothers are strictly forbidden to go in there, and, honestly, are not interested. Piles of books, random sweaters, an upended shoulder bag, even the lace panties, given that they belong to their sister—who cares? I am tolerated because I deliver stacks of clean clothes. "Put those away in your drawers," I always say, and she never does. It would be so much easier for me to do it myself, but this standoff has become a part of our relationship, my attempt to teach Ruby responsibility, her attempt to exhibit independence. And so much of our lives together consists of rubbing along, saying things we know will be ignored yet continuing to say them, like background music.

Somehow Ruby emerges every morning from the disorder of her room looking beautiful and distinctive: a pair of old Capri pants, a ruffled blouse I bought in college, a long cashmere cardigan with a moth hole in the sleeve, a ribbon tied around her hair. Ruby never looks like anyone else. I admire this and am a little intimidated by it, as though I had discovered we had incompatible blood types.

Alex wears a T-shirt and jeans. Max wears a T-shirt and jeans. Max stops to rub the dog's belly when he gets to the kitchen. She narrows her eyes in ecstasy. Her name is Virginia, and she is nine years old. She came as a puppy when the twins were five and Ruby was eight. GINGER says the name on the terra-cotta bowl we bought on her first Christmas. Max scratches the base of Ginger's tail. "Now you'll smell like dog," says Alex. The toaster pops with a sound like a toy gun. The refrigerator door closes. I need more toothpaste. Ruby has taken my toothpaste. "I'm going!" she yells from the back door. She has not eaten breakfast. She and her friends Rachel and Sarah will stop at the doughnut shop and get iced coffee and jelly doughnuts. Sarah swims competitively and can eat anything. "The metabolism of a hummingbird," says my friend Nancy, who is Sarah's mother, which is convenient for us both. Nancy is a biologist, a professor at the university, so I suppose she should know about metabolism. Rachel is a year older than the other two, and drives them to school. The three of them swear that Rachel drives safely and slowly. I know this isn't true. I picture Rachel, moaning again about some boy she really, really likes but who is insensible to her attentions, steering with one hand, a doughnut in the other, taking a curve with a shrieking sound. Caution and nutrition are for adults. They are young, immortal.

"The bus!" Alex yells, and finally Max speaks. This is one of the headlines of our family life: Max speaks. "I'm coming," he mumbles. "Take a sweatshirt," I call. Either they don't hear or they don't care. I can see them with their backpacks getting on the middle-school bus. Alex always goes first.

"Do we have any jelly?" Glen asks. He knows where his own things are, but he has amnesia when it comes to community property. "It's where it's always been," I say. "Open your eyes and look." Then I take two jars of jelly off the shelf inside the refrigerator door and thump them on the table in front of him. I can manage only one morning manner, so I treat my husband like one of the children. He doesn't seem to mind or even notice. He likes this moment, when the children have been there but are suddenly gone. The dog comes back into the room, her claws clicking on the tiled floor. "Don't feed her," I say, as I do every morning. In a few minutes, I hear the messy chewing sounds as Ginger eats a crust of English muffin. She makes a circuit of the house, then falls heavily at my feet.

After he has read the paper, Glen leaves for the office. He has early appointments one day a week and late ones three evenings, for schoolchildren and people with inflexible jobs. His office is in a small house a block from the hospital. He pulls his car out of the driveway and turns right onto our street every single morning. One day he turned left, and I almost ran out to call to him. I did open the front door, and discovered that a neighbor was retarring the driveway and a steamroller was blocking the road to the right. The neighbor waved. "Sorry for the inconvenience," he called. I waved back.

I put on a pair of khaki pants, a white shirt, and soft flat slip-on shoes with rubber soles. "Those are such . . . mom clothes," Ruby sometimes says. It is not exactly an insult. I am wiry and tan from work, or perhaps from genetics. My mother taught English to high school students, not exactly a physically taxing profession, and she, too, is wiry and tan. At seventy, she still wears tennis clothes without thinking about it.

At eight-thirty a dump truck pulls into the driveway. On its side is a trio of primitive painted flowers, the kind that second-grade girls draw in their notebooks in colored markers. A blue flower, a pink flower, a yellow flower, and to one side the words LATHAM LANDSCAPING. One day I was a freelance copy editor, then I had three children, then I took a master gardening class, then I started a landscaping business. The business is successful.

"Hey, Mary Beth," says Rickie from the truck. He's wearing his Latham Landscaping windbreaker, but the zipper strains over his big hard belly. The truck is tidy, but I know that the glove compartment is filled with candy wrappers and greasy waxed paper. Rickie runs the equipment; he's past being able to use a shovel or do the weeding. We are going to see a copper beech two towns over that is losing its bark. It's probably a fungus that's been going around, moving slowly and silently through the forests and the front yards, the way a cold does through the kids' classes at school: first one, then another, then a half dozen or so. This tree is probably a hundred years old, and it's probably not going to get much older. It's a shame; it's a glorious tree, the kind that looks immutable.

That's the humbling thing about doing what I do for a living: You can look at the pin oak in a front yard, or even the daffodils you put in the autumn before, and know that long after you are gone there will be shade, and color, and you won't be there to see it. In many ways it's a soothing feeling, like telling your daughter that someday she will have your diamond earrings, without ever spelling out what "someday" means.

"Want to stop for coffee?" Rickie says. What Rickie means by coffee is a box of assorted doughnuts.

"Sure," I say. "There's never enough." I rummage in my bag. "Wait, I forgot the phone again. I'll be right back."

We might still have a nighttime frost, so there's not much we can do yet in people's gardens. Last year around this time, a woman hired us to put in hundreds of flowering plants for her daughter's outdoor wedding. God had smiled on her. The spring afternoon had been sunny and warm, and the delphiniums, the lobelia, and the sweet-faced purple and blue pansies glowed against the green of the grass, vying with—overshadowing, I would have said—the Dutch blue of the bridemaids' dresses. The next night there was a hard freeze. Those pansies were the saddest things imaginable the next morning, splayed on the ground. I hated the sight of them.

"We got a call for a big job around the courthouse," Rickie says. "The county clerk wants you to give them a proposal."

"Oh God, save me from the county clerk. No matter what I come up with they're going to want geraniums."

Rickie hits a pothole and the tools jump in the back of the truck with a jangling sound. I take a tissue from inside my bag and blow my nose. A woman I only vaguely recognize waves as we

wait at a red light. Every day, with few variations—snow, minor illness, the failure of the paper to arrive, a lost backpack, a sleepover
that's left us one, or two, or sometimes even three kids shy of the
usual full set—every day is like this. Average. Ordinary. More or
less.

I am sitting on a small padded bench outside the dressing rooms at Molly's Closet. The dressing rooms look like shower stalls. In fact, I suspect that Molly's dressing-room curtain is really a shower curtain. It is a lively print of flowers that I know are not found in nature. The bench outside is far too low for even a middling-sized woman in good physical condition. My back hurts, I'm hungry, and I have to go to the bathroom. The trifecta of the over-forty female crowd. At least I don't have cramps. Ruby does. "I so need chocolate," she said in the car, which is a warning not to talk about school, or her friends, or anything else of moment. Tears hover.

Ruby is trying to find a dress for the prom. This has become her life's work, along with a short story that I have not been permitted to read but which apparently may be the lead story in this year's literary magazine. Ruby will edit the literary magazine next year. She is also president of a club that concerns itself with what they call the enslavement of the people of Tibet, and a member of the council that meets with the principal once a week to tell him what is going on at school. "Oh, you're Ruby Latham's mother," people sometimes say to me when I introduce myself. She is not what I envied in high school, the popular girl. She is something I'm not even sure existed then, the sure-footed girl. She gives the impression of being completely herself, and only a part of that impression is false.

"No way," I hear her groan from inside the dressing room, and yet another dress is thrown over the bar that holds the curtain. The bar looks as though it's a shower bar, too. Molly's husband, who is a builder, built her shop, but on the cheap, she always complains. "Anything that didn't make it into another job, I got," Molly says, but with that mock irritation that means it's not a big deal.

"Can I see?" I say.

"There's no point," Ruby replies.

Two weeks ago, Ruby went to look for a prom dress at the vintage store in the next town. The doodles on her desk suggested that she had hopes of finding one of those dresses my mother wore for important occasions when she herself was young: a snug bodice, a belted waist, a long full skirt. When I was a child, there was a trunk in the basement with my father's name stenciled on it, but instead of old suits and books inside there were dresses of my mother's that we wore to play princess. My mother didn't care. She was usually upstairs at the kitchen table, drinking tea, correcting papers, looking up toward the yellowish fluorescent fixture, then down to scribble comments in the margins. "Oh, Mary Beth, I have no idea where those dresses got to," my mother had said when I called her in Florida the other day to ask about them.

Nancy told me with a faint air of superiority that Sarah bought the second dress she tried on. And Rachel said sadly last week that she'd ordered a dress from a catalog and didn't really like it much. But Ruby is incapable of being either casual or resigned. I can see her feet beneath the curtain edge, the nails painted blue, the tiny baby toe curled in like a comma, just as it was when she was born. I was doing copyediting at home then, in the apartment in Chicago that we rented while Glen was finishing his ophthalmology training. I knew no one, did nothing but read textbook manuscripts and make careful marks in pencil, hieroglyphics of error. My left hand worked the ledge of my belly, back and forth, feeling toes beneath my skin, like pebbles under a layer of loose sand. You don't feel so silly, so stupid, so sad, talking to yourself if there's someone inside you that you can pretend you're talking to instead.

When Ruby came back from the shopping trip to the vintage store two weeks ago, her hands were empty and the big tapestry bag slung across her body looked flat and sad. The sound Ruby's feet make on the stairs is the window of her soul. "She's pissed," Alex had said, sitting at the kitchen table. "Language," I said mildly. "Pissed isn't a curse," he said. "It's vulgar," I replied, taking chicken out to defrost.

My back is aching as Ruby tries on two more dresses. She will never find anything at Molly's Closet. They're pretty dresses, but they're ordinary, made of ordinary fabrics. Ruby loves panne velvet, moiré taffeta. She appears in a beautiful cream-colored satiny dress. I'm pleased to realize that it is one I took off the rack.

"Imagine this if I took off the sleeves and made the neck square. And maybe, I don't know, added some kind of inserts in the skirt. Maybe lace, so that part of the dress you could see through? Does that make any sense?"

I breathe and try not to make my breathing sound like a sigh. If Ruby hears me sigh she will say, "I told you you didn't have to come." Everything for Ruby is an either/or. I think this may be a keystone of her personality, although it may be her age, too. My mother says I was the same, but she seems to refer to most of motherhood as a martyrdom. Her widowhood, her real martyrdom, we have never really discussed. "It must have been so hard for you when Daddy died," I said one evening when we had been watching the sun go down over the golf course behind the condominium where she and Stan live. She waved her hand, a gesture of dismissal. "That's life," she said. "And everything turned out fine." She waved her hand again, this time at the green on the fourteenth hole, water diamonds arcing from the invisible sprinklers buried belowground. We could hear Stan in the kitchen, doing the dinner dishes. Maybe he was what she thought of when she thought of having a husband, not the man I could only vaguely remember: longish sideburns, a heavy jaw, the smell of citrus cologne, a dry kiss on the crown of my head. For some reason, my father liked to call me Mary Elizabeth Ever After, one of those nonsense names parents make up. I had one for Ruby, too: When she was small I used to call her Ruby Tuesday, and she would frown and say, "That is not my name." I had done the same to my father, hands on hips, brows knit together: That is not my name. Oh, your mother was willful, my mother says to my children sometimes, shaking her head and exchanging glances of complicity. I am so middleground these days that it seems impossible to believe, but I suppose that is the progression: the sharp edges of youth ground down by life. A razor becomes a knife becomes a paperweight. It's difficult to believe it will ever happen to my own children, especially my daughter.

"I'm having a hard time seeing it, but maybe that's just me," I say.

Ruby sighs loudly. "I don't know," she says.

"Did you try the blue one?" I ask.

"It's such a magazine dress," Ruby says. When I was a girl, I used to sometimes rip a picture of a dress from a magazine and take it into town to see if anyone had it, or something like it, something like it but cheaper. If Ruby sees a dress, or something like it, in a magazine, this means it is devalued by ordinariness.

The phone rings. It is my oldest friend, Alice, who was my college roommate and now lives in New York City. "What does chicken pox look like?" she says, without greeting or identification.

When we were in college, Alice divided men into three categories: boyfriend material, husband material, and father material. Since we graduated twenty-two years ago, she has met many of the first and almost none of the last two. Her son, Liam, is three now, and was fathered by Donor No. 236: medical student, sandy hair, tall, mathematical, methodical. Because I am a good friend, I've never mentioned that the shorthand description of the nameless Donor No. 236 sounds something like a description of my husband, who Alice called "the straightest guy on earth" until she realized I was serious about him. Sometimes there are people you love because you learned to love them a long time ago, because when you say, "Remember the night we went skinny-dipping in the dean's pool?" she does.

Alice and I had a period of frost when my children were small. When we talked, the sentences were empty—how's work, where did you spend the holidays, how are your parents? "You've lost yourself," she'd finally said. Of course, I had. Now Alice has, too.

"How large an area does the rash cover?" I ask, while Ruby taps one foot insistently and tugs at a long ringlet.

"There's just one blister, but it's very red and angry. And he's been out of sorts all morning."

"Let me call you back. There's never only one chicken pock. He's probably out of sorts because he's three. I'm shopping for a prom dress with your goddaughter."

"Call me back as soon as you're finished," Alice says, and hangs up. "I am not one of those crazy older mothers," she often says. She is one of those crazy older mothers. It's good of me not to say so, especially since she told me I was certifiable when I was just twenty-six and discovered I was expecting Ruby. "He rushed you into it," she'd said of Glen. "He absolutely did not," I replied at the time, and it was true. Ruby was an accidental baby. We had been thunderstruck when I got the news three months after our wedding, as stunned as teenagers who had skipped sex-education classes. I have never been able to decide whether I should tell Ruby this someday, perhaps when she has children of her own. My firstborn, my girl, my happiest accident.

Molly has a dress over her arm and holds it up for Ruby. It is a high-waisted dress in some filmy coral material. Ruby says so sweetly, "I have a problem with that color because of my hair, but thanks so much, Mrs. Martin, it's really pretty." Ruby likes to say that her hair is red, but it's really brown with auburn highlights, a big wavy mass that she pulls at when she's thinking and that makes a hair curtain around her pointed, slightly elfin face. She has outside manners and inside manners, company manners and home manners. Or lack of manners. You can see it in her brothers' faces sometimes, as they think to themselves, Will Ruby offer to take me to the diner for breakfast or scream at me for leaving the shower dripping?

Only with her father is she always the polite and thoughtful Ruby she presents to the world. Last year her favorite word was *authentic.* She says that Glen is utterly authentic. I suppose that this is true, and may have something to do with why I married him in the first place. Or maybe it was the loneliness, when college was over and Alice had found a place for herself in New York. I remember a weekend when I visited Glen at medical school, and we went to an Italian restaurant and walked back to his apartment through a fine mild rain and made love that night and the next morning and had pancakes and bacon for breakfast. I laughed at the tiny earthquakes the elevated train made every few minutes as it silenced our voices. "I wish every day was like this," I'd said, and Glen said, "Why couldn't it be?" How young we were.

The shopping trip is a failure. Ruby is putting on her own clothes, a long flowered skirt, a tank top, an Argyle sweater. From inside the dressing room, muffled by the sweater she is pulling over her head, I hear her say, "I'm thinking of breaking up with Kiernan."

"What?" I say. Because of the surprise, I have let my voice rise and sharpen.

"Nothing," Ruby says. "Forget I said anything. I knew you'd make a big thing out of it."

"All I said was 'What?' "

"Never mind," Ruby says. "I don't want to talk about it."

It's hard, almost impossible, to imagine Ruby without Kiernan. It's not just that he has been her boyfriend for more than two years but that they have been playmates since kindergarten. His mother, Deborah, was once my closest friend; Kiernan's family once lived next door to ours. From time to time my husband says, "Does Kiernan ever actually go home?" But he says it in that weary indulgent way that men take note of things they think should bother them but really don't. For his birthday, Kiernan bought Glen a pair of very old spectacles he found at a flea market, and although the rest of us thought it was a peculiar gift—the boys making faces, Ruby saying, "Aren't they great?" in the extravagant fashion of someone trying to make it so—Glen spent a fair amount of time examining the lenses, the construction, the material, and the old glasses wound up on his desk at work.

I should have realized something wasn't right that morning when Kiernan missed breakfast. Last night he and Ruby had gone out to the yard at eleven to watch for some comet that was supposed to sweep across the sky. When we were getting ready for bed, I saw him adjusting the telescope, then going inside to turn off the house lights so the darkness was deeper, the stars brighter. Standing to one side of the curtains, I heard him say something to Ruby, who was lying on one of our old quilts, but she turned away from him. I saw a spark of silver from behind the curtains and turned back to see if the comet was visible, but when I looked down I realized it was the flash of Kiernan's camera, that he was taking pictures of her. "Please, stop," I heard her whine. When I woke in the morning she was in the same position asleep, another quilt over her, but Kiernan was gone.

"He doesn't like to go to sleep," Ruby told me once when I mentioned that Kiernan had been at the house early, before anyone was up. "He says if he stays up all night it's never yesterday." She had been charmed by the idea, I remember. But this morning she'd merely looked exhausted.

She sweeps by me out of the dressing room and toward the door, stopping to smile at Molly. "I just can't make up my mind today, Mrs. Martin," she says sweetly.

"Do you want to go for tea and muffins?" I ask on the street.

"I'm not hungry," she says. "I have to go home and work on my story." My window of opportunity for more information is gone, snapped shut. I will have to wait.

I am in the car alone, picking up Alex from his friend Ben's house. The street is an Impressionist painting: *Azaleas and Rhododendrons in Full Flower.* These are the shrubs of the suburban neighborhood in which I grew up, but most of our clients have turned their backs on all that. How many women have asked me for English gardens? We are in New England, which is not the same as England at all, but perhaps wishing, and viburnum and hollyhocks, will make it so.

All the twin books say that it is a good thing that Alex has different friends than his brother has. But Alex has more of them, too, many more of them. His friends are other players in the soccer league, boys who plan to join the lacrosse team at the high school next year, friends from the sports camp where he refines his skills each summer. In July Alex will go to a place in Maine where all the boys wear uniform polo shirts and have mixers once a week with the girls who attend camp across the lake. The girls wear polo shirts, too. Theirs are pink, the boys' blue.

Max will go to the camp in Pennsylvania where he has learned to tie-dye, throw a pottery bowl, and play the drums. He is known there as Max the Mute, but not in a mean way, not the way he would be known by that name at the middle school. M & M, some of his camp friends call him. Max has two school friends, Zachary and Ezra, who are just what you would expect: shambling, graceless, brilliant boys who feel as though they've been plunked down on a planet to which they are not native. They come over, go into Max's room, and play computer games, staying on the lime-green side even when Alex is not home. Neither of them is much for eye contact. They are the kind of boys who may well grow up to invent something astonishing, to teach in a prestigious college, to cure cancer. Right now, they have hard lives.

Alex has an easy life. I try not to mother him any less for that. It's odd: Glen and I are conventional people, neither quirky nor creative, although we once had faint pretensions to both. Yet the child who feels the most like the cuckoo in the nest is the one who is most like us, bookended by his always eccentric brother and his confidently distinctive sister.

Ruby is going to a college summer program for promising writers. She leaves as soon as school is over. When she talks about it there is an odd strangulation to her voice, which sounds like excitement but is tinged with fear. "You can stop bragging now," I heard Rachel say, but that's a misreading based on Rachel's own anxieties. Sarah and Ruby are both excellent students; the list of colleges to which they will apply and to which they are likely to be admitted has been implicit since they were both reading in kindergarten while the others were trying to figure out the difference between orange and yellow. Rachel has struggled along behind them, sitting at our kitchen table as Sarah tried to explain quadratic equations and Ruby read John Donne's sonnets aloud. "I wasn't an A student, either, and I'm fine," says Rachel's mother,

Sandy. She and Rachel's father divorced when their daughter was a toddler. Seeing college swim coaches at Sarah's meets, paging through the catalogs about writing programs on Ruby's desk, Rachel sees on the horizon the dissolution of the safe circle she has had in lieu of a happy family. She calls my daughter Opal, Garnet, Pearl, sometimes Amethyst. She calls me Mom. Sometimes late at night when I am cooking for Ruby and her friends, Rachel will put her arms around my middle and lay her head on my shoulder. She is one of those big jokey girls with broad shoulders and flushed fair skin who is always hiding a great sadness, as though it were an egg she carried around cupped in her hands, with their chewed nails and cuticles. It's a great weight for Ruby to carry, knowing that Rachel depends so on her affection.

The house where Alex's friend Ben lives is up a winding road from town, down a long drive, sitting in a bowl made between a sharp wooded ridge and a berm covered with creeping chrysanthemum. Ben's mother's name is Olivia, and she is actually English, so it makes perfect sense that she has never asked me to create an English garden around her stone house in Vermont. Her house sits surrounded by several large fir trees, with a hedge of burning bushes around its foundation, and little more. There is a small carriage house at the foot of the lawn, off to one side, wreathed in old privet. The whole thing looks exactly right, as though nature did it. So many of my clients want their yards to look like their living rooms, like carefully groomed and color-coordinated arrangements that are neither to be changed nor used. "They are such boys!" Olivia says emphatically as she opens the door. She is small and very fair, but her voice, with its precise consonants, is carrying. Her blond hair is held off her face with a barrette and she is wearing one of her husband's sweaters, so that, overwhelmed by gray wool, she looks a bit like a child herself.

"Oh, no. What did they do?"

"Nothing. They were perfectly lovely, but they are so astonishingly male. Not a word about anything. How is school? Fine. How is your mother? Fine. When does your sister leave? I dunno. Like blood from the bloody stone. Quite another species, don't you agree? Or do you? My sister says her daughter drives her mad with her disapproval. Ruby doesn't seem a bit like that, I must say."

Olivia's house is pretty and unpretentious, with sports equipment in baskets in the corner of the den, the kitchen, and the front hall. Masks, balls, sticks. Her husband, Ted, is as American as she is British, with a big grin and a firm handshake and a long stride. She met him at Oxford when she was an undergraduate and he was a Rhodes scholar, and he still plays soccer with a men's league in town. They have four boys, Ben the eldest, and, unlike my children, Olivia's all seem to be cut from the same cloth. "Someday," she said to me once, "there will be five hulking men in the house, and one small woman." I'm not certain why Olivia and I are not friends. It's just one of those things that happen. "Tea?" she asks, and I say, "I would love to, but I have to get home and make dinner." Perhaps that's why we haven't become closer: We are on different schedules. So much of friendship is about being in the right place at the right time. That's how Kiernan's mother, Deborah, and I found each other, both young mothers of young children, both a little overwhelmed, a little lost. Alice is the friend who knew me when I was young and uncertain, Nancy the friend I acquired when I needed someone sure and straightforward and sane to a fault. I'm not sure I have room now for any more friends, even one as nice as Olivia. I'm vaguely sorry about that every time I see her.

Ruby is home working on her prom dress. She is now happy about her prospects. Somehow she had remembered a photograph of my mother in a long dress with a bright swirling psychedelic print. Somehow my mother had unearthed it and sent it up to us. Ruby has removed the cowl collar and created a scooped neckline, has made a sash from some bright pink satin. "An obi sash," she repeats when she describes it. A few days ago, all of this looked like wishful thinking, pieces spread across Ruby's desk and desk chair, her short story momentarily forgotten. Now I am beginning to see what it will look like.

"Your daughter has the oddest taste," my mother says on the phone. "She should go to design school."

My mother told me I should go to nursing school. I assume she had my best interests at heart. "What in the world can you do with an English-literature degree?" she had asked, a high school English teacher always scrabbling to make ends meet. She was so happy that Glen became an ophthalmologist. He had majored in philosophy, then decided to spend the rest of his life peering into other people's eyes. "The windows of the soul," said my mother. "It does make you wonder what we'll talk about at dinner," I'd replied. "What do you think writers talk about at dinner?" my mother asked, before Glen could say anything. "Or artists? Whether they're out of milk. Whether the basement's flooded. Don't delude yourself." Later, Glen said a little sulkily, "You can be an ophthalmologist and still read." He doesn't read. He watches the news and the History Channel. He leans forward to peer at the screen as they show the building of the pyramids, the bombing of Hiroshima, the construction of the railroads. "Come in here and take a look at this," he calls to the children, and as though they have actually flocked to him, hovering behind the wing chair, he points at the screen and provides his own narration: three thousand men, ten tons of dynamite, three decades, thousands of deaths. Somehow it all sounds the same to me no matter what the municipal project or the government initiative or the natural disaster.

Once I asked him about the enormous variety of eye colors he must see every day. It was years ago, when I'd spent the morning at the kitchen table, staring into the eyes of Kiernan's mother, Deborah, a clear watery hypnotic green. "And you must see some amazing blues, too," I'd said to my husband. "Eye color's not clinically significant," he said, bent over the newspaper.

"Kiernan gave me this," Alex says now, in the car on the way home from Ben's, holding up a key ring with a large yellow compass dangling from one end.

"When did you see Kiernan?"

"He was at Ben's. He, like, babysits for them sometimes—not babysits, because Ben is too old, but, you know, hangs out. Whatever. You know. They know him from day camp."

Last summer and the summer before, Ruby and Kiernan were counselors at the day camp at the community center. In the evenings, they sat at our kitchen table and cut out construction-paper stars and planets. They chose books for story time, and decided which rainy-day games were least likely to end in tears. Kiernan would develop grandiose ideas, and Ruby would talk sense into him. He wanted to do a production of *Our Town*. "K, they are five and six," Ruby had said. "They'll get it," he insisted. "People always underestimate little kids." Ruby found a dramatic version of "Jack and the Beanstalk" to do instead. Kiernan sulked through the rehearsals. Ben's brother Aidan was Jack.

"Is he your boyfriend?" Aidan asked Ruby accusingly one day, staring at Kiernan.

"What do you think?"

"I think he is." Aidan didn't sound at all happy about it.

"I think you're right," Ruby said with a small smile.

My boys both like Kiernan, but I should have been paying closer attention lately when they talked about him. This is how I learn most of what I know about my children and their friends: by sitting in the driver's seat and keeping quiet. Behind the wheel I am invisible, a chauffeur. A month or so ago the boys were in the car, their backpacks between them, and my reverie on whether we had lettuce and which day lilies would have a second bloom had slowly given way to the muttered discussion behind me.

"All I mean is that he can be weird," Alex said.

"You think everybody's weird," Max replied in his low, almost inaudible voice.

"Remember that time he was listening to that same band over and over for, like, months? He would take off his headphones and you'd hear the same song. They weren't even a good band."

"They were an okay band."

"Okay, they weren't a popular band. Nobody knew about them but Kiernan."

Ruby will not discuss Kiernan with me. She is sorry she said anything at Molly's Closet. "You make such a big deal out of things," she says. When I refer to Kiernan as her prom date while she is foraging for food with her friends, she slices fiercely through the sandwich she is making. She is not a vegetarian this year. The sandwich is turkey. Sarah is having turkey, too, and Rachel is picking at ham and cheese. Rachel has had a manicure, and her bitten nails are sad little stubs of magenta. She keeps raising her fingers to her mouth, then putting them down again.

Sarah says, "We don't really date the way you guys did when you were young." She makes our youth sound like something Glen might have seen on the History Channel. Sarah's sport reflects her character; she spends her afternoons swimming a straight line, her stroke unvarying, her body shaped like a garden spade, her hair a neat bob of silky brown that dries cleanly in place. She is Ruby's reality check. "Am I overreacting?" Ruby will sometimes say to Sarah, and Sarah will smile and say, "Yes." As in most triangular friendships, both of them feel deeply protective of Rachel because she is not the best friend of either.

"I get that about dating," I say to Sarah. "But each of you is going to the prom with a specific boy, even if you're all going together." Sarah is going with Eric, the boy she has been seeing since ninth grade. It would not surprise me a bit if I could fast-forward the film of all their lives and find Sarah and Eric married and moving into a house a block or two away from both their families. Sarah wants to be a nurse. When Nancy said, "You could be a doctor, sweetie," Sarah looked at her mother and said, "And you could be a dean, not a professor. They're two entirely different jobs."

"Well," Nancy said to me as she recounted it. "I guess I got told."

I don't know what I would see for Ruby on that film of the future. I fear that what I would see for Rachel would be unhappiness or discontent. Ruby has specific aims and desires. Rachel just seems to have a big yearning for something unnamed, perhaps never to be named.

"Kiernan is obsessed with prom," says Rachel, opening the fridge to get the mustard. "Just obsessed."

"He needs to grow up," says Ruby. "It's just a dance. Big deal."

Sarah's mouth is full. The swimming coach once figured out that Sarah needs five thousand calories a day just to stay at her current weight. Around a mouthful of bread she says, "Eric only cares about prom so he can get to breakfast, and the lake. French toast and tanning. Doesn't that make me feel special? I think you should be nicer to Kiernan, Rubes," she adds, cutting her eyes sideways toward me to make certain she is not giving too much away.

"I am nice to him," Ruby says.

I start to fold towels in the adjacent mudroom, hoping that they'll become talkative when I'm out of sight, but instead they begin a serious conversation about pedicure colors. Kiernan found a sky-blue tuxedo at the thrift store at which Ruby struck out on a dress. It came with a ruffled shirt, a cummerbund, and an enormous bow tie. Ruby says the bow tie looks like a butterfly. I know exactly what Kiernan will look like. He will look like James

McGhee, the boy who took me to my prom. He wore that self-same tuxedo. I remember finding an old photograph of the two of us posed in front of two freestanding Styrofoam Corinthian pillars that had been set up in the hotel hallway, and thinking what a good thing it was that the classic black tux had come back into style, and that the sort of Empire-waist dress I was wearing had gone out of fashion. Now Kiernan is wearing the blue tux, and Ruby and all her friends wear dresses with Empire waists. I am trying to learn to take nothing for granted.

It's raining hard and I am parked at the curb, waiting for Max to be finished with his drum lesson. I'm so tired that I can't tell whether my foggy vision is the rain, or lack of sleep. Through the fine mist thrown up by the water hitting my hood I can occasionally see a strange *woosh* of movement in the picture window on the second floor of the hardware-store building. Weeks ago I had to park across the street, and from there I could tell that the odd blur of movement was Max's shaggy head. It's why he doesn't want to cut his hair. He hurls it around when he plays the drums, and a small smile pops the dimples I've seen so rarely in the past year. When Max's voice began to change, so did his mood. Both are low most of the time. The students moving up from middle school to high school were asked to fill out a questionnaire. "Describe yourself in one word," one of the questions said. Ruby said Max left the space blank. "Maybe he couldn't come up with just one word," I'd said. "Mommy, be real," Ruby replied, shaking her head.

   "He looks like a homeless guy," Glen says sometimes after Max has cleared his plate and put it in the sink, his bare feet silent on the kitchen floor. "I try to be tolerant." Glen believes this, but it's not really true. He confuses silence with tolerance. A young man came into his office to interview for a job as a part-time bookkeeper, and Glen almost didn't talk to him because he had a shooting star tattooed on the back of his hand. He has turned out to be a hard worker, but most of the time, when Glen mentions him, he adds, "I hope he's socking away his salary, because it's going to cost him a couple thousand dollars when he decides to have that thing removed."

One night Ruby put down her fork and said, "Daddy, he probably has more than one. You just don't see them. Most people who get inked have a saying: not where a judge can see it."

"You'd better not have any thoughts along those lines," Glen said, his chin set sharp as an arrowhead.

"Oh, Daddy," Ruby said airily, twirling her spaghetti. "My body is a temple."

Max and Alex laughed in unison, the way they had when they were little. It made me happy to see them of one mind again for just a moment. They were never alike, even as infants, one bald and moonfaced, the other all eyes and long parentheses of legs, but when they were small they complemented each other. Max would build with Legos, and Alex would hand him the blocks. Alex would kick the soccer ball around the yard, and Max would go back into the woods to retrieve it. Alex only began to be unkind to Max when other kids did. They would look at the baroque doodles on the front of Max's notebook and say, "What's that supposed to be?" and Max would say, "It's a microscopic organism found in the water on Mars. It glows in the dark." The ones I secretly called the Polo Shirt boys would make a face. And the girls would go where the Polo Shirt boys went. And Alex became one of the Polo Shirt boys himself.

"People at school don't believe me and Max are twins," Alex said one day.

"Max and I," I say, and then, "I was there, sweet pea. You absolutely are."

"Just fraternal," he said, as though that wasn't the same, perhaps not even closely related.

I can see Max's hair going back and forth, back and forth, like a wheat field in a windstorm; can very faintly hear some thumps. I don't think Max plays the drums very well yet, but I'm not sure exactly how you recognize good drumming. If he continues, we will build him a soundproof room in the unfinished space above the garage and buy him a set of drums. For now, he takes his sticks and plays on the surface of his bed, the kitchen counter, the dashboard of the car. When he drums he seems happier, or at least less sad. The rest of the time he seems absent, as though he's gone somewhere else and left his body behind. "Earth to Max," Alex says sometimes to get his brother's attention. At least they are beginning to reach puberty at the same time, caught in some odd middle ground of metamorphosis. Their legs have become long and muscled and suddenly covered with hair. The bones beneath the skin of their faces have come into sharper relief. Ruby says I should pay no attention to the porn on their computers. "It's the tech version of *Playboy* under the bed," she told me.

"When my mother found *Playboy* under your uncle Richard's bed, he was grounded for a week," I said.

"I dunno, does that make sense to you? Plus, are we suddenly going to decide that Nana was the perfect mother?" Sometimes I wonder if there is such a thing as being too honest with your children, or at least your daughter. My boys wouldn't think to pass judgment on my upbringing unless I told them I'd been beaten in the basement. But Ruby has parsed my childhood stories and come up with a fairly accurate portrait of a mother who believed clothing and feeding were the same thing as loving. At least, unlike Glen's father, my mother didn't believe in corporal punishment.

The plans for a terrace garden are on my lap. "Hyssop," I write in the margin, then erase it. I put my head back and close my eyes. After a few minutes, I force myself to open them again. "Bee balm," I write, and then say aloud, "Jesus God." How can I make a garden for a woman who has told me she hates bees? When I asked my client how she felt about butterflies, she made a rocking motion with her hand. "I'm not a big bug person," she said.

Ruby left the house early this morning, said it was to work on the literary magazine. I think she wants to avoid being alone with me. In the middle of the night on Saturday, I awoke to a sound from downstairs and realized that it was the teakettle whistling. Ruby and Sarah were moving swiftly around the kitchen, taking milk from the refrigerator, reaching for the sugar. I stood in the doorway watching them before Ruby saw me and startled slightly. "Go back to bed," she'd whispered to me.

"Pearl," wailed a voice from the den. "Pearl, I'm gonna puke."

"Oh, God," Sarah said as I pushed past her.

Rachel was lying on the couch, covered with a blanket. There were twigs and some leaves snarled in her long dark hair, and I pulled them off. "I hate myself," she whispered, and then louder, "I hate myself."

"Shh," I said. When Rachel opened her eyes and saw me standing over her, she wailed and rolled onto her side, hiding her face in the cushions. I could see a smear of dirt on her shoulder, and what looked like a bruise on her throat. It reminded me of a night in college when Alice had staggered in at dawn and fallen onto her bed opposite mine. "So many men, so little time to go to the arboretum with the wrong goddamn one," she'd muttered. It was the one time I'd taken care of her rather than the other way around.

"Please go away," Rachel cried into the cushions.

"Mommy," Ruby hissed from the kitchen.

"Where were you tonight?" I said, standing between Ruby and Sarah at the stove.

"At Tony's," Sarah whispered, picking up a tray with the tea and some crackers.

We have a steak house, and a pizza parlor, but the kids like Tony's, an ice-cream place two miles outside town that puts its picnic tables out in May and stores them away in October and has a menu of microwave breaded things to supplement the sundaes in waxed paper cups. The kids sit on the picnic tables—not on the benches, atop the tables themselves—and call comments to one another and make one root-beer float last until it's just a muddy puddle in the bottom of the go-cup. One girl after another pulls a friend aside, into the filthy ladies' room, behind the storage shed, to whisper. They broke up. He's home from college. Her period is late. He got suspended. Like a broadcast in another room, we mothers hear about some of this after the fact—in overheard calls, or conversations at the kitchen table. The kids know we will keep quiet, not out of tact but out of shame. We know that our children are having sex, smoking pot, drinking beer, but it is easier to say nothing. "Ruby looks good!" some of the other mothers said when my daughter began to eat again, the closest they ever came to acknowledging that there was a time when Ruby looked terrible. Even when we're honest with one another, we tread carefully; the quickest way to lose a friend is to suggest that she is a bad mother, or to suggest that her children have problems, which amounts to the same thing. (Well, maybe not the quickest way to lose a friend. I know the quickest way.)

"Since when does Tony's serve beer?" I asked Ruby in the kitchen.

"Mom, let us handle this."

"Make her leave," Rachel cried from the other room. "I don't want her to see me." I could hear Sarah's quiet murmur. Sarah will be a good nurse. Even I felt a little calmer at the sound of her voice, until Ruby suddenly leaned toward me and closed her eyes. We swayed together like slow dancers at a high school mixer.

"Oh, Mommy, she's so messed up," she whispered.

"How bad? Do we need the police?"

The moment had shattered. "What?" Ruby said. "Oh, God, no. God. She just makes . . . bad decisions. Really bad decisions." She'd shivered then. "Please go back to bed. Let us take care of this. I promise I'll call you if we need you." Back upstairs, I lay awake until the sky lightened. By morning Ruby was asleep in her own bed, and Sarah and Rachel were gone, the mug on the counter and the blanket on the floor the only signs that I hadn't had a nightmare. If they had made coffee instead of tea, if I had not been awakened by the whistle of the kettle, I might never have known that anything had happened.

I lean back in the car and will myself to stay awake. Perhaps tonight I will take a sleeping pill, just to catch up. "Boxwood," I write on the plans. Main Street is almost deserted because of the weather and the time of day. It's just after 6 P.M., and while the city fathers have done what they can, with the historically accurate streetlamps and the free parking, no one stays in town once evening comes. The small Middle Eastern restaurant that opened two years ago, run by an immigrant couple with two sons who are already poised to be the valedictorians of their respective classes, gets a couple of tables of diners on weekday nights.

I see a woman in a glistening yellow macintosh pass in front of my car. Her hood is up, she's holding an umbrella, she looks like an altogether generic person hurrying to an errand in a heavy rain, but I'm certain that it is Kiernan's mother, Deborah. There is a particular lilting motion to her walk, as though her toes were turned out and she were on the balls of her feet even in rubber rain boots.

Deborah was once a dancer. We were once the closest of friends. I'm fairly certain that in the downpour she has not noticed or recognized my car, which is a dark heavy hatchback like those belonging to half the mothers in town. But it may be that she has and is refusing to look my way. This happens with some regularity, Deborah pretending to see nothing but air where I'm standing. It always makes me feel a little sick to my stomach. Last year I was at a backyard party for the Lawrences' twentieth anniversary, and Deborah came through the patio doors, and there I was, facing her. Without a word she was gone, as though she had been a hologram of herself, projected for an instant and then dissolved.

"Give my love to your mother," I used to say to Kiernan, and then "Give my best to your mother," followed by "Say hi to your mother," until one day Ruby said, "Mom, that's beyond pathetic. Just stop."

I wonder what Deborah will think if Ruby breaks up with Kiernan. I wonder if it's even possible for Ruby to break up with Kiernan. It's not just that Kiernan is in love with Ruby, although I know he is; sometimes he looks as though his eyes are going to begin to spin in his head as she moves around the room, picking up the phone, picking up a magazine. He would like it best if Ruby stayed still and talked to him, but since that's not how Ruby is, especially these days, he takes second best, asking Alex about soccer and Max about some animated movie he's seen, Glen about the local minor league baseball team, me about whatever I have cooking on the stove. Kiernan is not just in love with Ruby; he's in love with our family.

It's twenty-five after six when Max opens the car door. Despite my best efforts, I've fallen into a doze. "You scared me," I say. Max doesn't answer. He passes me a note with his drum teacher's strange crabbed handwriting.

"Please call me," the teacher has written.

"Is everything all right?" I ask.

"Is that Kiernan's mom?" Max asks.

The rain has slowed to a gray drizzle, and Deborah has hurried past, a bag in one hand. I catch a glimpse of her big eyes, so like her son's. She wears her dark hair very short now, a ruffly inch or two all over, as though she is daring you to avoid those eyes. Her face looks like a room with no drapes or shades. She angles her umbrella sharply. There's something undeniable about the posture of a person trying not to acknowledge your existence.

"I can't wait until camp starts," Max says, playing imaginary drums in the air.

We are standing outside a house on Winding Way, Rickie and I, and John, and Tony, who runs the backhoe.

"This is so bad," says Rickie. He's chewing hard on his bottom lip. John is shaking his head. Tony is walking back and forth, swearing under his breath. I try not to cry. The boss shouldn't cry.

It is the Friday of Memorial Day weekend. Two days earlier, we finished a big job: six tiers of shrubs, a small copse of flowering plum and pear, a long hedge of weigela. Almost all of it is gone. The property is pocked with holes. A few of the shrubs have been tossed down a steep slope behind the house and are lying in the creek below, their roots raised to the sky like fingers. Please, please, save us, they seem to plead. Rickie says some may be salvageable. The fruit trees and the bigger bushes are gone, nowhere to be found.

Rickie has already called the police. A patrol car pulls up as I stand there, arms folded across my chest. I know the officer who gets out. His daughter plays peewee league soccer on the field after

Alex and his team are finished, and we have exchanged polite remarks about footing. Somehow this makes it worse. Whatever community impulse those soccer games stand for, this is its opposite.

"There were really plants in all those holes?" the cop asks. His nameplate says his last name is Jackson. We shake hands. The men nod.

"Plants, hell," Rickie says. "Thousands of dollars' worth of trees, too. This is more than vandalism. I'd say we're looking at twenty thousand dollars' worth of plantings in all. That's not even counting the labor."

"I have invoices back at the office," I say. "Where are the guys?"

The guys are the Mexicans who work for me from spring through fall. They live in an old decommissioned motel out on a back road that was once the best way to drive through this part of the state. When the interstate was finished, the motels along the old road died. My guys live a shabby, makeshift life in a cinder-block rectangle with windows so small they barely let in light and air. They make coffee on a hot plate, eat fast food. Rickie says they live better here than do their families in Mexico, where they send money each month. I've decided to believe it. The wages we pay them shame me. That, and the fact that the only one who really registers as an individual with me is a short thick man named José. Or that's what he has told me his name is. Nancy says they all use names they think white people can recall and pronounce. José, Manuel, Juan. José is a soccer maniac and first spoke to me when Alex, in uniform, was dropped off at a job site. He has shown me pictures of his children, two little girls photographed in white dresses holding pink carnations.

"All our people are doing that big sod job at the club," Rickie says to me. "Why?"

"I want to get this fixed right away. These people will be back by the end of next week. I know it sounds crazy, but I'm going to feel better if by next week this place looks like nothing happened." I look up at the house. It is a large place, not pretty but impressive. It might as well have a sign at the end of the drive: COSTASMALLFORTUNE. The owners are new to the area, one of those couples who confuse me: prosperous disproportionate to their ages, which I guess to be early thirties. They are away in the south of France and so decided that this was the perfect time to have their place landscaped. Now it looks as though it has been savaged by a storm. What sort of people steal trees? "I don't mean to sound hysterical, but I am really freaked out by this," I say.

"It doesn't sound hysterical at all," says the police officer. "This is pretty horrible."

"I think they have lights with motion detectors at the corners of the house," said Rickie. "If we put those on, maybe it will help keep anyone from coming back and doing it again."

"We might put everything back in and have this happen again?" I ask.

Rickie shrugs. Officer Jackson says, "I can have a car go by once or twice a night." He makes some notes. "Your insurance will cover the cost of the plants, right?"

"Is that all anybody thinks about nowadays?" Rickie says, his voice verging on a shout. "Somebody comes in here—or somebodies, because this was a lot of goddamn work—and steals all this stuff that we spent days putting in, and I'm betting just junked it. I'm betting every one of these plants was tossed in a field somewhere and is lying there dying in this heat." It's unseasonably warm for May, in the high eighties, and the policeman has big rings of black beneath the sleeves of his dark-blue uniform shirt.

"Hey, I'm with you," he says. "This is really sick and sad. If one of my kids did something like this, he'd be on lockdown for a year. I just asked because if the insurance will cover it, I'd like to get this lady a police report fast so she can file what she needs to file and recover some of her losses."

"You think it's kids?" I ask.

All of us look back at the holes in the ground. The teenagers in town traditionally go a little crazy as the weather warms. When Ruby and the twins were younger and my business hadn't yet taken shape, I was entranced by the notion of long, formless summer days, hiking the hills, going to the county fair, putting up tents so they could spend the nights in the yard peeking out at the stars. But the tales of older kids racing their cars on the outlying roads or smoking pot in the woods scared me off, and by the time the twins were six they had joined Ruby in day camp, making mosaic ashtrays and playing badminton. Max would throw his long arms around my pelvis and bury his face in my side as though he were longing to return to the womb. "Come on," Alex would say in the soothing voice he had once used with his brother. "We can paint." That was before Alex began to understand that Max's behavior reflected on him with the other kids. It was strange that it never went the other way, that Alex's ease and prowess never cast a sliver of sunshine over his twin.

"I don't have a clue," says the officer. "I mean, we do get some vandalism, but this seems pretty over the top. Not to mention a lot of work. Maybe you could see if you can get something out of your kids?"

"It's not them," I say, then sigh. "I bet you hear that all the time—'It's not my kids.'" I know he does. The big end-of-the-school-year debacle in town was two years ago, when half the baseball team played too much beer pong and set fire to a ramshackle barn at the edge of what had once been a dairy farm. All the parents spent days denying that their kids had been involved, although two of the boys had bad burns on their hands. There were two fallback explanations: the legendarily destructive and vindictive kids from the next town (who, when we played them in athletic contests, looked and behaved exactly like our own children); and the Mexicans, who were always being suspected of petty theft but, as far as I could tell, never did anything worthy of official notice except fight among themselves.

Then a construction company building houses across the road produced a security-camera video that showed eight boys siphoning gas out of the SUV that one of them had gotten as a graduation gift and pouring it around the barn doors. The parents divided into three groups: the ones whose boys just stood there and watched, which made them innocent; the ones whose boys did the siphoning and the lighting, which made them "misguided," according to the attorney representing the wildest one; and the two decent sets of parents who made their sons perform hours of community service, picking up trash along the road, even before the court said they had to do it.

"My kids aren't angels," I say, "but their friends are all pretty attached to me." I point to the sign we'd posted: ANOTHER LOVELY LANDSCAPE BY LATHAM. "That's a whole lot of alliteration," Ruby had said when I first came up with it.

"I hear you," the cop says. "But maybe the word'll be going around, you know? Ha ha, guess what me and Jason did—that kind of thing."

"I'm going to kick somebody's ass," says Rickie. "Kids or adults or whoever. I'm going to kick somebody's ass to hell and back."

I'm not sure the kids would tell me if they knew. They were good about informing when there were little things involved: which eighth-grade boy carried condoms, which girl had had a summer-camp boyfriend that her boyfriend at home didn't know about. But they kept the big things to themselves. Sarah and Rachel had kept Ruby's secret for six months of freshman year, until I walked into her room one morning and saw her bare back, a xylophone of spine and ribs with not a bit of fat for buffer.

"It took you a long time to figure things out," Rachel had said to me accusingly when Ruby started eating again.

Just this morning, I had run into Rachel's mother while picking up coffee. Sandy was wearing a sundress and platform sandals, her toes lacquered a dried-blood red. I knew she thought we were friends, but I had never liked her. When Rachel was twelve, a stocky girl tortured by bad skin and full-on orthodonture, her mother sent her to fat camp. Worse, that's what Sandy had called it—to the girls, the mothers, everyone: fat camp. "As you can tell, she doesn't get it from my side," she'd said.

"Is Ruby giving you a hard time?" Sandy asked, her hand on my forearm. "Because Rachel is making my life miserable."

"It's a hard time," I said. "College, the course load. They're all under a lot of pressure. Junior year is probably the hardest year of high school for these kids."

"Isn't it?" Sandy always spoke as though she were delivering lines from a crucial scene in a soap opera. "It's so hard. I don't know if I'm going to get through it. I keep asking her, What about Sarah? What about Ruby? Why don't they have these issues?"

"Oh, they have issues."

"It's my dating. She should be old enough to have come to terms with it." After Sandy divorced Rachel's father, she'd married a real-estate broker, then lived with the man who built pools in the area. Now she's seeing a vice president of the local bank.

"Well," I say, "I think that's got to be hard on a teenage girl, you know?"

"I know she wants me to feel guilty. But I just won't. I think guilt is a useless emotion. They need to understand that we have to have a life, too."

I had sipped at my coffee in lieu of speaking. I was afraid that, like the princess in the fairy tale, frogs of candor would leap from my lips and I would reply: "We don't have a life. We had children instead. Your daughter is sad and insecure and in some kind of trouble. Grow up. Stop thinking about yourself. Forget about men. Buy some appropriate clothes."

I am a coward. Instead, I had agreed that it was necessary that someday soon we have lunch.

After the police officer pulls away, I see that I have a message from Alice on my phone. "I really need advice on potty training," her recorded voice says. And it's almost irresistible to call her back and say, Oh my God, it makes no difference—preschool, playdates, sharing, reading readiness. I remember Ruby and Kiernan, both of them five, playing side by side in the grass behind the little house where we lived when the children were small, squabbling, pulling toys out of each other's hands, calling the twins dumbbells and stupid heads. Deborah was worried that Kiernan would resent the baby she was expecting. Someone had said at the time, "Little children, little problems; big children, big problems." What did we know?

That evening I have dinner with Nancy. The girls have taught us what they call the small-town look-around: Before you begin to speak, you look all around you to make certain there is no one within earshot you wouldn't want to overhear the conversation. Even at a restaurant a half hour out of town, we both do it.

"I have had the day from hell," I say.

"Please," says Nancy, rolling her eyes. "You have no idea." Her elder son, Fred, the one in college, had his wisdom teeth out the day before. Her youngest, Bob, fell trying for a ground ball and broke his ankle. "If Sarah pulls a muscle swimming, I'm running away from home," she says.

Nancy's crises always seem to trump mine, but I still tell her about the stolen plants, and about my encounter with Rachel's mother. "Sandy says Rachel doesn't understand that her mother needs to have a life. She says guilt is a useless emotion."

"Oh, please," says Nancy. "Guilt is what separates humans from animals."

"Fries or a salad with that?" the waitress asks as she takes our orders.

"Fries," Nancy says.

"Me too," I say. "I'm so sick of salads."

Nancy had Fred before I had children, and Bob before I had the twins. When we first met, we discovered that Sarah and Ruby were born within two days of each other, and that we both believed natural childbirth was the big lie of our time. (Sandy once told me that she had had an elective Caesarean to keep her tone "down there.") Nancy learns more about Sarah from me than from Sarah, and I learn more about Ruby from her than from Ruby. Although there always seems to be less to learn about Sarah.

"I have this situation with Kiernan and I'm at a complete loss," I say as our burgers arrive. "He's always at the house, which was always fine, except that now Ruby doesn't seem to want him around."

Nancy's mouth is stuffed with food, and she is signaling that she wants to speak but can't. She always eats too fast. Once I had to Heimlich her in a Chinese restaurant.

"I only know this from eavesdropping on Sarah—" she finally says.

"Of course—"

"But apparently he's been doing this routine where he bought

Ruby this ring and he wants her to make some kind of promise about how they will stay together, and they'll go to colleges near each other—"

"Which is an idea he might have gotten from Eric and Sarah—"

"Which you know," Nancy says, "makes me completely crazy. I feel as if I was a bad role model for her, getting married so young, and you know, ultimately, I have no regrets, but still the idea that she might wind up with someone she met when she was fourteen . . ." Nancy is eating my fries because she has finished her own. She and Bill met in eighth grade. Fred is twenty and still with his high school girlfriend, and Bob is only fifteen but has had the same girlfriend since high school began. They grew up with a family mythology, and they're sticking to it.

"So what should I do?" I ask. "I mean, in the natural order of things your daughter breaks up with a boy and afterward you see him a couple of times a year on Main Street or at a game. But Kiernan has practically lived at our house since the Donahues moved back, what, four years ago?"

"Five. They moved back the week I became department chair." Nancy is a biology professor at the state university campus an hour north of town. She is apparently a recognized expert on some single-celled organisms. Since we are all, in some fashion, single-celled organisms, this makes her an expert on everything and everyone. My friendships have a certain symmetry at the moment: Alice is always asking me what she should do, and Nancy is always telling me what I should do.

"I don't know what to tell you," she says. "If Kiernan was a different kind of kid, he and Ruby could break up and he could still hang around. But if he were a different kind of kid, she wouldn't have been with him in the first place. She's moving on, and he's not. The thing about Ruby, she's so mature that she understands all this."

"I don't think you should assume that Sarah is immature because of Eric. It's worked out all right for you and Bill."

Nancy eats my last fry. "I suppose," she says flatly.

Bill and Nancy will have a big silver-anniversary party next
year. He runs an insurance agency, and Glen thinks he's great. I
think he's fine. Nancy and I have an unspoken agreement not to
talk too much about our husbands. We tell ourselves that it's because of the danger of disloyalty, and because the two men are
friends. But we also have a vested interest in making certain that
the infrastructure of our lives seems more or less intact.

"I think if Ruby and Kiernan broke up, Glen would be relieved," I say.

"I thought Glen liked him. Glen likes everybody."

"He doesn't like either of Kiernan's parents," I say. "He never
has."

"Well, they're not Glen's kind of people. Kevin Donahue talks
big and screws around, and Deborah's completely nuts." I feel my
face go flat. "I know you hate to hear that, but it's true. I've never
understood how you could have been friends with her."

I say nothing. I'm not going to submit Deborah to Nancy's
harsh judgment, or tell her why the friendship ended.

"So what should I do about Kiernan?" I say.

"I have no idea," Nancy says.

Neither do I.

I am in the kitchen cooking when Ruby calls me from her bedroom. Usually I find this irritating, since I know the point is that she's too busy or exhausted or important to come down one flight of stairs, while it is simple for someone with as little to do as her mother to come up them. I'm always reminded of Alex's question about a female judge he met on one of our rare visits to my brother Richard's home in the New York suburbs: "But if she doesn't have any kids, what does she do when she's home?" His father and I had cackled wildly in the front seat, shrieking answers: Sleep! Read! Talk to her husband! When we had exhausted our sarcasm, Ruby said in a creamy tone of voice, "You both are so completely full of it the car might flood."

Today I know that Ruby doesn't want to come downstairs because Kiernan is sitting in the kitchen. He works on the high school paper and has just brought Alex the last edition of the year, which has a story about the soccer squad in which Alex and Ben are mentioned. "With the departure of five varsity seniors," Kiernan reads aloud, "including goalie Chris Argento, the Hawks face an uncertain future next year. But first years Alex Latham and Ben Cooper, co-captains of the undefeated middle-school squad, may help to fill the gap."

"You wrote this," Alex says.

"Dude, I didn't," Kiernan says, his hand over his heart. "I'm the picture guy. Strictly visual. The sports editor wrote it."

"You lie. You wrote it."

"I swear. I'm barely literate."

"Mom! Mommy!" Ruby cries from her room, and Kiernan lifts his head and tracks the sound like a dog listening to a high-pitched whistle.

There are peppers in a sauté pan. I am going to finish cooking them before I go upstairs.

"This is really great, Alex," I say. "You have to show this to Daddy the moment he walks in the door."

Alex looks down at the paper again. "When they say 'may help to fill the gap,' do you think that means Ben and I make varsity?" he says.

"Dude," says Kiernan, raising his hands palms up, a you've-got-it-made gesture. I give him a look over Alex's head.

"Oh, honey," I say, pushing peppers around in the pan. "I think a lot depends on who else is playing and what positions need to be filled. Besides, if you play JV you get a lot more playing time when you're a freshman."

"Mo-meee!" Ruby shrieks.

"Shut up," Max mutters. He is on the window seat, eating cherries and reading a comic book.

"You're a jerk," Alex says. "Just because no one ever mentioned you in the paper doesn't mean you have to act like a jerk. Jerk."

"What?" Max says.

"Dude, I think he was remarking on your sister's banshee wail," says Kiernan.

"What he said," Max mutters again.

When I'd called Max's drum teacher, he said he thought Max was seriously depressed. "That guy can't even stand up straight, and he's qualified not only to teach music but to do psychological analysis?" Glen said as we talked in bed. There were four panes of bright light aslant on our ceiling from a white June moon. The light through this window, the smell of the air, the witchy line of a tree branch that has insinuated itself into the sight line of my side of the bed: this is how I track the seasons. I can't say why, but when I see those squares of light on the ceiling I feel as though all will be well.

"We should find another music teacher," Glen had said. He was really annoyed, mainly because he is as worried about Max as I am. Two of his teachers say they will fail him for lack of class participation. One of the two says she has never heard his voice.

Upstairs, the house smells like hot olive oil and gym socks. When I open Ruby's door, a puff of incense mixes with the other two and makes me feel faint for just a moment. The dog is lying at the foot of the bed. Ruby is sitting cross-legged at the head, tapping at the keyboard of her computer.

"I called you, like, ten times," she says without looking up.

"I am cooking dinner and talking to your brothers. And Kiernan. Who is waiting downstairs for you, I assume."

Ruby lets down her hair, winds it around her hand, puts it up in a bun that looks identical to the one she just dismantled. Her reconfigured prom dress hangs from the back of her closet door. It's beautiful, a swirl of primary colors with a deep U-neck and trumpet sleeves. No one will have anything like it.

Above her bed is a photograph of the hands of a girl wearing dark nail polish holding an ornate silver pen. Ruby writes, and Kiernan takes pictures. There were many reasons that they became a couple, including the fact that he has always been in love with her, with the specificity of her appearance and her personality. "That's so Ruby," Sarah says sometimes about a movie, a book, a dress. But Kiernan finally won her with a series of black-and-white photographs. She had written a short story about a high school student undone by writer's block, and Kiernan gave her a series of photos to accompany the story—a close-up of a hallway locker, a half-erased blackboard covered with a plot outline of *Anna Karenina,* Ruby's own hands as she wrote in her journal. The last had run in the literary magazine alongside the story, and by that time Ruby's hand was most often woven tightly into one of Kiernan's, on the street, in the lunchroom, in our den, where the hands told a story Ruby and Kiernan's decorous public behavior belied. If Kiernan thinks in pictures, Ruby thinks in stories, and I can imagine her making up one in her mind now—one that begins, "When I was in high school I had a boyfriend."

"Can you just tell him I'm surfing the crimson wave?" she says. "He knows not to bother me then."

I find it astonishing how open my daughter and her friends are about menstruation. Ruby, Sarah, and Rachel talk as though there is no reason the world shouldn't share in their moods, cramps, and back pain. It's not that they're insensitive: I remember one afternoon at our kitchen table when Sarah started to weep because of some fairly mild criticism from Eric, and Ruby and Rachel put their arms around her, draped themselves over her the way they do, and said, "Oh, honey, we'll make you some hot chocolate." It's just that they are open to knowledge and immune to shame. The other day I found the box for a pregnancy test in Ruby's bathroom. I'd hesitated and then held it up wordlessly. The air seemed to vibrate. It's so odd that, depending on the circumstances, pregnancy is either the thing we embrace most wholeheartedly or the thing we fear most. Ruby's eyes had narrowed. "Rachel," she'd said flatly, adding, "It's fine." I'd stood in the doorway, holding the jamb with one hand. "It's. Fine," Ruby said without looking up, in a voice that told me that was as much as I was going to learn.

"I don't have to make excuses for you," I say. "Sometimes Kiernan stops by just to stop by. He brought Alex a copy of the *Newshawk* with Alex's name in it."

"It's just that he's always here, whether I want to see him or not."

"I think you're the only one who can put a stop to that, honey," I say, scratching the spot where Ginger's tail meets her hindquarters. Dreamily, the dog raises one cocked back leg. It twitches in the air, as though she were dreaming that she is doing the scratching herself, then falls heavily back onto the bed.

"Ya think?" Ruby says harshly, and then she rearranges her hair again. "Seriously, don't you think that with all three of us away for the summer he'll get used to not stopping by?"

"He might stop by just to say hello."

"He's so intense, Mommy. So intense. Like, nothing is casual, everything is so—" She searches for a word, pounds the keyboard, sighs so that her whole slender rib cage rises and falls. "Intense."

I don't reply that Ruby is intense as well. She has so much in her life—Sarah, Rachel, her brothers, her father, me. Her writing, her politics, unformed though they may be. Kiernan doesn't see his father much since the divorce, and, I've heard, or overheard, that he doesn't talk much to his mother. He has no brothers or sisters. He has Ruby, and everything that Ruby carries with her: the confidence, the happiness, the brothers, the parents.

"Do you want dinner?" I ask.

"I'm working on my story." I have begun to think that Ruby's story is less a piece of fiction than the flotation device that is buoying her and carrying her away from here.

Downstairs, I add chicken to the peppers and start the rice. Kiernan is telling Alex a story about a soccer league in which his father once played that allegedly toured Europe. It may be true; it may be Kevin Donahue's invention. Kiernan's father is the sort of charming and irresistible man who is always only one remove from the big moment, the big idea, the big score. "I can taste it," Kevin used to say to Glen when he was coming up with yet another scheme, and I could feel my husband's disapproval and disbelief as though it were a change in temperature.

"K, are you having dinner here?" Alex asks. I don't turn from the stove, and I imagine Kiernan staring at my back. Finally I say, "There's plenty." Kiernan has heard me say this hundreds of times, but I'm afraid that there is now something crabbed and reluctant in my voice.

"Nah, dude," he says, and the chair scrapes against the tiles. "I've got stuff to do."

"Ruby is working on her story," I say.

"I know," Kiernan says. "I'll see her later."

"Why is Ruby being mean to Kiernan?" Max asks over dinner.

"Really mean," says Alex.

"You just like him now because he brought over that stupid paper," Max growls.

"What? I like him. I just think he can be weird sometimes."

"Who?" Glen says. He has arrived home late from work, and he is abstracted.

"Sometimes your sister just needs to be by herself," I say. I overcooked the peppers. They're khaki mush around the pieces of chicken. No one notices. If, in an hour, I asked them what they had for dinner, they wouldn't remember except that they would agree it had been good.

"Where's Ruby?" Glen asks.

"Upstairs. She's working on her story. She says she'll have yogurt later." Glen makes a face. He still worries about what Ruby eats, how often, and how much.

Alex hands Glen the copy of the school paper, folded to a small square so that it is nothing but the soccer story.

"Wow!" Glen says. "This is pretty impressive, buddy."

"I don't know," says Alex. "Like, do you think it means I'll make varsity?"

"Mom!" Ruby calls from upstairs.

I pull into the driveway late, as the sun is beginning to smear lilac and fucshia across the horizon, turning the tops of the green hills candy-colored, mocking the pale blue of the fading evening sky. The long hours now that the days are warming make up for the lackluster pace of the winter months, and I'm often exhausted, sore, and grubby. But occasionally I stop and sit at the wheel to look at my house. It's nothing much: medium blue, white shutters, a Dutch Colonial with little to set it apart but a steeply sloping roof with three sharp dormers. The trees around it were planted long before I knew an elm from a beech: two large oaks at one corner, a flourishing blue spruce at the other, and a Japanese maple to one side of the front door. There were topiary yews around the foundation; I hacked them down within three days of taking title. The children were little then; they sat cross-legged on the front lawn, mesmerized by the suggestion of violence in my behavior, and my borrowed chain saw. "Mommy really, really hates those trees," Ruby had told the boys solemnly.

I imagine that the house looks happy, but I suppose that's because it's what I want to believe. But it never looks happier to me than it does at twilight on a warm night when the lights come on. It's pretty when it's frosted with soft snow in the blue haze of a winter evening, but it's usually too cold in my car then to do more than leap out and hurry into the welcome of a good furnace. But on a mild night like this one I can afford to sit for a while and watch the windows, rectangles of gold. A spill of lamplight through a pane of glass spells home to me. When the kids were babies, I used to sing nonsense songs as I rocked and nursed them, and suddenly, out of nowhere, I remember one of them: Safe and sound, safe and sound, all around is safe and sound.

And then the other night Rickie drove me home, and looked up at the house, and saw something else. "Maybe you want to put in some of those motion-detector lights yourself," he'd said, and, with the best intentions, tainted it all.

"Oh, come on," I replied.

"That cop said they've had some things going on—break-ins, that kind of stuff. And that thing with the trees—I just don't like the way it feels."

I don't like the way it feels, either, whether it was vandalism or theft, teenagers or adults. But I patted Rickie's arm and said, "There are always lights on at my house. Glen complains all the time about our electric bill."

Even as I sit watching, a lamp comes on in the den, and I wonder who is in the room: Glen with the front part of the paper, Alex with the sports section, Max with a letter from one of his friends from camp. Or maybe it's Ruby, who has learned to walk through the house and turn a switch here and there to make the dim corners bright. I feel as if I'm watching my life. I feel as if I'm not in my life. I get out of the car and go though the door so that feeling will pass.

I pause in the mudroom to hang my big canvas bag on one of

the pegs. The three of them are in the kitchen, making s'mores if the smell of singed graham crackers is to be believed. I wonder if anyone actually makes s'mores, or whether everyone pretends that's what they're planning and then does what we do: put the Hershey bar and the marshmallow between the graham crackers and swear softly as the crackers snap in two, try again, abandon the graham crackers, toast the marshmallows, eat the Hershey bars. I can see Ruby in profile, a square of chocolate in her hand. She eats with tiny bites, like a small animal, a mouse maybe. The therapist said she would probably always eat that way. I slip off my rubber clogs, mud thick in the treads after another long day restoring the vandalized property on Winding Way. The workmen were truculent and fist-faced about repeating a job they had already done. When they were finished and got into the van to be dropped off at the shabby motel, none of them responded to my "Good night!"

I want to run upstairs and get into the shower, but I like to watch my children when they don't know I'm there, convinced that they'll reveal themselves to me in some essential way. They're so different when it's just the three of them, together. "Three people united against a common enemy," Nancy says of her own kids. "Or enemies." But it's not that. My brother, Richard, and I were two people related by blood, with little in common. When he left for college, it was as though the pond of our family had rippled slightly, then closed around the disturbance and become smooth again. We went from two adults and two children to one adult and one child with scarcely a thought, or at least a spoken one. And I went to college and left my mother, and she married and left me, and I moved East and she moved South. She and I talk once a week by phone, and she sends me news clippings, and occasionally a book that her book club has enjoyed. I have no idea what she felt when my father died, how she feels about me, what terrifies and what moves her. I remember spending most of my college vacations at Alice's house, a big confusing old place with two staircases and four brothers and parents who worked side by side in real estate. They told smutty jokes and drank whiskey sours, and her father said that when the kids were away he and his wife went skinny-dipping in the lake, and her mother said that was a nice thing to say in front of me, I would get the wrong idea about all of them, and the boys spit beer at one another at the table, and Alice said, "Oh, grow up, all of you."

They were a clan, not, as my family had been, people sharing a house and a name. Somehow my own children have become a clan, too, even when they are mean to one another, even when Ruby is short with the boys or Max is ignoring Alex and Alex is picking at Max. I think they are perfect at the same time that their inadequacies terrify me. Two years ago, I was worried all the time about Ruby. Now it's Max. I don't think it will ever be Alex.

"No, you're right, Mrs. Ruffino is hard," I hear Ruby say sympathetically, putting down her square of chocolate.

"Like, my grades are okay in every other class," Alex says, "and she says she's going to give me a C. And I'm like, Mrs. Ruffino, what? I show up, I read the stuff, I write the papers. I think she's always on me because, like, I'm not that good a writer, and I'm getting trashed because of you."

"So it's my fault you're failing English? That sounds like a lame excuse," Ruby says, licking her finger.

"Are you gonna finish that?" Max says, and Ruby pushes the rest of her chocolate bar across to him.

"I'm not failing," Alex says.

"A C," Ruby replies. "The parents will not be pleased."

"Duh."

"What are you reading?" she asks.

"*Scarlet Letter*," Max mutters.

"And Melinda Bernstein is like, Oh, Mrs. Ruffino, I love this book—it's so good." Alex has pitched his voice falsetto. Ruby laughs.

"You both have Mrs. Ruffino? I thought Mom made sure you were in different classes."

"Two sections," Max says, unwrapping another chocolate bar.

"And, anyhow, Max is in genius math and I'm in dummy math," Alex says.

"It's not genius math," Max says. His voice has become so indistinct that I feel as though at any moment it may disappear entirely, and we will have to read his lips on the rare occasions when he speaks.

"When we get to the high school it's going to be completely bogus, because every English teacher will be like, you're Ruby's brother?"

"No, they won't."

Max mutters. He has a marshmallow in his mouth. "What?" Alex says.

"You're the favorite," he says.

"Me?" Alex says.

"Ruby," says Max.

"Oh, don't be stupid, Max," she says.

Ruby drops her eyes to her lap and frowns. I can tell she doesn't believe what she is saying. She's scratching at something on her painter's pants, probably a blot of chocolate.

"Bullshit," Alex says.

"You'd better not let anyone hear you talk like that."

"You say it all the time."

"I do not say it all the time," Ruby says. "I use profanity very little, actually, compared to most people I know. And I'm three years older than you."

"It's because you're a girl," says Max.

"That's sexist," Ruby says primly. "Why shouldn't women swear as much as men do?"

"Not the swearing thing. The favorite thing."

"It's because she's the oldest," Alex says.

"It's not true," Ruby says.

It is, in a way. I'm often distressed by the difference between my feelings for Ruby and those I have for her brothers. Perhaps it's because she's the oldest, and I was so young, and I discovered myself as I learned to know her, discovered that I could do without sleep, without stimulation, could subvert myself to a greater good. I felt triumphant when I survived her colic, her fall from the bed, the morning she caught her tiny pink finger in a closet door.

But sometimes I think part of the problem is that I've never really seen the boys as two distinct people. I hadn't even known I was expecting twins until the very end of the pregnancy. Ruby had been a large baby—"nine pounds," I once told the therapist desperately, when her weight was down to ninety, as though that would show there had been some terrible mistake—and the enormous ovoid belly that preceded me into every room could be explained away until we heard the dissonant heartbeats.

It's hard to care for two infants at once—to nurse them, comfort them, make certain you know each of them individually. I used the word *wait* so often. Nancy says that I'm fooling myself, that she never gave Sarah and Bob the time she gave Fred, her firstborn, that it would have been the same had Alex and Max been born three years apart. But she's wrong, in part because I can't tell her what I really feel—that in some peculiar and shameful way I think of my sons as two halves of a single whole, as though they were Siamese twins inextricably joined together by their differences. I wonder if that's the reason they seem to have moved to opposite ends of the gene pool, become the athlete and the artist, the conventional and the quirky, whether I'm responsible for the fact that Alex is almost annoyingly energetic and Max is sinking deeper into a pit of torpor. Each occupies the place not taken up by the other.

"Okay, so which parent is your favorite?" says Alex, and my throat closes.

"Oh, please," Ruby says wearily. "That's stupider than the other." I realize that, like a small child, I am thinking, Pick me, pick me, and then I'm ashamed of myself. Poor Glen, spending day after day gently lifting bifocals onto the seamed faces of retirees, asking wriggling kindergarteners to read the fourth line on the chart, comforting teary teenage girls who have just been told they need glasses for the classroom, who has uncomplainingly taught skating and bike riding while I waved from a window, who cried in the delivery rooms and drove cautiously to the ER even when there was blood and screaming—he deserves to be more than first runner-up. He's a good man, a good husband and father, and I emphasize this extravagantly for the sake of the kids. "Look at your father out there," I say when he throws a thumbs-up as he whizzes by on skis. "Your father did that surgery," I say when Ruby comes home from school and narrates the miracle of some girl seeing the board without glasses for the first time in her life. "We'll eat when your father gets home," I say when they're swarming the kitchen, opening and closing the refrigerator door as though, like a fairy-tale cave, the contents will have magically changed in the past three minutes. And in making him central to their existence, and their happiness, perhaps I am doing the same for myself. I can't quite recall, or evoke, that strange and powerful feeling that made me yearn to be with him every moment of every day, that made me think "till death do us part" sounded wonderful instead of simply like a very, very long time.

"No, but, like, if the house was on fire would you save Mom or Dad?" Alex insists.

"I would save Max, because he wouldn't even notice that anything was wrong," Ruby says, licking her fingers like a cat.

Max yawns, and the other two laugh.

Pick me, a voice inside cries again, and then the three of them look up as one. I see the resemblance: the glossy hair, although Alex's is trimmed short and Max's is too long now; the dark brown eyes, although Ruby's tilt up at the corners like my own do. They make her look flirtatious, along with the habit of ducking her head and looking up through her lashes. That look has led to many misunderstandings, and a number of Kiernan's thunderstorm rages.

All three of them smile—even Max, a little bit—and the front door slams shut with the whine of stiff hinges. "Didn't anyone notice this poor old dog sitting by the door?" Glen says, and I hear Ginger's toenails on the tile, and then the soft rhythm of her drinking.

"We never use the front door," Ruby says. "Ginger knows that."

"She didn't bark," says Alex. "She needs to bark if she wants us to let her in."

"She never barks, do you, Ging? She doesn't want to put anyone out. She is the perfect puppy, the most perfect puppy ever in the whole wide world." Ruby is using her dog voice, which is not dissimiliar to her baby voice.

"Dad," says Alex, "which kid is your favorite?"

They all grin. This is a setup question. Glen has had the same answer since they first asked this question on a family trip to visit their grandparents, when Ruby was eight and the boys were five.

"Ruby is my favorite on Sundays and Thursdays, Max is my favorite on Mondays and Fridays, and you are my favorite on Tuesdays and Saturdays."

A silence, with the sound of Ginger panting, then the familiar coda: "And on Wednesdays I can't stand any of you."

"That is so old," Alex says, but he is still smiling. He is glad he didn't have to choose between us. One tree, two trunks. That is what we are to our children. And that is the way I will make certain it stays.

It is that dolphin-gray hour just before sunup, and there is the sound of wailing from outside. In the first fuzzy moments of waking, I think it's that tom cat from the house behind us, but there's a powerful emotional undertone to it, and finally I realize that it's someone repeating a word: No, no, no, no, high-pitched and terrible.

"What the hell?" Glen says.

I look outside onto the lawn. Kiernan is standing looking up at Ruby's window, his hair askew, his bow tie a tired snarl of satin hanging around his thin neck. He sways, so that it looks as though he is being buffeted by the wind, although it is a still morning. He is crying, so that the consonants flatten and disappear.

"It's Kiernan," I say, taking my robe from the foot of the bed.

"I don't care if it's the president of the United States. If that noise doesn't stop, I'm calling the police."

"Go back to sleep," I say.

The last I saw of Ruby and her friends was just after 2 A.M., when a big group had come back to our house to have breakfast after the prom was over. Rachel's date had disappeared. The girls had had to convince Rachel not to call him, although it was unclear whether it would be to beg him to come back or to tell him that he was the lowest and should expect never to be acknowledged again.

I knew better than to ask about this as I stood at the stove, scrambling eggs. Rachel's mascara was a dirty shadow beneath her eyes, and I heard Sarah say "That is so not acceptable" several times in a peremptory tone much like her mother's.

"The DJ sucked a big one," one of the boys said, too loudly, and I smelled something sweet and yet astringent—maybe bourbon— on his breath.

"Dude," Kiernan said reproachfully.

"Sorry."

Ruby's glossy head was bent over Ginger, who had been given special dispensation to leave her kennel in the middle of the night. Eric was passing bits of corn muffin under the table. "You're not supposed to feed her," said Sarah. They already acted like a long-married couple.

At eight o'clock, burnished to a fine sheen, flawless, untouched, they had tolerated photographs in the front yard. Sarah wore a white strapless dress, her shoulders a sharp muscular shelf above the band of eyelet. Rachel had on a black satin halter dress too old and too snug for her. Kiernan had brought Ruby a beautiful nosegay, tiny roses of a bright pink that matched the obi belt. He bowed ceremonially as he handed it to her, and when he lifted his head his eyes were yearning, pleading. I've seen his father, Kevin, with that same look. "Dance with me?" he'd said once when we were all younger, at a backyard party by the Donahues' pool. Glen, who doesn't like to dance, had watched the two of us as we jitterbugged barefoot. He's a good dancer, Kevin Donahue, I'll give him that. Ruby says Kiernan is a good dancer, too.

By the time the stretch SUV had delivered all of them back to the house for breakfast, Sarah's hair had begun to slip out of its upsweep in the back, and she had a faint spot on one side of her dress. Rachel's gown was creased from sitting through the banquet-hall dinner of prime rib and mashed potatoes, and, I suspected, watching her date dance with others while she sat alone.

Kiernan, too, looked as though the evening had been a disaster. His suit was streaked with dirt in spots, and he sat at one end of the long table in the kitchen, legs spread, arms crossed on his chest, eyes down. "No thank you, Mommy," Ruby had said when I put a plate of eggs in front of her. The edges of her roses had begun their slow, sad deterioration.

Glen thinks I am overinvolved with our children's inner lives, especially Ruby's. Before Ruby stopped eating during freshman year, he used to complain loudly that his parents never worried, and he was right. Neither did mine. Our children still find it astonishing that my father died and no one went to a therapist. Instead, my brother, Richard, turned into an adult overnight, standing at the head of an oak casket with his uncles behind him. He also became one of the least emotional people on earth, which I suppose may be something of an advantage for an oncologist. His patients die, and he prevails. Everything, as they say, is a trade-off.

The wailing rises and falls from outside. "Somebody has to talk sense to that kid," Glen says through clenched teeth. "Some of us have to get up for work." I almost reply, "Both of us do," but decide this is not the moment. Glen throws the covers aside. "You cannot go out there," I hiss. "I'm going to take a shower," he says.

The grass is cold and wet on my bare feet. I fold my arms over my chest, conscious of the fact that I am wearing only my nightclothes. As I come outside, the noise stops, and the early-morning silence is resonant with nothing in it. A light goes on in our neighbor's kitchen. He is a widower who liked our children better when they were small and went to bed at eight o'clock.

Kiernan is sitting cross-legged on the grass. His tuxedo jacket is thrown over one of the wooden chairs in the backyard. The knees of his pants are sodden. I pat him on the shoulder. His face is all puckers, the way it was when he was little and he'd skin a knee and his mother would pour peroxide on it. "This will hurt," Deborah always said, as though knowing would make it better, when it only made him cry more. First the promise of hurt, then the hurt itself.

He sobs into his hands. His emotions are adult, his behavior childish. And then I realize that his emotions aren't really adult at all. They're too unguarded, too undiluted. In the words of Ruby Latham past, they are too authentic. If he were forty, and this woman he loves had left him, he would never sit in her yard and sob. He would say she'd always been a bitch, never been much. Or he would get drunk and try to turn another woman into her in a bar and then in bed. Or he would work too many hours, or play too much golf, or find some other way to swallow whatever he was feeling, preferring a rock in his gullet to his heart on his sleeve, preferring anger to grief, resentment to bereavement. Anything but this, this undisguised despair.

"Honey, I think it's time for you to go home," I say softly. Kiernan puts his arms around my legs and presses his face against the side of my knee. I can feel him shaking beneath my flattened palm. I remember when I first saw his little moon face, when the Donahues moved in next door to us, when we all lived in smaller houses, little Cape Cods across town. "Hi!" he'd chirped, standing in a break in the scraggly hedge fence between the yards. "My mommy says I can play with you. This is my new house. I have a green room." Even then his eyes had followed Ruby around the yard as she danced in her pink tutu, her eyes half closed, singing to herself, conspicuously ignoring him.

They had both been ready to enter kindergarten. The twins were toddlers, and Deborah was pregnant and not certain that she was happy about it. Long afternoons we sat on her back deck drinking iced tea and giving the kids Popsicles. Instead of bathing them all, we let the sticky stuff wash off in the shallow end of the pool, let Kiernan and Ruby paddle down to the diving board in their bright-colored tubes. How lonely we would have been without each other!

And all those years later, this: Kiernan sobbing into the muted florals of my robe, the smell of alcohol coming off him like a disinfectant, a smear on his tuxedo shirt. He had always been an emotional little boy, prodding dead birds with his lip trembling, or stamping into the house, head lowered, if he were teased too much. I had warned Ruby about the strength of his feelings when they were much younger, before they became more than friends. I had warned her that the pendulum of his emotions swung wide. "Oh, Mommy, Kiernan? Like kissing my brothers," she'd said in eighth grade. But then she'd become an injured bird herself, and Kiernan had helped her heal, heal so well that she had flown away.

"I love her so much," Kiernan says, his words slurred by sorrow, and drunkenness, too, so that it's hard to understand him.

"You'll feel better after you get some sleep," I say.

He looks up at me and squints. "You need to talk to her," he cries, loudly. "She'll listen to you. You tell her this is a mistake. A big mistake." He makes the word last forever, and his head drops again. "She's making a big mistake," he says into his hands.

"Let's get you home, Kiernan," I say.

"Tell her!" he screams suddenly, and the sound echoes off the house, the ridge, the sky.

"That's enough," I say sharply. "You need to go home."

He slumps over, elbows on knees, head down. "I love her so much. You tell her."

The sun crests over the edge of the pumping station on the hill, turning its bricks from brown to red the way it does to Ruby's hair, and I realize I am afraid to move. Kiernan will finish his senior year in high school, and he will go away to college, and he will become something fine and true: a beloved teacher, perhaps, or the sort of lawyer who represents the indigent. He will have a life in which this one seems merely like the sort of dream that is vivid at the moment of waking and has vanished by the time you've had your coffee. But this day my daughter has cast him out of the closest thing to paradise he has known, our kitchen. To us it seems so ordinary, so little to have, but I have seen in his eyes, and in Rachel's, too, the glitter of yearning, and felt sad that the best we could offer was a kind of borrowing. Kiernan had believed he could turn the borrowing into ownership. And from time to time as he grows older, he will remember Ruby Latham, and how he loved her, and how he lost her. Every other girl will have a Ruby ghost hovering over her without her knowing it.

When I go into the house, Glen is sitting at the table, eating cereal. I expect him to chide me for the time I've spent standing barefoot on the lawn, for my failure to simply put my foot down, which is an expression handed down from his father to him and well worn in our house. Instead, he looks up briefly and makes a rueful little curve of the corner of his mouth. "Poor guy," he says. There was a Ruby Latham in Glen's life, too, a girl with whom he went to high school named Betsy. We ran into her once when we were first married, and I could feel the push of the past as she and my husband talked in front of his parents' house. It goes without saying that she looked a bit like me. Or I like her.

The coffeemaker comes on with its customary click, and I put on water for oatmeal. Glen steps outside and in a moment I hear a

car door slam. I realize that my husband, always practical, had figured out that Kiernan had no way to get home and had taken him
in the car. I hope he won't tell Kiernan that he will get over it.
Later, Glen says that they didn't speak at all, except once when
Kiernan asked him to pull over. Even as he threw up at the curb of
the Sunoco station, Kiernan was still crying.

Upstairs, Ruby has climbed into our bed the way she did when
she was small and there was a storm. "I feel like a terrible person,"
she whispers, her voice breaking, and I know she does, and I know,
too, that there is some part of her that is going to enjoy this, enjoy
being so beloved and so mourned. I go into the bathroom and
when I emerge she is sound asleep, a long piece of hair twisted
around her finger. Down on the lawn, there is some flattened grass
where Kiernan sat, and the pale blue tuxedo jacket left behind.

Ruby's writing program begins the week after school ends. The night before she leaves, Sarah and Rachel crowd into her bed for a sleepover. "Why do they call it a sleepover when they never sleep?" grumbles Glen, who says this at least five or six times a year. In the morning they gather in the kitchen and weep, but it is the pleasurable weeping of girls to whom nothing really bad is happening. Ruby doesn't cry. She's been quiet and sad since the night of the prom. I saw her smile genuinely only once, when at the awards assembly she won the prize for writing, a red Webster's dictionary with her name embossed on the front cover.

"Kiernan's mom told my mom that it will turn out that this is the best thing that ever happened to him, that he needs a fresh start," Rachel says while Ruby is upstairs getting her bags.

"God, Rachel, you have the world's biggest mouth," Sarah replies. Outside in the driveway, the three girls hug. "I'll find you a surfer guy in California after I find one for myself," says Rachel, who is spending the summer with her father.

"You just be careful," Ruby replies.

"Always," Rachel says, putting Ruby's bags into the back of the car while Sarah and Ruby exchange glances over her bent head.

"Are you worried about Rachel?" I ask as we drive out of town.

"I'm always worried about Rachel," Ruby says absently.

She is mostly silent for the rest of the drive, looking out the window, playing with her hair, bundling it up, taking it down. She is tolerating the classical-music station. She's nervous, I know—not that she will feel out of place but, oddly, that she won't, that she is now the strange and beautiful girl in the vintage housedresses whose story takes up the front third of the literary magazine, and that this summer she will find herself among dozens such, and lose her sense of determined self-invention. It's been several years since she began to develop this assured persona, and in retrospect it seems that I didn't handle it well at the beginning without really understanding that I was handling anything at all. There was a period just before I turned forty when I grew my hair and traded my pants and sweaters for dresses that swirled atop my knees. "You're wearing that?" Ruby had said one night, wrinkling her nose.

"What's wrong with this?"

"It would be fine if you were my age," she said.

Was I ever her age? Sometimes I put her music on in the car and step hard on the gas and I can feel it from somewhere deep in my body, a double yellow line atop the asphalt egging you on and a bass beat throbbing in your midsection, that feeling of being young. But I was never that girl when I truly had the chance. My mother liked everything just so, and neither my brother nor I wanted to rattle her. There are two kinds of tempers, hot and cold. The second is worse. My mother had a cold temper, silent and hard. I was never pierced or inked, never wore strange jewelry or provocative clothes. I went to the prom with a boyfriend who was as much an accessory as a person. Our relationship faltered when I was at college and ran out of stamps for my increasingly infrequent letters. My senior year at a party I met Glen, who was already in med school and was visiting one of his brothers. The two men walked me back to the shabby garden apartment I was sharing with Alice and two other friends, and then they flipped a coin to determine who would call me in the morning. Whenever Glen's family gathers for holidays, his brother Doug will flip a quarter in the air and slam his hand over it. "Too late, Dougie," Glen likes to say. Sometimes I remind myself that I almost skipped the party, that I almost went to a different college, that the whim of a minute could have changed everything and everyone. Our lives, so settled, so specific, are built on happenstance.

Ruby knows that I majored in English, and she once asked why I had not decided to be a writer myself. "I just found it way too hard," I'd said. She looked away. It seemed that the notion that there was something she could do that I could not was disconcerting. "How do you know what to write about?" Rachel once asked her when the girls had read aloud a story Ruby had written. "I just know," she replied.

The college at which Ruby will spend the summer looks nothing like the large state university where I went to school. It is designed along familiar lines: iron gates, stone columns, red brick, a quad with some old-growth trees. Ruby says there is air-conditioning in the dorms and frozen yogurt in the dining hall. Her roommate is a girl from New York City named Jacqui LeBoutillier. "I am deeply jealous of her name," Ruby had told Sarah and Rachel. "I think you would just take seriously anything written by someone with that name." It turns out that both Ruby and Jacqui like Robert Lowell, Flannery O'Connor, vintage shops, and almond butter.

This morning, before we left, there was a bag at our back door, and inside was a collection of Lowell's poems called *Life Studies*. Ruby picked it up and paged through it, put it down on the table amid the dishes, the mugs, and the papers. "Are you going to take that?" I'd asked as I grabbed my keys. "I already have it," Ruby said. "I don't know how anyone could not know that I already have it." Poor Kiernan. He can't seem to do anything right.

When your children are away for the summer, public expectations are twofold. Other mothers assume you will feel incomplete or liberated, depending on their own situations. I feel neither. I feel that my children need to be gone this summer, Ruby to grow, Max to heal, Alex—well, because the other two will be away.

Glen always feels their absence more than I do. "Wow!" he says on the first night that all three are gone. "It's really quiet in this house." He suggests that we go out to eat, take in a movie, although he doesn't really like to go to restaurants, and he's rarely entertained by anything at the multiplex. But after a day or two he settles into his usual routines, and I into mine. The other fantasy of childless summers is romance for the long-married, epic sex, and household nudity. Once I hinted at this to Nancy, at the missed opportunities because Fred and Bob and Sarah all stayed home for the summer, and she rolled her eyes and said, "The kitchen-floor thing? Please. Spare me."

Instead of leisure I'll be out at work, in yards and gardens, long after the time I'm usually home. This is the busiest time of year for me: endless pruning, planting, weeding, listening to whining from homeowners who are enraged at the vagaries of nature, the appetites of Japanese beetles, the ravenous deer, the unreliable weather that brings down trees with a single gusty storm or cripples tender flowers with a searing sun.

After I drop Ruby off at the dorm I drive three hours home,

over roller-coaster roads, stopping to oversee the work at a week-end place outside town. "How we doing here?" I ask Rickie. The man we're working for cleared a hilltop with a shockingly beauti-ful view of a string of mountains and valleys so that he could build a gargantuan faux cabin. His builder bulldozed dozens of trees, and now the owner wants to replace them. He is not a patient man—he is apparently one of those people who make money by making money, one of those people whose work I don't understand and don't care to—and he likes big trees. He doesn't want anything to grow; he wants it to appear. I hate the notion; what I love about my work, and I suppose my life, is the slow inevitable progression. I count my years in small bushes grown broad, climbing vines that snake over fences and roofs, saplings that are spreading trees.

"We got the English walnuts," Rickie says. "They're really nice. But we're going to have to work out the watering. I'm hoping we'll get some good rain the next couple of days. Plus, we're down one guy. Luis took off."

"Aw, no," I say. "We can't afford to be shorthanded right now. Can you get me a couple of other guys?"

"I got three college prospects home for the summer. One used to be a stoner, one worked for the quarry last summer and only lasted a week because he says he pulled something in his shoulder, and one is apparently your pal Nancy's oldest kid."

"Fred? What?" I dial my cell phone and wait. "Nance? Is Fred looking for a job? Why didn't you say anything? Oh, for God's sake—well, of course. Of course. Is he over his wisdom teeth? Tell him it's a done deal. No, I'll tell him. I'll call him now. Or have him call me." I snap the phone shut. "You'll love Fred," I tell Rickie. "You know the type—former three-sport athlete, never com-plains, always on time."

"That'll be a nice change," Rickie says. "Look, go home. We're almost done here. We'll clean up and drop the guys off. I'll reset the irrigation system in the morning."

I pull into our driveway and the phone rings. It's Alice, and I sigh. Heat rash? Allergies? Instead she says, "Hey, babe, you okay?" Somewhere she has written down that today was the day I was to drop Ruby off. Having a child has both softened her center and made her sharper at the edges.

"I'm fine," I say. "It's an amazing moment, watching her get ready to be whoever she's going to become."

"I'm terrified just thinking about it, and my kid's only three," Alice says. "Remember us?"

"I remember you. I can't really remember me. Was I as vague as I think I was?"

"Oh, come on. You were so calm and sane. Like your life, no surprise. I was the one who had delusions of grandeur and ricocheted around for all those years before I got it right. Or semi-right."

"How is the boy king?"

"He's with my parents. My mother says she's sick of hearing me talk about sunscreen, and that she raised five kids without it. Promise me we'll be deeply, deeply critical when we're grandparents. Not to the kids, because then they'll shun us and withhold our grandchildren and ruin our lives. But when we talk to each other."

"Promise."

Max is at the kitchen table when I go inside, eating ice cream from the container. "Did you have dinner?" I ask, opening the fridge.

"Yes?" he says.

I can't help it, I start to laugh. "Oh, Maxie, Maxie, what in the world is going to become of you?" I say, and suddenly his face falls.

"Don't say that, Mom," he says.

"Oh, sweetie, it wasn't existential. I was just fooling around. Where's Alex?"

"Ben's?" he says. The question mark goes everywhere with him nowadays.

"Are you packed?"

"Sort of."

"Is Alex packed?"

"Sort of."

I take a spoon to the ice cream. It's the kind with cookie dough in it, and all the cookie dough has been picked out. "It was like that already," Max says as I dig around. "I swear."

"Where's your father?"

"You have a lot of questions."

"You can say that again."

"You have a lot of questions."

I put the ice cream in the freezer. "How early can we leave to-morrow?" Max asks. Maxie, Maxie, finally heading to where he feels at home. I run my hands through his shaggy hair, kiss the back of his bristly boy-man neck, wrap my arms around him. He looks like a dandelion, with his skinny stem and his ruffled head. Once he used to run to hug me; now he suffers me to hug him.

"As early as you want," I reply.

"Dad's asleep in the den," he says.

Right after the Fourth of July we drive Alex to camp, although Olivia and her husband have offered to take him along with Ben. The two boys run off together, and we have to chase them for the farewell kiss. The soccer field is already full. Olivia is a bit weepy. "There are three more at home just like that," her husband, Ted, says, reaching for her hand. She sniffs, then smiles, but the smile won't hold. "Ridiculous," she says to herself in her clipped English voice, but even that sounds uncertain.

"They'll all be gone before you know it," Glen says, as though that is a helpful observation.

"Yeah, you people with older kids always say that," Ted says. "Want to borrow ours?"

On the ride home, I'm making a shopping list in my head when I realize that we're passing the motel where my guys live. A sign that says ROOMS teeters atop a metal stanchion. I've rarely been there. Once one of the men was ill and wouldn't see a doctor, and I brought one of Glen's friends out to examine him. Once the police called me because there had been a fight, and I told the men, arranged in a small knot in the gravel parking lot, that I couldn't employ workers who made trouble. Rickie translated as the men looked down at the toes of their work boots, their arms folded over their grubby T-shirts. They have one rusty pickup truck among eight of them, five who work for me and three others who help out at a dairy farm. I have no idea how they manage groceries or laundry.

From inside the motel I hear music, and I listen for some pleasant Mexican song, a plucked guitar, a tambourine. Instead I hear hard rock, and the rumble of faintly raucous voices. It's after seven, and they have had enough time to start drinking in that way men do when they are really tired, which is not a way I want to interrupt.

"I worry about the guys who work for us," I say to Glen.

He slows slightly and looks at the building. It could not look more cheerless if it were a prison. In fact, compared with this, the county jail looks country-club. In spring, the yellow rockets of forsythia obscure the razor wire.

"I don't know what to tell you," Glen says. "You need the hands. They need the cash. It's mutually advantageous."

Once José told me that to visit his daughters he drove through the night in January and June to a Texas town near the Mexican border. Each day the girls would arrive in his motel room, and they would play video games at the local diner or go to an amusement park nearby. The girls had special identification papers so they could attend school in the Texas town and go home each afternoon to their mother in Mexico. Two years before, after José had spent only two days with them, the immigration guards at the crossing said, "It's school vacation this week, isn't it?" The next day the girls stayed on the other side with their mother and waved at José, and the day after that he drove north again, back to the ski resort where my guys work in the winter, running snow blowers, cleaning concession stalls.

Whenever I see him at the work site I think of this, particularly with our children away. Without them the days drag and fly, ponderous and yet gone before we even have a chance to notice them. "Is today Wednesday?" I sometimes say at the breakfast table, peering at the top of the paper to check. Glen goes to a three-day conference on laser surgery in Boston and brings me back a necklace I don't like. "It's gorgeous!" I say. I go to an extension service seminar at the university on pest control and buy ladybugs and nesting boxes. I wonder if this is what the rest of my life will be like.

Nancy and Bill have a barbecue, and everyone gets a little lit on vodka gimlets. The whole house smells like lime. "A retro drink," Bill says as he passes them around. In the kitchen a group of women gather around the table, picking at a plate of cold shrimp. The men are in the backyard. "Warming themselves in the flame of the gas grill," Nancy says, raising her eyebrows. Fred is in the den watching a baseball game. "How's it going at work?" I ask him as I meander in.

"He's sore as hell, I can tell you that," Nancy says, coming up behind me and handing me a fresh drink.

"Thanks, Mom," Fred says. "Mrs. Latham asks me a question, and you answer. It's like ventriloquism."

"How's it going?" I repeat. I can see part of the answer: his forearms are covered with scratches and bruises.

"I'm okay," he says.

"The guys are being tolerant?"

"I mean, let's be real," Fred says. "I'm the resident gringo. They think you're paying me double what they make."

"They told you that?"

"They talked about it the first day. None of them know I speak Spanish."

Fred spent a semester and a summer in a village two hours from Barcelona. Nancy told me that he's become so fluent in Spanish that at college he's tutoring kids in a housing project full of new immigrants.

"Yeah, and now I'm stuck," Fred says. "I start to talk to them, they'll remember that they said stuff in front of me the first couple of days that maybe they shouldn't have said. They'll figure I narced them out."

"I think once high school is over that term no longer applies," Nancy says.

"Whatever. I should have just used my Spanish from the beginning. *Buenos dias* from the get-go, you know?" He rises gingerly to his feet. Fred has always been fit, but there's running-five-miles-in-expensive-shoes fit, and there's enlarging-a-six-foot-hole-with-a-shovel fit.

When we hear the shower running above us, Nancy says, "You're not paying him any more than the others, are you?"

"How can you of all people ask me that?"

"Spare me, Saint Mary Beth. He's my son, you're my friend."

"Everyone's making fifteen dollars an hour." I stop, multiply, check my math. "God, I'm a terrible person, aren't I? That's six hundred a week."

"You're right. Your landscapers are being paid only what the teachers at the elementary school make." Nancy looks sideways, then down. When she wants to say something unpleasant, it is always absolutely clear. "What?" I ask.

"Besides, at least one of them was ripping you off. The one who quit? He took all those plants at that big new place on Winding Way. Apparently, they all know it. Three truckloads' worth. He sold it all to some nursery."

"Luis? You're kidding? He seemed like such a good guy."

"Apparently not. Are you going to tell the police?"

I envision having my remaining workers questioned, having them vanish and leaving all my jobs undone. I feel ill, as though I had a party at my home and someone stole from my jewelry box or my medicine cabinet, except that I have never even invited my workers to my home for a party, not once. And now I never will. I gave them an end-of-season party last year, with pizza and beer, but it was at a job site, and I never thought about how dirty their hands would be, after a day of work, until I watched them scrub at them ineffectually with paper napkins.

"Food's ready!" Bill calls from the kitchen. We join the men outside. "I heard someone may rent the Donahue house," one of the women says. "Apparently, Deborah's mother is ill and she's moved up to her mother's place to take care of her."

Glen looks across the patio at me. I take a gulp of my drink and promise myself that it will be my last. I know that Deborah's mother lives in a little town about an hour north of us. I'd been there a couple of times with the kids when Kiernan and Ruby were eight. Deborah had moved in with her mother then, too, not because her mother was ill but because Deborah was. "A complete breakdown," Kevin whispered. "Catatonic." Her mother's house was small, and we sat outside on a porch swing while the kids played on the scrubby front lawn. The light faded and the sun set while I talked about nothing and Deborah stared at the street. Her hands shook in her lap. Kevin told me as we walked to my car that it was because of the medication. "She really needs you," he'd said, holding my hand. Kiernan stood at his side, and I pulled my hand away. "Daddy, when are we going back to our own house?" Kiernan said.

They'd rented out their own house while they were away, then later sold it, then bought another and moved back to town. Kiernan was twelve when they moved back. Deborah had thrown her husband out the following year, screaming at him late at night on the lawn as the neighbors stood behind their curtains and listened. For a while, the episode hurt Deborah's business. When the kids were young, she and Kevin opened a coffee shop on Main Street; he handled the finances and she did all the baking. They sold it when they moved north, and when Deborah came back she set herself up making wedding cakes. The cakes were astonishing things, with quince branches of spun sugar circling the layers or calla lilies made of frosting in a lifelike bunch on the top. But for a few months people thought it was bad luck to buy a wedding cake from a woman who had tried to hit her husband with her son's Wiffle bat. "Can you ever keep it in your goddamn pants?" she had screamed, so that everyone on the block heard. Kiernan heard, too, and then he heard it again from the boys at school. Ruby was sweet to him then.

"A couple of those guys are going to go to the Keys to go sportfishing," Glen says as we walk home from the barbecue. "I might go."

"You don't like to fish."

"I don't?" Glen says, making a crazy face, and we both laugh, and then because we're drunk and our kids are away and it seems like the obvious thing to do, we go home and have sex. Neither of us seems to want to do it much anymore, but when we do it's fine. I do things I've been doing for years. He does, too. They still work. They just seem a little beside the point, like rereading a book for the sixth time. Another thing that I could never have imagined when I was Ruby's age, when my boyfriend would edge his fingers up inside the leg of my shorts and my knees would fall open like a physical reflex.

The next morning, Glen smiles at himself as he shaves. "I hope the kids are okay," he says at breakfast, as though to show that we are interested in the same things.

We both know that's not true. Maybe it's not even important. Sometimes, driving home from a job in the gloomy summer dusk, shivering in the air-conditioning, I find myself crying for reasons that are overwhelming and mysterious. When I was young, my mother used to stay up to watch old movies on television, and when I crept down the stairs, my legs scissoring my nightgown into a trap around my thin calves, I could peek through a narrow sliver of banister and see her hunched forward on the couch, crumpled tissues on the table like white carnations. She cried at *Stella Dallas, Mildred Pierce, Dark Victory, Waterloo Bridge.* I think she used the movies as a plausible excuse to weep in a way that would have seemed indulgent to her otherwise. Her husband had died, leaving her with a houseful of ashtrays, two young children, and enough life insurance to throw a dignified funeral and pay off a five-year-old car. But she still somehow believed she needed to hitch her grief to someone else's tragedy.

I have no excuse for my own tears. In the way of women my age, I increasingly count my blessings aloud, as though if other people acknowledge them they'll be enough: three wonderful children, a long and happy marriage, good home, pleasurable work. And if below the surface I sense that one child is poised to flee and another is miserable, that my husband and I trade public pleasantries and private minutiae, that my work depends on the labor of men who think I'm cheating them—none of that is to be dwelled on. Besides, none of that has anything to do with my tears. If I were pressed, I would have to say that they are the symptom of some great loneliness, as free-floating and untethered to everyday life as a tornado is to the usual weather. It whirls through, ripping and tearing, and then I'm in the parking lot of the supermarket, wiping my eyes, replacing my sunglasses, buying fish and greens for that night's dinner. If anyone asks how things are, I say what we all say: fine, good, great, terrific, wonderful.

Even among women, we don't speak of this. Only once did I catch Nancy, sitting on her patio with a glass of wine as the first leaves did a whirligig from the elm shadowing the yard. Fred had just left for college, and Sarah was at swim practice. I said, "Oh, Nance, Thanksgiving will be here before you know it." But when she turned her face to me her eyes were blank, as though she couldn't understand what I had just said. The next day when we drove to a brunch together she said, tartly, "At least you didn't ask if I was having my period. When I was a teenager, I thought women were only allowed to cry every twenty-eight days."

How foolish we are sometimes. When we were first together, I once said to Glen, my hand on his thigh in that way that doesn't survive marriage, "Do you ever just cry for no reason?" We were so alike, so compatible. Everyone said so.

"I don't think so," he said, his face creased with thought. "I can't remember ever doing that." Now I wouldn't think twice about that response. Now I wouldn't even ask.

"How was your day?" I ask.

"Fine," Glen says. "Did you have someone take a look at the roof?"

"They're coming tomorrow," I say. "Do you want some wine before dinner?"

"I think I'll have a beer," he replies.

What if I were to tell him that that night, driving home late from weeding a garden, heading into a line of darkening pink and mauve where the sun had settled below the ridgeline, I had sobbed as though brokenhearted. "Why?" he would have said, and what would I tell him? Could I sit opposite this open-faced man, with his pink cheeks and his warm brown eyes (not clinically significant), and say, "Loneliness?" Worse still, what if he said that he had done the same, felt the same? Then where would we all be?

"There's a six-pack in the fridge," I say, taking dill from the crisper drawer.

On and off during July, we've gotten hang-up calls in the evening. "Hello," I say, and then, louder, with a sharp edge of anger, "Hello?" There are three in quick succession one night in late July. Glen gets the third as we are undressing for bed and says, "Next time we call the police." The fourth call comes just after eleven and wakes us both. "What?" Glen says like an expletive, sitting up. The phone is on my side of the bed.

"Mom, don't freak out," Max says in a shaky voice, and I hear noise in the background and make out the symphonic blare of a hospital, a sound still familiar from Glen's residency.

"I'm so sorry he got you on the phone before I did," says the camp director, who calls as Glen and I are deciding which of us will make the long drive.

Max has fallen from a tree. His arm is broken. The X-rays look bad. Glen calls our orthopedic surgeon.

"No, it's Max, not Alex," I hear him say. Alex has separated his shoulder, broken his collarbone, and had his knee repaired. Max has had stitches only once. "This is the second time he's fallen out of a tree," I say to Glen.

I drive through the night, a cup of bitter coffee from the gas station beside me. In the hospital waiting area Max is slumped in a chair, his arm in a sling, a twitchy young man who I assume is a counselor beside him.

"Hey, honey," I say, sitting next to him and putting my arm around his shoulder. There are grubby paths on his cheeks from tears. The counselor leaves for the bathroom.

"I have to go home, don't I?"

He does. His things are already packed. At the steps to his ramshackle cabin stands a tiny girl, a little Tinkerbell of a person, with hair dyed a horrible harsh black. She has a diamond on one side of her nostril. Max disappears around the side of the cabin with her while I load the car with his duffel bags and his boxes of drumsticks. Despite the arm and the tears, I'm thrilled. Max has a real girlfriend. They embrace in the shadow of the cabin, and I look away.

"You should come visit us," I say, turning as we get into the car, and the girl sobs by the passenger door.

"Mom, chill," Max mutters.

The next day the orthopedic surgeon repairs the arm, which has broken in a way that requires a pin. I can tell by Max's breathing, short and shallow, that he's afraid. His hair is almost to his shoulders, and his shoulders are squaring off in a way that looks familiar, that reminds me of Glen. But once the sedative has taken effect and his full lower lip has relaxed, he looks almost exactly as he did when he was a toddler, waking on a summer day like this one, his eyelids heavy over his dark eyes, his small bandy chest glossy with sweat.

"I love you, baby boy," I whisper as they wheel him away.

"Love you, too, Mom," he whispers back.

It is almost the last nice thing he says to me for the rest of the summer. It is almost the last thing he says to me for the rest of the summer. He lies on the couch in the den, watching nonsense TV, ignoring the stack of required school reading I've put on an end table. He grows thin, grows thinner, and becomes sullen and sad. The girlfriend's cell phone doesn't work at camp, and when she calls from the pay phones by the canteen he can hear the raucous sounds of the life he's missing. Dishes pile up on the coffee table beside him, and he leaves them there until someone else puts them in the sink.

"He's not a paraplegic," Glen hisses angrily one evening in the kitchen.

"He'll hear you."

"I hope he does," replies Glen.

"I hate my life," Max says one day as I leave for work. It's a sentiment I've heard from Ruby before, but Max says it as though he really means it. I call the therapist who helped Ruby to see if she knows someone for Max.

"He's depressed?" she asks.

"I'm no expert, but I would say yes." Max has no writing on his cast. What could be more depressing than that? The fingers curling out of the plaster look as though they had been living in some underground burrow, as though, exposed to direct sunlight, they would shrivel.

"Any suicidal thoughts?" the therapist asks.

"Do kids who have suicidal thoughts share them with their parents?" I say angrily. I was always angry when she was treating Ruby, too, always sure she was passing judgment on us, on our family, on our happiness. Always afraid of what she was going to say.

"Come to work with me," I say to Max. "You'll feel better if you get some fresh air." I have become Glen's father, who thinks and talks always in clichés: A little hard work never hurt anyone. Make hay while the sun shines. Early to bed, early to rise.

Max shakes his head. Glen wants him to start cleaning up after himself, to get a haircut. "He's not going back to school looking like that," Glen says.

"He's depressed," I say.

"I understand that. He can be depressed with a haircut. He can be depressed loading the dishwasher."

That night I arrive home and there is a pizza box on the kitchen counter. From the den I hear a sound; it is Max's deep goofy chortle, so long unheard. Smiling, I take a slice of pizza from the box and go into the den. "Hey, Mom, look," Max says, and Kiernan stands up, puts his arms around me, and squeezes, hard. "I missed you guys," he says.

I've missed him, too. He draws the solar system on Max's cast, then makes a black-and-white photograph of it; in the center there is a star, and on the photo he handcolors the star a deep, deep yellow, so that it glows amid the monochrome. Max hangs the photo on the wall of his room, above his bed. I ignore the fact that Ruby's return is approaching and put the list of therapist's names I've gotten in the desk drawer.

Kiernan is driving a rusty clunker with a burgundy matte paint job that he says belongs to his uncle. He is mowing lawns in the early mornings, just after the dew has burned off but before the sun is too high. "It's really good money," he says, selling himself to me with a peculiar edge, as if he's looking for work.

He and Max are a pair, both thin and mop-headed, almost like brothers from the back. This makes me nervous, that and the fact that while Max is still mostly quiet, Kiernan can't stop talking. But after a while I recognize something about his behavior. It is a little like the way I was when I was home with an infant and would go out to a party. I was crazed by human contact, chatting relentlessly, conscious that before long I would be back in my cage. I realize that Kiernan has no one to talk to.

"Senior year," says Glen at dinner one steamy August night.

"Really!" Kiernan says. "Talk about the end of an era. And you, dude. High school! It's the first day of the rest of your life."

"I want this cast off," Max says.

"Think positive! You can make it happen! It's all about attitude!" Kiernan sounds like an inspirational speaker. Glen looks at me across the platter of spareribs. The doctor has said Max will likely have to keep the cast on until the end of September. He's eating spareribs awkwardly with his one good hand, and I mentally remind myself not to make them again until he can use both hands. Kiernan is eating almost nothing. He's like one of those young religious aesthetes I used to encounter in some of my comparative-literature readings, all limbs and eyes and fervor. If he were a medieval monk, he would be flaying himself before bed every night.

"You need to talk to him," Glen says quietly as we finish the dishes. "Ruby will be home next week." There is the faint rumble of deep voices in the next room; Kiernan and Max are watching television together.

"You can't speak for yourself?"

"Mary Beth," Glen says. "You know I won't say what you want me to say. You know you want to do this yourself. You live for these mother moments."

"That's a terrible thing to say. I hate this. I hate it. He's such a nice kid. He's been like a part of our family." I think of all those early evenings, Ruby reading her work aloud, Kiernan sprawled on the couch listening, shaking his head at the end, saying, "That is so good, Rubes. Do you know how good that is?" I remember the two of them eating sandwiches on a quilt in the yard, lying on their backs afterward and dreamily naming the constellations. Last year Kiernan gave Ruby a star for her birthday. She has a certificate. I wonder where it is.

A part of our family, I think again, as Kiernan helps me with the garbage and puts a hand out to stop me at the end of the drive.

"I need a big, big favor," he blurts out. "Can I live here this year?"

I'm stunned. It must be apparent in my face, because he continues, the words tumbling from his mouth so quickly that I can barely keep up. "My mom is staying with my grandmother because she's getting worse and worse, she hardly knows anything anymore, she doesn't even know who I am, sometimes she screams when I walk in the door, she goes, who is that man, and my mom has to say, that's your grandson, and my mother keeps saying she needs my help with her and that I'll adjust but, like, it's my senior year, my senior year! And she wants me to go to school up there, she says it will be better, a fresh start, a fresh start—I don't need a fresh start, I don't have friends there, I don't know anyone, I'm going nuts. I promise I won't cause trouble, you won't even know I'm there, I don't even have to come in the house if you don't want me to, I've got it all figured out—there's that room over the garage, there's that toilet downstairs, you won't even know I'm there." His eyes are wild, and he's breathing as though he's been running, and I put up my hand, palm out.

"Kiernan," I say, and he stops.

"Breathe," I say.

"Really," he says, inhaling sharply. "Really. I promise I won't be any trouble. To anybody. I can help around the house. I can shovel snow or run the leaf blower. Or I can just disappear. I can live here and no one will even know I'm around." We both know who he means.

"There has to be another way," I say softly. "You've got the truck. It would be a long drive, I know, but you could drive down here to school every morning. I'm sure the school district would look the other way."

"No," he says, shaking his head. "I won't have the truck every day. Or a car. My mom says she needs her car for deliveries. Or in case there's an emergency with my grandmother."

"You've already discussed this with your mother?"

"If you can call it a discussion."

"And she said no."

"She laughed at me! She said, 'Like hell.' "

"What about your old house? You could live there by yourself. I could look in on you."

"She already rented it to some guy. She says she needs the money."

"And your dad?"

He just shakes his head.

"I can't go against your mother."

"I'll be eighteen in three weeks. I can do what I want. I just need a hand for a little while."

He turns and locks the lids on the garbage cans. "Kiernan," I say again, but he won't look at me.

"Never mind. It was a stupid idea. I'll think of something."

"Kiernan, I'm so sorry."

"Never mind," he says, and walks to the truck and gets in.

Glen is finishing his glass of wine when I go back inside. "I don't know what the hell Deborah is thinking," I say heatedly, sitting down beside him. Through the doorway I can see Max, the reflection from the TV screen a flickering shadow across his face. He has five books to read before school starts in three weeks; they're in a pile on the floor, the spines still stiff. "Alex didn't do it yet, either," Max said when I mentioned it.

"How do you know that?"

"Mom, get real," he replied, pointing the remote.

"I'm way too tired to have a Deborah conversation," Glen says, looking straight ahead.

We were never really couple friends, the Donahues and the Lathams, even when we were neighbors. Glen and Kevin would stand in the adjoining driveways and chat occasionally, and sometimes they would come to our house for dinner, and sometimes we would go to theirs.

But it wasn't like it is with Nancy and Bill, when, over time, the men started to describe themselves as friends quite apart from the friendship between their wives. It was mainly Deborah and me. She was so vivid, so unequivocal. She wore Indian-print tunics, ornate silver earrings, cuff bracelets. She could stand on her head. I don't know why that impressed me so.

She was the one who told the abusive peewee baseball coach that he was a sadist, and followed it up with a letter to the county athletic league. She demanded that they get rid of the separate boys and girls soccer leagues, and it happened, too, although too late for Kiernan and Ruby, who wouldn't have cared much in any event. "I'm not fighting for my kid, I'm fighting for all the kids," she had said in a fury. Glen said that she reminded him of a bumper sticker he had seen that said, "I love mankind. It's people I can't stand."

Once, in the parking lot of the supermarket, I watched her rip into a guy whose pickup truck had a pair of fake rubber testicles hanging from the back hitch. "We have children in this car!" she yelled, while the man kept repeating, "Lady, you're nuts." The argument got so loud that the twins and Ruby, Kiernan and his baby brother, Declan, all began to cry, and someone in the store called the police. The police made the guy take the things off the truck. In a minivan full of sobbing children, Deborah had been triumphant. But when seven-year-old Ruby told the story at the dinner table—"And Kiernan's mommy yelled and yelled, and it

was so scary, Daddy, and the police came, and they had GUNS"—
Glen gave me a look, and that night he said, "I don't really want
our kids in that kind of situation."

"She doesn't take any crap," I'd said.

"There's a difference between being assertive and looking for a
fight," Glen replied. "I don't know how Kevin stands it." Maybe
that was why Glen didn't particularly like Kevin, that and the fact
that there were already rumors that Kevin liked other people's
wives better than he liked his own.

It was Glen who heard Deborah screaming, that summer
evening, when Kevin was gone somewhere, probably to someone
else's home, to someone else's queen-sized bed and waiting wife.
We were eating at the patio table in our backyard, and Deborah
was next door, in the kitchen, with the sliding doors open to the
deck so she could keep a close eye on her two boys. Kiernan was
floating in a tube in the pool, and Declan was in some flotation device shaped like a boat with a canvas harness inside. He was two
then, Declan, a placid little fair-haired boy entranced by the bigger
kids. No one ever figured out exactly what happened, although it
seems likely that he somehow wriggled free of the harness, shifted
his weight, and silently, suddenly, slid south. One moment, Deborah cried afterward, she was making faces at her baby boy, and the
next he had vanished.

I remember the day in stutter-stop images: Deborah shrieking
high and loud; Glen standing up at our patio table so suddenly that
his chair fell over onto the concrete; our three kids staring as he ran
into the Donahues' yard and up the steps of the deck to the pool.
All the while, Kiernan floated in the tube in the deep end, frozen
as Glen dove in, then lifted Declan to the deck and knelt over
him. There was a moment of deep silence before Glen began to
work on the little boy, a moment broken, as Ruby said, in her

fluty, unknowing, precocious little girl's voice, "Mommy, is Declan drowned?"

The day after the funeral, Deborah followed my car to the garden center. Her voice sounded funny, as though it were coming from the bottom of a hole. "Can Kiernan stay with you?" she asked, her words slurred. "He says he wants to stay with you."

"Oh, sweetie, that's not a good idea," I said, stepping away from the car so that Ruby couldn't hear. "He needs to be with you and Kevin."

"Just for a little while, Mary Beth. I can't take care of him right now. It would be good if he could stay with you just for a little while."

"Deb, you know that's not a good idea." I reached out to hug her, but she stiffened and staggered back, and then she pushed me in the center of my chest with the flat of her hand, and those green eyes had flared. "Fair-weather friend," she spat.

"Deborah, you know that's not true."

They had a construction crew fill in the pool. In less than a year, you couldn't tell there had been anything in the backyard but grass. And when they moved back to town, to a different house, Kiernan walked two miles to ours, although he was only twelve.

"Everybody's exactly the same," he'd said when he sat down for lunch. But Deborah and I were never friends again, not really, and after a while we were not even friendly.

Ruby's different when she returns from the writing program. To begin with, she asks that I not come to pick her up. Instead, a young man brings her home, helps her unload her things onto the driveway, gives her a chaste kiss and a long hug, and drives away. It's only once he is gone that I emerge and follow his hug with one tighter, longer, from which my daughter divests herself slowly, with a smile, as though she were taking off a heavy coat on a hot day.

"He's just a good friend," she says. "In answer to your question."

She seems quieter, and happier, too. She has two journals full of poetry. She says her teacher disapproves of writing poetry on the computer. She says she has sent three poems to small magazines and that she is waiting for replies. "As soon as I get the rejection letters, I'll send them out again," she says evenly. Ruby is using her make-nice voice with me, and I don't like it. It's as though she has outgrown the need to oppose me, which I fear is only a few beats away from outgrowing me entirely. Sometimes I feel as though the entire point of a woman's life is to fall in love with people who will leave her. The only variation I can see is the ones who fight the love, and the ones who fight the leaving. It's too late for me to be the first, and I'm trying not to be the second.

At dinner, faced with Max's cast and its unmistakable model of the solar system, a little of the old Ruby resurfaces. "Nice," she says to Max, tapping the plaster, recognizing Kiernan's handiwork. "Really subtle."

"Did you hear from Kiernan while you were away?" I asked Ruby, and she replied, "Every single day."

She tells the boys about her summer as her father and I listen. She talks about her roommate and her teachers—"brilliant," she says reverentially, her voice tremolo, of her poetry professor—and an aspiring short-story writer with whom she seems to have spent much of her time. "He starts Yale next week," she says, and I suspect that he is the young man who brought her home. Max scowls. It's not just that he is loyal to Kiernan but that he has never liked the idea of either his sister or his brother having intimates he doesn't know. Last year Alex visited Colin, his friend from camp, and then Colin came to our house for a few days. Max was so truculent that the two boys moved into the guest room to avoid him. "I didn't do anything to him," Colin had said, and Alex replied, "Sometimes he's just like that."

He has been like that for weeks, except for the times when Kiernan was at the house. His hair is ratty, two weeks away from white-boy dreadlocks. "Who cares?" he mutters. I pray that among the kids moving up to the high school from the other middle school there will be someone who loves comic books, Japanese animation, and drums.

"So how, exactly, did you do that?" Ruby says to Max, cocking her head at his arm, after asking both boys about their time at camp.

"I fell out of a tree."

"Figures," says Alex, his mouth full of spaghetti. His story is that he has eaten nothing but cereal and peanut-butter sandwiches since July.

"Why?" Max says.

"Why don't you just tell people that you were playing soccer or something? Who falls out of a tree?"

"People who don't give a shit about soccer," Max says.

"Whoa whoa," says Glen. "You're not at camp anymore, buddy."

"Yeah, like I don't know that."

"Max!" says Ruby.

"You don't talk to your father like that, Max," I say.

"I'm sorry, but can someone make Lacrosse Boy shut up about how great he is. You know what, never mind, I'm done anyhow." He picks up his plate with his free hand, starts toward the sink, and drops it. There is chicken cacciatore, lettuce leaves, and bits of Italian pottery all over the floor.

"Oh, not those dishes," I hear myself say, and wish I could snatch the words from the stuffy summer air and shove them into my pocket, to be whispered later when no one is around.

Ginger begins to snuffle excitedly around the food, grabbing a chicken bone and trying to run into the next room. Ruby wrestles it from her mouth as the dog breathes heavily. "No, no, Ging," she says. "Not chicken."

"Shit!" Max yells.

"Upstairs," Glen shouts, and Max leaves the room with the sound of a battalion of boys. A moment later, the detonation of his door slamming seems to shake the house, and Ginger runs, her tail tucked, into the mudroom.

"I didn't do anything," whines Alex.

"He's just hormonal," says Ruby.

"Uh—news flash? He's a guy?"

"Uh—news flash? Guys have hormones, too? They just happen to be different hormones?"

"I don't care who has hormones," Glen says, gulping down his food the way he does when he's unhappy. "We're going to keep the profanity under control in this house. I'm not giving an inch on this."

"It's just lazy," Ruby says airily.

"What is?" Alex says.

"Profanity."

"Are you really going to be a writer?" Alex says.

"Yes."

"Are you getting back with Kiernan?"

"I prefer not to discuss that," Ruby says, taking her plate to the sink.

"Max'll hate you if you don't."

"Max doesn't hate any of us," I say.

"Max won't hate me," Ruby says. "He'll just be upset. He's having a tough time. I had a tough time starting high school, too." Ruby's dark eyes slide across the table and into the air above, away from me, away from Glen, into the middle distance of uncomfortable memory. This is her material. She's shown me one of the poems she's written. It says:

Together they eat as the sun sinks behind them.
But he is eating his fears, and she is eating her cares.
He is eating his exhausted hours
And she is eating nothing at all because there is too much to swallow.
Her throat is thick with her selves.
Nothing can squeeze by them.
Only one of them eats what is on his plate, not what is in his mind.
But they all smile at one another as the chandelier makes silver
    demitasse of light on the polished pine.

Black past the windows, yellow inside.
Plates empty.

"Oh, Ruby," I said. "The demitasse."

"I know," she said, dancing in place, a jig of joy—the sort that she did so often as a little girl and seems to have outgrown. "I know. As soon as I wrote that, I thought, yes." It was as though she were talking about someone else, some other family, as though the person in the poem with the cares was not me, the exhausted one not her father. Where is the joy that I worked so hard to create? Perhaps it is in the demitasse of light, or in the fact that she can even invent the demitasse of light.

"Do you want to drive over to Tony's and get ice cream?" Ruby says to Alex. We have gotten her her first car, an elderly Volvo wagon Glen bought from a patient who was retiring to some small town in the South where it is always warm. "Volvos have the best safety record in the business," Glen had told Ruby, but her face had been alight the moment she saw the boxy car in the driveway. "It is so completely me," she said. What she means is that it is retro, un-expected, that no other student at the high school will have one. She has hung a blue crystal rosary from the rearview mirror; it snags the light and sends it back in shards across the dashboard. Ruby will drive the boys to school each morning so they won't be reduced to taking the bus, which I'm told is populated entirely by losers.

"Uh, yes?" Alex replies, as though he is trying to figure out the trick behind this new solicitous sister. He goes upstairs for Max, comes downstairs alone. Ruby shrugs and takes the car keys from the dish by the door.

"Maybe Mr. Huntington was right about Max," I say. "Maybe something really is wrong."

"Who?" says Glen.

"His drum teacher. Maybe he was right about Max. Maybe he needs to see a therapist."

"Oh, for God's sake, Mary Beth," Glen says. "Ruby's right. It's hormones. His face is a mess, he could use a shave, he smells like the zoo in summer. He'll get over it." This is a step up for Glen. His own father had a veritable Bartlett's of stoicism sentiments. "I'll give you something to cry about" was his favorite.

"He told me he wants his own room," I say. When I asked Max whether he had discussed this with Alex, he'd replied flatly, "He won't care." I think he's right about that.

"Spoiled," Glen says, shaking his head. "These kids are so spoiled. I shared a room with two of my brothers until I went to college. I got to that tiny little dorm room with a twin bed and thought I'd died and gone to heaven because I had it all to myself."

"And you walked seven miles through the snow to school," I say.

"You're such a hater," Glen says, and I burst out laughing. This is one of his favorite things, to co-opt the children's slang and de-nature it with adult use. Two years ago he said "That is major" so often that it was excised from kid-speak forever.

"I love that term, and now they'll never use it," I say.

"That's their problem."

Max has mentioned moving to the room above the garage, but this seems a terrible time to turn it over to either of the boys. I envision Max cocooned in solitary disaffection, refusing to come into the house, slipping into the kitchen at night to make a pouch of the front of his T-shirt and fill it with food from the fridge. I envision Alex watching the glow of the lights on the second floor, waiting for us to turn off our reading lamps and then sneaking out for a spate of pool hopping. It's too late to move Ruby. She's already nervous about her territory. "You're not going to turn my room into an office when I go to college, are you?" she has asked.

Apparently, Rachel's mother already has plans to turn her daughter's bedroom into a home gym.

Glen goes to bed early, and I look at some garden plans at the table. I'm drowsy when I hear the car door slam outside. Alex goes upstairs to shower, and Ruby puts the kettle on. "The ice cream wasn't enough?" I ask.

"I didn't have ice cream," Ruby says. "Alex ate enough for both of us." She sits down opposite me, her face cupped in her hands. Her hair is in a braid down her back, and she wears silver stars in her ears.

"Has Kiernan been here?" she says.

"When?" I ask.

"Any time," she says.

"I don't know how often he stops by, honey," I say, putting my hand over hers. "Max likes to see him. Kiernan was a big help when he came home from camp."

Ruby stands and reaches into the pocket of her overalls. She takes out a silver ring. Like her car, or the polka-dot chiffon shirt she is wearing, or the mixture of anger and sadness in her brown eyes, the little silver circlet of lopsided hearts is so Ruby.

"I found this on my bedside table," she says, dropping it on the counter, where it makes a high note of a noise, then spins and falls.

"What should we do?" I say, and for the first time I am looking at her, talking to her, one woman to another.

"I don't know, Mommy. I feel so bad for him. His mother is crazy, and she's such a bitch, I'm sorry, I know you hate that word, but it's true. To make him go to a new school for senior year when he's already in such bad shape? He leaves me messages and he sounds like he's been crying, or he's going to cry, or he's pretending not to cry. I want to be his friend. But I need him to let me be, you know? I just need him to let me breathe. He doesn't let me breathe."

"He thought it was going to be more than you did," I say.

"I don't think that's it. It was a big deal for me, too. But after a while I started to think that Kiernan didn't really want to be with me, the way I am now. I think maybe Kiernan just wants to freeze everything forever. Like, like—like Peter Pan."

"And you're Wendy."

"See, that's it. That's the problem. I'm not Wendy. I'm Ruby. And I'm not Ruby when she was five, or fifteen. I'm a different Ruby." And she starts to sob, the kind of sobbing that refuses comfort, and all I can think is, Life is hard. Life is hard.

Finally she reaches for a paper towel, blows her nose, and wipes her eyes.

"Should I tell him he's not welcome?" I say.

"How can we do that? It would kill him."

How deeply she feels, my grown-up girl. I can remember the moment when I realized that. We had gone to London together, the five of us. It was just before Ruby began to waste away, but she was already starting to concern herself with odd things, to plumb the scope of the universe: ocean life, the constellations. In retrospect, I wondered if she was immersing herself in notions that made her feel small before she took the next step of actually making herself smaller.

Before our trip, she had read a half-dozen books about the Tudors and the Plantagenets, and she wandered the aisles of Westminster Abbey carrying a royal family tree. The boys were eleven, bored and hungry, sitting in the back banging the heels of their sneakers against the bottom of a bench until I had to hiss a warning. Ruby and Glen were standing together by a pale marble tomb, and as I joined them I saw that atop it was the figure of a woman.

"It's Elizabeth," Ruby had said. "Isn't it terrible, to think that she's under there, dead? And Shakespeare, and Charles Dickens, and Henry VIII, and everyone else I read about? They're all dead."

Her voice was rising. A tour guide at another tomb paused, then resumed in a slightly louder voice.

And then Glen began to speak as though his whole heart were in his words. He turned to Ruby and said, "All that tread the globe are but a handful to the tribes that slumber in its bosom."

"What?" she whispered.

"All that tread the globe are but a handful to the tribes that slumber in its bosom," he repeated. " 'Thanatopsis,' by William Cullen Bryant. I wasn't always an eye doctor, pumpkin." The lines from the poem were still on an index card in the center of Ruby's bulletin board. I was betting they would wind up on her yearbook page.

I cover the ring with my palm, feel it warm under my skin. "I'll figure out how to handle this," I say.

"No, Mommy," Ruby replies. "I have to give it back myself. I just hope he'll listen to me. I don't think he really listens to me anymore." We both look up as Max tromps across the floor above us. "I'll take Max some nachos," Ruby says, putting the ring back into her pocket. "He didn't really get much to eat at dinner. I'm worried about him."

"I know. Bring him up something to eat. Just make sure he brings down his plate after."

"Yeah, right, that'll happen," she says, not yet completely transformed.

We're sitting side by side in a small office that was clearly once the best bedroom in a Victorian house one block over from the hospital. It has a bay window and a tin ceiling. There are tea-colored lace curtains, but all the rest is standard doctor's office: a slab desk, some framed diplomas, two armchairs covered in a brown-green nubby fabric, the kind that no one uses in the home, the kind that is designed to endure.

I cross my legs and smile. I am wearing a dress and carrying a real purse, instead of a canvas tote bag filled with shears and spades. This is my good-mother apparel. I may have been wearing the same dress when we met not far from here with the woman who helped Ruby begin eating again.

"I think this is a remediable situation," she had said.

"Who uses the word 'remediable,' " Glen said angrily in the car afterward.

"This is less about body image than about Ruby's sense of autonomy," she said.

"She's a kid," Glen said as we pulled away from the curb. "She needs autonomy?" When Glen is afraid, he loses his temper. "Where's the goddamn doctor?" he'd yelled when I abandoned my rhythmic breathing and started to wail as Ruby was being born. "The goddamn doctor is right here, Dr. Latham," the obstetrician had said, pulling on her gloves.

I am breathless with anxiety. Once, when I was thirteen, I broke a bottle of perfume that sat on my mother's bureau. I could never remember her wearing the perfume, which looked like old scotch and smelled as dark and exotic as its amber color suggested. But I couldn't remember a time when the heavy cut-crystal bottle was not on the right-hand corner of the lace doily, balancing a set of silver-backed brushes on the left. I'd yanked open a drawer, and the bottle wobbled and crashed to the floor, filling the room with the suffocating odor. I left the pieces there, and when later my mother called sharply, "Mary Beth!" I sat on one corner of her bed, the smell making me sick and faint, and said I couldn't imagine how such a thing had happened. Many years after, it occurred to me that perhaps my mother had made so much of it because my father had given her the perfume, but at the time I simply insisted I'd done nothing wrong, even in the face of the evidence.

That feeling is the same feeling I have in this doctor's office.

His name is Pindaros Vagelos. Nancy told me he was the psychologist who treated a girl in Fred's class who had tried to kill herself her junior year, although the girl's mother insisted that it was an accident. "An accidental wrist-slitting after thirty Xanax—you don't see that very often," Nancy had said in her harshest voice. Apparently, the young woman was now doing brilliantly at one of the most prestigious liberal-arts colleges and was planning to attend medical school. "She'll probably go into psychiatry," Glen had said on the drive over to Dr. Vagelos's office. "All the nuts do. The beautiful girls go into dermatology. The jocks do orthopedics."

"And the ophthalmologists?" I said, but it was not a day to try to jolly him.

"I guess," Max had said when we asked him if he would talk to someone about how he was feeling. The painters had finished turning the guest room a mustard color that Ruby said might as well have been called Depression Yellow, and Max's furniture had been moved from one side of the hall to the other. He got the old bunk beds, since it turned out that he didn't care about a double bed the way Alex did. There was something so sad about those bunk beds, the lower all tumbled and untidy, the top one neatly made, waiting for the kind of sleepovers that, at least for the moment, were unlikely to take place. After only two weeks of school, a counselor had called to say that Max was a "student of concern" and that several of his teachers had reported that his homework was not complete. His cast had come off, but he still held his arm at a right angle by his side, and his handwriting was crabbed and illegible. "Did somebody go in my room?" he would say if I emptied the hamper or cleared the crusty dishes from the night table. Sometimes I swore I was in an empty house, and then I would hear the faint creak of a floorboard. The week before he had finally left his room after school to come here, to see Dr. Vagelos, to pronounce him acceptable.

"What's he like?" I had asked.

"He wears glasses," Max said, carrying a slice of pie upstairs. I put a hand out to touch him, and it slid along the length of his arm as though I had stroked the banister.

Glasses, a beard, a slight stoop, a cardigan: It was all in the name. So Glen and I are both surprised when a young man in a striped shirt unbuttoned at the throat opens the varnished oak door. He smiles as he shakes hands and settles us both. Thirty-five, perhaps a very boyish forty, wearing the rectangular black-framed glasses I associate with fashionable architects. My heart sinks.

"We've had two useful sessions," he says of Max, leaning back in his chair slightly.

"I don't want to sound insensitive, but all this just reads like puberty to me," says Glen, lacing his fingers together in what I take for a doctor-to-doctor gesture. "I was depressed for most of high school."

"That's interesting," Dr. Vagelos says.

"Not clinically depressed. But you know what I mean. The girls don't like me, I don't like algebra, my parents are a pain in the butt."

"Do you think Max might be clinically depressed?" I say. Nancy has told me the medications are wonderful nowadays, although how she knows I can't imagine. Her children run on endorphins and milk.

"Is there anyone in either of your families who suffers from depression?" the doctor asks evenly.

My stolid mother, his peripatetic brother, my brother the workaholic, his father the alcoholic.

"No," says Glen.

"Maybe," I say. "Undiagnosed."

"Look," says Dr. Vagelos, "why don't you give me some time to really get to know Max? He and I have had two good conversations. He seems willing to talk."

"Not to us," I say.

"It could be he's worried about upsetting you."

"He's upsetting us by not talking," Glen says, and I hear a slight quaver in his voice. So much for puberty, girls, and algebra. For purposes of our union, he carries the stoicism, I carry the concern. At times like this, I want what he's having.

"He loves you both very much. And he loves his sister and his brother."

"He said that?" I ask.

"He did. But he also said—and I tell you this because he said I could—that he feels like a loser. Especially compared with his brother." He looks down at a legal pad on his desk. "His brother, Alex."

"That's ridiculous," says Glen, his voice strong again. "We've never indicated in any way that Alex is superior to Max."

"The twin relationship is complex," the doctor says, and suddenly I remember a day when I was sitting in the rocking chair by the window, trying to nurse both babies at the same time. Their legs were entwined, and each was trying to push the other away with his splayed feet. "They don't like each other," Ruby had said solemnly, standing by the side of the chair with her thumb in her mouth, twisting a curl.

"Of course they do, pumpkin," I said. "They were inside together all this time."

"If they like each other, then how come they're kicking?" she replied.

"They're fraternal twins," I tell the doctor. "If you saw them together, you wouldn't even think they were related."

"And that carries its own particular set of issues, doesn't it? In the twin relationship, issues of difference can be even more significant than issues of sameness."

"I'm just not sure that's at the root of his problems now," I say.

"What's your best guess?" the doctor says, looking into my eyes.

"I think he feels like he doesn't belong anywhere anymore," I say, and, shocked and dismayed at my own words, I begin to cry. "I love him so much. I don't want him to feel bad about who he is." Glen pats my arm gently. I look, and he is crying, too.

"I actually think he knows that," Dr. Vagelos says. "I think we're ahead of the curve here in terms of how Max feels valued by the two of you. But how the world values him may be a different matter, and that goes to how the world values his brother." Dr. Vagelos picks up a newspaper clipping from beneath the legal pad. I know what it is, even though I am still wiping my eyes. "Latham First-Year Soccer Standout," the headline says. It's a feature from the local paper called Player of the Week, and two weeks ago they chose Alex. Glen sent the clipping to his father, and his father sent Alex a copy of the story laminated onto an enormous wooden plaque.

"Did Max tell you he plays the drums?" I ask.

"Yes, he did. And that he's an ace computer programmer. But you should know that at some level he doesn't feel that his gifts are important. And he doesn't feel he's entitled to his negative feelings. That's another reason he doesn't feel comfortable discussing them with you. He says that he has a great home, great parents, great siblings, and that he should be happy because of all that. In some ways, he's as distressed by what he sees as the wrongness of his emotions as by anything else. I think one of the phrases he kept repeating was 'I just can't help it.' "

"So maybe it's chemical," I say.

"That's certainly something I'll be considering. But we have a lot of ground to cover. I wanted to talk to you, and he wanted me to talk to you, to let you know that we think we can work together."

"We appreciate that," says Glen. "You come highly recommended. I'm impressed that you thought to clip the newspaper story."

"I didn't see this myself, Dr. Latham. Max brought it to me, I think to show me what he was up against. He has another copy that he kept himself."

"I swear," I say, trying to laugh, "I never dressed them alike."

Dr. Vagelos smiles again. He has a warm smile; his whole face is in it, especially his eyes. "As I said, sometimes difference can be more of an issue than similarity."

"You obviously have given the fact that he's a twin a lot of thought," Glen says.

"It's my area of expertise. I'm sorry, I assumed you knew that. I assumed that's why you sent Max to me as opposed to someone else."

"I had no idea," I say.

"It's a strange and mysterious relationship," he says, looking down at the pad again. "Think about it—both twins hear the maternal heartbeat in utero. But, because of simple positioning, one sometimes hears it more faintly than the other." And at the thought I begin to cry again.

He stands to hand me a tissue from the box on the corner of his desk. Both Glen and I rise simultaneously, as though we were doing calisthenics. Instead of the outstretched hand this time, the doctor reaches to touch each of us lightly on the forearm.

"I think Max and I can work together well," he repeats.

In the doorway, Glen turns back and says, "How did you come to concentrate on twins?"

"I'm a twin myself," Dr. Vagelos says, and he gestures to a photograph on the bookcase of two men standing side by side, their arms around each other. At this distance I can't make out faces, but it's easy to see that one is a full head shorter than the other.

"Your brother taught you about differences as well as similarities?" I say with a laugh.

"My brother has Down syndrome," he says, "so that would be a yes."

Neither of us speaks in the car as we drive past the hospital and turn onto Main Street. Someone beeps, and we both raise our hands in a wave. "Who was that?" Glen says.

"I have no idea." We edge around roadwork and then turn onto our street. The back of my truck is filled with mums, a blanket of yellow and orange.

"What was he, about sixteen?" Glen says, looking straight ahead as the car idles at the curb.

"He's younger than I thought he would be," I say. "Did you like him?"

Glen nods. His shirt collar is askew in the back, and I pat it into place. "All I care about is whether Max likes him," he says.

Max is responsible for our Halloween party, which has become such a tradition that when I once suggested we skip it my family behaved as though I had blasphemed in church. "Mom," Alex had said in a peremptory fashion, "if we don't have a Halloween party, what will people do for Halloween?"

Of course, everyone in town does not come to our Halloween party, although in recent years, as friends of the kids brought their own friends, and their girlfriends, and sometimes even their parents, it began to seem that way. As I drive down to the minimart to buy more ice, or some extra marshmallows for the cocoa, I see lots of families doing what we once did, many years ago: adults walking slowly down the sidewalk, sometimes with a baby dressed as a pumpkin or an angel on one hip, while ahead run princesses, pirates, skeletons, and ghosts. I can tell how long they've been out and about by the gray shadow at the hem of a white satin dress, by the slow plod as the bag full of candy grows heavy, by the tempers of mothers and fathers standing on the street: Just four more houses and, I swear, we're going home.

Ruby loved Halloween, loved to dance up the front walk to strangers, to announce, her consonants precise, "I am Sleeping Beauty." Or the Little Mermaid. Or a ballerina. Glen and I each carried a boy that first year—one a bunny, the other a cat. "Dr. Latham!" one or two of the older people had said as they looked over Ruby's head to the two of us waiting across the lawn. "I'll see you next month."

But when Max was four our routine altered. He would no longer approach a strange house. He stood on the sidewalk, dressed as a fireman with a hat so red and shiny you could see your own fun-house face in its surface, and refused to go farther. From time to time during the next few weeks, he would feed us a clue at the dinner table or at bedtime: We were not supposed to go to strangers' houses. We were not supposed to speak to strangers. We were not supposed to take candy from them.

"Halloween you can," Alex said. "I got good candy, and I don't know how come I had to give you some 'cause you were too scared to go."

"Maxie, I've been going out on Halloween for a long time, and nothing bad ever happens. It's fun! You'll like it!" seven-year-old Ruby had added brightly, in the same voice she used to tell him how wonderful school would be.

Max shook his head. The next year, he put on his costume and stayed in the house. I stayed with him as he handed out Hershey bars to the other children. Afterward he put three Hershey bars in his own bag, then traded Alex for a peanut-butter cup. Ruby refused to trade. She had lost patience.

Thus, the Halloween party was born. That was not how we explained it to others. A disaster provided cover. When the boys were in first grade, on Mischief Night—"which is such a lovely poetic name for horrible mass destruction," said Nancy, who had just become my friend at the time—four juniors at the high school had decided to try to bring down a lamppost by chaining it to a trailer hitch. They had indeed brought the lamp down; it smashed through the back of the truck and grazed the head of one of the boys, who went on to spend nearly eight months in a rehab facility learning to tie his shoes and recognize the alphabet. The town council imposed a Mischief Night and Halloween curfew of 8 P.M. for anyone under the age of twenty-one.

"That so has to be unconstitutional and, like, completely illegal," some teenager will say in our kitchen at some point during early fall. But no one has done anything about it in the years since it first went into effect. The parents of the little kids, weary of complaints about sore feet and heavy bags, have them home long before then. The parents of the older kids are happy to have someone else assume the burden of getting them off the streets at a reasonable hour. The parents of teenagers are delighted that the opportunity for mayhem is curtailed by law.

And it was a godsend for us, because it enabled us to create the Halloween party without having to explain that it was because our son was terrified of trick-or-treating. Our friends brought candy and their costumed children. There was a pumpkin piñata and apple-bobbing. We set up a benign haunted house in the basement, with an illuminated witch who cackled on a continuous loop and a ghost that swooped on a zip line. Max was allowed to see everything in daylight before the evening of the party so that he wouldn't be afraid.

The children are all old enough to come on their own now, but most of their parents still arrive, bearing plastic pumpkins full of Milky Ways and Swedish Fish. Some of them even dress up. Glen wears a dark suit and a mask of whoever happens to be president at the time. Alex always wears what I think of as a man-of-action costume; this year he is a member of the Boston Red Sox, which hardly seems to count as a disguise. Ruby's outfit is always more of a fashion statement: This year she is a turn-of-the-century news-boy, with her hair under a flat cap and knickers set off by red sus-penders. She already had everything she needed in her closet.

Max seems a little better these days, or, at least, no worse. There have been no more calls from school, and now that they are in dif-ferent rooms, he and Alex seem more civil to each other, although Ruby says that Alex still ignores his brother at school. "I guess just because they're twins everyone thought they would always be friends," she said ruefully.

"Did you talk to Max about that?"

"He barely speaks to me, Mommy. I hope he outgrows this be-fore I leave for college."

I felt a terrible twinge at the thought. "Oh, Lord, I hope it hap-pens long before then," I replied.

I am relieved to peer out the dining-room window at dusk and see a silver robot at the end of the walk, handing out Hershey bars to small children, a few of whom pat his big boxy body. Max still likes to be the one to dispense candy to the smallest trick-or-treaters. The box costume is his specialty. One year he was a set of dice, another a box of crayons. His greatest achievement was a re-frigerator, with a door that opened, although it seemed ready to tear free any minute. Inside were cardboard shelves with some empty containers—milk, yogurt, a discarded pickle jar—and, atop the foodstuffs, Max's face, peering out from what would have been the freezer compartment.

The robot lumbers toward the house to get more candy. I wave. He raises a hand in an old ski glove painted silver. He is walking stiffly, an authentic automaton. He must have made this in the garage or the house would have reeked of spray paint.

"Great costume," I call.

Muffled by the box, I hear "Thanks."

The lawn is studded with cornstalks twined together with raffia and large piles of gourds and pumpkins. There are big terracotta pots of gold mums on either side of the front door. I'm glad we do this. I sometimes think of having grandchildren who will believe that people always have Halloween parties, who will gently mock Grandpa in his presidential mask and wonder why Grandma doesn't wear a costume. "She never has," one of my children will say. I know this may well be a delusion, that it's possible there will be no grandchildren, or they will live half a world away, or their parents will be too busy to give more than the most cursory notice to Halloween. It's only before the realities set in that we can treasure our delusions.

Almost as soon as I put the trivets on the table and the spiced nuts in the bowls, the guests begin to pour in, until I am not sure I know who is here and who is not. Nancy is always dressed as a witch. "Totally appropriate," she says at some point every year, her black synthetic hair falling around her face. Sarah is dressed as a nurse, perhaps to annoy her mother. I am surprised to see Ben's mother, Olivia, with her blond hair in ringlets, wearing a girlish gingham dress. As small as she is, she looks like a child. Ben has disappeared out back with Alex, but her three younger boys surround her. They are dressed in bear suits. "Goldilocks!" I say, laughing, and hug her. "This porridge is just right," she says airily, and we both laugh. This is the first year she has come to the party, and I'm touched that she made such an effort.

Sandy comes with Rachel, and is dressed—barely dressed—like a Playboy Bunny. Rachel is wearing a Wonder Woman costume, which is really just a Playboy Bunny costume in red, white, and blue. "Wowwee," I say to Rachel, who blushes fiercely. Here is what I know about dressing like your teenage daughter: She will always look better than you. I look around for Ruby.

"Have you seen your buddy?" I ask Sarah, who is listening to Eric's heart with her stethoscope.

"I think she went upstairs. Her hair keeps falling out of her hat. Maybe she's going to braid it up."

"How's his heart?"

Sarah listens carefully. "He doesn't have one."

Eric says, "I gave it to you."

"Ooooohhh," Sarah and I groan together. "You are so slick," Sarah adds.

The macaroni and cheese is running low, and I take another pan from the oven. Glen is eating ham with his fingers. "Make yourself a plate," I say. "I'll just pick," he says.

I carry the trash out back and see that most of the children of a certain age are standing around in the yard, only half costumed. Ben has unzipped his bear suit and pulled it down to his waist. For once it hasn't rained, the great Halloween catastrophe. "Noooo," Ruby would wail if we made her wear a slicker over her sequins and satin. Both my boys are talking to a pirate with an enormous gold hoop earring and long dark curls half hidden by a knotted headscarf. Through the eyeholes of his black mask, I see the glitter of green.

"Aaarrrggh!" Kiernan shouts in a pirate's voice. "Fifteen men on a dead man's chest. Dude, is that right? Fifteen? Sixteen?" He is brandishing a long plastic sword. He pokes Max in the front of his robot box. "How many men on a dead man's chest?"

I put the trash at the side of the house and come back and touch his arm. "Shiver me timbers!" Kiernan says.

"And yours," I reply. "How's school?"

"It's all right," he says.

"How's your grandmother?"

"Kind of crazy. Whoops, sorry, I'm not allowed to say that.

She's the same." Eric and Sarah come outside. "Ahoy, mateys!" Kiernan calls.

Suddenly, like the sound of a door closing, we have run out of conversation. All the years I've known this boy, and now there is nothing for us to talk about that is not dangerous: his mother, his future, his father, his feelings, my daughter.

"Did you eat?" I say. This is what mothers say when they don't know what to say: Did you eat?

"Nah, I'm not really hungry. I'm going out later. I just wanted to stop by. You can't fool around with tradition. I told Max I think I've been coming to this party from the beginning." Almost, but not quite. The year of the first Halloween party, Kiernan and his mother were still living elsewhere. Nancy told me she heard afterward that during those years he had had night terrors and begun to wet the bed. I remembered he had once told me that what was so difficult was knowing that his former life was so close by and yet so far from him. At least now he can drive.

"I'm working on a big, big project," Kiernan says.

"What's the subject?"

He puts his finger dramatically to his lips, and leans toward me. Suddenly I realize that he's drunk. Yo ho ho and a bottle of rum. "Top secret," he says.

Night is beginning to fall, and someone inside turns on the backyard lights. Illuminated, Kiernan looks thin and bony, more skeleton than pirate. Ginger lumbers over and he scratches her ears.

The back door slams sharply, and Ruby scans the yard, her hair wild around her face, no newsboy now. She finally finds us with her eyes, sets her jaw, and strides over.

"Honey—" I say, but she interrupts, shaking her fist in Kiernan's face. She flattens out her hand suddenly, like a slap without hitting, and there is the ring with its lopsided hearts. I look from one of them to the other.

"Stay . . . out . . . of . . . my . . . room," she says so loudly that everyone in the yard stops talking.

Kiernan blinks behind the mask. "What?" he says.

"Don't play innocent with me. I've tried to be nice about this, but now you're making it impossible. I come out of school, you're standing on the sidewalk. I leave Sarah's house, you're across the street."

"It's a free country," Kiernan says. Ginger whines and bumps against his leg.

"You're right, it is. So you can be anyplace you want if you just want me to get madder and madder and madder. But you can't go into my room. I've tried to be nice about this, but I'm done."

"You've tried to be nice? Like I'm some charity case—oh, poor Kiernan, I have to be nice to him?"

"Kiernan, just leave me in peace. We used to be together. Now we're not. I wanted to be friends. Now I don't." Even I flinch. Ruby pushes her open hand toward him. "Take it," she says. "It's not mine."

"It's yours."

"Dude," says Eric. He and Sarah are standing behind Ruby now.

"Yeah, whatever, I'm leaving." Kiernan taps the plastic sword against his leg.

"You need to get on with your life," Ruby says, turning her back on him. Slowly, he raises the sword in the air and points it at her, narrowing his eyes.

"Dude," Eric says again.

"I'm sorry, Kiernan," I say. "I think you need to leave now."

"She needs to watch how she treats people," he says.

"You need to leave her alone. I'm sorry."

"You don't know sorry," he says with a sharp snarl, and I step back. Then he disappears into the darkness.

Next morning when I go to wake Ruby, the photograph of her hands is gone from above her bed. In the center of the wall is a brighter rectangle of paint, and a nail. The boys come down to breakfast before she does. Max has had to cut a chunk of hair off to free himself of a lollipop that somehow wound up on his pillow. "You were sleeping on a lollipop?" Alex says.

"Is Kiernan bothering Ruby at school?" I ask.

"She's a bitch," Max mumbles.

"Hey!" Glen shouts. "That's it. No more of that."

"He's a psycho," Alex says around a mouthful of cereal.

"Maxie, you can't let him into your sister's room," I say.

"What's going on?" says Glen.

My mother and her husband, Stan, are visiting us for the entire Thanksgiving week this year, with Alice and little Liam arriving from New York on Thursday for dinner and staying until Sunday morning. I am trying not to feel overwhelmed with comings and goings, shopping and meals, displacements and undercurrents. To accommodate my mother, Alex has moved into Max's new room, giving up his new double bed for four days. He is only mildly annoyed. My mother and Stan are coming early because Alex is playing in a big tournament soccer match. We are all going to the game together. Alex and Ben are the only freshmen on the team, and Alex is the only one who plays.

"Can you get Max to come to the game?" Ruby asked me.

"Does Alex want him to come?"

"I heard Alex and Ben talking about it, and Alex said Nana and Poppa were coming, and then Ben asked about Max, and Alex really sounded like he wanted Max to come."

"What, exactly, did Alex say?"

"Mom, trust me. He wants him to come."

So I went to Alex and asked, "Do you want Max to go to the tournament game?"

"If he wants to."

And then I asked Max, who said, "You think Alex wants me to go? No way."

The night before, Glen said offhandedly, "So we'll all go together to the soccer game."

"Of course," Ruby said.

"I guess," Max said.

"Cool," said Alex.

"This is just terrific," says Stan, sitting in the bleachers at the high school, his big hairy hands on his knees. He and my mother have been married for almost twenty years, longer than she was married to my father, but he still has the perpetual good humor of one who knows he will always be a newcomer.

"Bleachers are very uncomfortable," my mother says.

It's hard to know if we are nicer to Stan than his children are to my mother. I hear only my mother's side. Stan's daughter has told my mother she is not emotive enough.

"I'm not sure that's even a word," my mother had said, sitting across from me in the living room, which we use only for uncomfortable company. Nancy, for example, has never sat in my living room, nor I in hers. Occasionally, I step inside it to change the stacks of magazines on the end tables. From time to time, Glen grabs a stack and takes the magazines to the office for his patients.

"Why in the world would she say that to you?" I asked. It is true, of course, but it's like telling someone they have a stutter, likely only to make the condition worse.

"She read a book." My mother the retired English teacher spit this out as though nothing could be more useless than reading a book. "One of those self-help books. She says you have to verbalize your feelings. Why do I have to verbalize my feelings? Especially if I suspect that she won't like my feelings?"

"Max is seeing a therapist," I blurted. Why do I always do this? When my mother was talking about the need to establish myself professionally, I told her Glen and I were getting married. When she told me we needed to live frugally until he got a practice up and running, I cut her off to tell her I was pregnant.

"The eating again?" my mother replied.

"God, no. Boys don't do that."

She shook her head authoritatively. "I saw a program on television. Boys do it now." She narrowed her eyes. "He looks thin."

"So does Alex, Mom. They shot up overnight. They'll fill out."

"So what's the problem?"

"He's depressed."

"What does he have to be depressed about, for Christ's sake?" It is my father-in-law's voice in my head. We are seeing him at Christmas. "He needs a haircut," he will say of Max. "I still have the clippers in the basement."

Instead, my mother said, "It's probably a phase. But better safe than sorry."

I blinked. "I'm not opposed to therapy," she added. "I think people should spend less time moping over their own problems. But you can afford it. It's fine." That's my mother's judgment on most things: It's fine. Stan thinks everything is terrific. I suppose between the two of them they reach a happy medium.

"I think he has to verbalize his feelings," I said.

"Ha," my mother said. "Very funny."

Alex has always been her favorite. He is like my brother, Richard, but without the burden of responsibility that made my brother so aged so early. At the soccer game, my mother leans forward and scans the field intently. Her eyes follow Alex. Max is sitting with his knees apart, his head down, his arms wrapped around his midsection. He is wearing a hooded sweatshirt with the hood up. I think it makes him look like a terrorist.

"You look like a terrorist," my mother says. She pulls the hood down and says, "You look good with longer hair. It could use a little shaping, that's all." Max mumbles something and pushes his hair around with his hand in a way that does it no good. I have a fantasy, that we will go to the pharmacy and buy some pills and it will be as it was when he had those terrible ear infections: overnight, a miracle—no pain, back to normal.

"I try to get parents to understand that medication is not necessarily a panacea," Dr. Vagelos had said kindly, as though he could read my mind but was not judgmental about its contents.

"This is terrific," says Stan again. "This is a perfect fall day."

"I'm freezing," says my mother.

Glen gives her a sweatshirt we brought with us. She puts it on, puts her hood up, and gives Max a level look. He grins, and suddenly I love her. She has made my Maxie smile. I put an arm around her shoulder and hug. It is like hugging a mannequin. She's not a toucher. Stan's daughter has told her that, too. But she turns to me and says in a voice only I can hear above a scream from the crowd, "Everything will be fine."

I walk behind the bleachers where Olivia is standing with her hands in her pockets as Luke, her youngest, plays with sticks. She hands me a cookie and chews on one herself.

"I haven't seen you in weeks," I say. "I keep meaning to stop by with pictures from Halloween. The time just gets away from me." Olivia is wearing one of those waxed jackets and big rubber boots, and I think how very English she looks, with her pink cheeks and outdoor gear. Her fair hair is held back with a tortoiseshell band.

"I know," she says. "I have four different school runs now. High school, middle school, elementary, nursery. Sometimes I can't say whether I'm coming or going. And this little man is driving me mad."

"Such a great age," I say, watching Luke try to drive a stick into the ground. I think he's four, or maybe five.

"Really?" Olivia replies with a particularly skeptical lilt.

"Oh, come on."

"Notice the shirt." It is a long-sleeved red polo shirt.

"He must be freezing," I say.

"He's been wearing that shirt for a month. He absolutely refuses to wear anything else. I managed to suss out a duplicate, and now I steal away after he's in bed and wash one and leave the other in its place. Occasionally, he will sniff it suspiciously."

"Ruby wore a tutu for two months."

"I'm certain you managed it better than I have."

"No, I didn't." I remember for a moment how it enraged me to see my tiny girl in what soon became a graying rag, the netting torn, a network of tiny pills all over the bodice.

"And in the end?" says Olivia, who stops to speak sternly to Luke, now trying to poke his stick through the bleachers into the shins of spectators.

"One day she came downstairs in purple corduroy overalls. I kept my mouth shut because I was convinced that if I said anything she would tromp back up and put the tutu on again. But when Glen got home he said right away, 'Ruby, what happened to your tutu?' And she said, 'I threw it away. It was yucky and I didn't like it anymore.'"

"From your mouth to God's ear."

"How's Aidan? Ben said he was sick."

"Strep," says Olivia dismissively. "Antibiotics, done and done."

I look at her staring off, abstracted, over the ragged gray fields of winter weeds and add, "You must miss home sometimes, especially during the holidays."

"I've actually finally begun to think of this as home, now that I live with a houseful of American citizens," she says. "Although I have yet to be persuaded of the charms of turkey. And it would be useful if people would stop remarking on my accent."

"What accent?" I say.

"Bless you," Olivia says, and then her voice disappears in the screams of the crowd. "We'd better go back," she shouts. "Maybe the coach will play Ben for a few minutes." She reaches for Luke's hand. "If Alex were to make a goal, and you not there—disaster!"

"I'd say I had been," I reply.

"Terrific game," Stan says.

"Where were you?" says Glen.

"I'm hungry," says Max, and I hand him a sandwich and put my head on his shoulder. All normal activity gives me hope: eating, sleeping, speaking. It is as though Max is a baby again, and I am charting his milestones.

"I love you, Maxie mine," I say.

"Love you, too, Mom," he says, letting his side go just a little softer. Behind his back I smile at Ruby, and she smiles at me.

"You want half a sandwich, Nana?" Max asks.

"I think I will," my mother says.

Alice and I are sitting on the floor of the den, laughing loudly. Luckily, the house is laid out so that sound from the den barely carries to the master bedroom, where Glen has been sleeping for the past hour. I know this because of countless mornings when I have been told that the kids' friends stayed until past midnight, playing Uno or watching movies or just talking, mornings when the last thing I remember is turning out the light at 10 P.M. and the last sound I heard was the coo of a wood dove from the back lawn.

"I can't believe we haven't heard any complaints from my son," says Alice, picking up her glass of wine. I raise mine to her. There are half-eaten turkey sandwiches on a plate between us. I love turkey sandwiches, but by the Saturday after Thanksgiving even I have grown tired of them.

"Repeat after me: Liam is fine," I say. "Liam can sleep without me. He can even breathe without me."

"All I can tell you is that at home he'd be out of his crib and into my bed," she says. "And don't tell me he's too old for a crib. I know he's too old for a crib."

"He's discovered someone more interesting than you."

"Impossible," says Alice, taking a drink.

"Someday he's going to marry somebody he thinks is more interesting than you," I say.

"Are you trying to make me feel bad, or have you had too much to drink?"

"Both," I say.

"I haven't had this much wine in years," she says.

"You haven't actually had that much."

"I know, but I hardly ever drink anymore. I picture having to go to the emergency room half-looped, or having the sitter smell something on my breath."

"What about when Liam was with your parents?"

"Worse," she says, staring into her glass. "I was convinced I was going to have to go get him in the middle of the night. My parents are both very casual about everything he does."

I say nothing.

"I am not one of those crazy older mothers. I'm a little type A, but you can't imagine what it's like to be the only one responsible. You have Glen. You even have the other kids. Look at how your boys were with Liam."

Alice and Liam had arrived an hour before Thanksgiving dinner. We could hear the sound of Liam screaming as the car door opened. "Oh, goodness," my mother said as she turned from the stove. This is why I made certain to have well-behaved children: so that my mother would not say those words in that tone.

"Will you go help Aunt Alice?" I had asked the twins. "I've got to get this stuffing into the oven."

Five minutes later there was silence, and Alice in the kitchen doorway, her cheeks pink and her long hair disheveled. Since we graduated from college, she has had many incarnations: business suit, cropped hair, leather jackets, enormous jewelry, stiletto heels. Now she looks much as she did when we were twenty—a big sweater, jeans, flat boots, long hair. She hugged my mother, then me. "Terrific to see you again, honey," said Stan. Glen handed her a tumbler of eggnog.

"Max and Alex went off with Liam," she'd said, looking around at all of us. "He was crying, and Alex said 'little dude' in a deep voice, and he stopped crying and walked off with them. What happened to your sons? They're men."

"That's an optical illusion," Glen said, picking at the turkey skin with his fingers.

Alice had watched with amazement as her son sat quietly through Thanksgiving dinner, built with Legos compliantly in the den with Max, watched football while lying atop Ginger, and then went without a whimper to Max's room, where he was installed on a futon on the floor. The company futon, we call it, for when the beds are full. The plan had been for Liam to share Ruby's bed with Alice, while Ruby slept on the couch in the den, but Liam has thrown himself completely into the big-boy camp. "Are you sure, Meensie?" Alice had said. "Won't you be happier with Mommy? Mommy has a big, big bed."

"I'm big," Liam replied.

"He needs siblings," Alice says in the den, absently fitting some blocks together. "Should I adopt?"

Alice is not going to adopt. Liam is not going to have siblings. This is simply one of those questions we ask one another so that our friends will say that everything will be fine.

"He'll be fine," I say. "He is fine. He's so cute."

"Your guys are wonderful. They're so grown-up. And they were so good with him. How many teenage boys would take that kind of trouble with a three-year-old?"

I say nothing. I hate women who meet a compliment with a list of their children's shortcomings.

I lie back on a pile of pillows. "What a day," I say.

The young man who drove Ruby home from the writing program had come to visit her. His name is Maxwell, but everyone calls him Chip, apparently because he comes from a long line of Maxwells.

"This is really great," he said over a lunch of open-faced turkey sandwiches layered with gravy and stuffing. "I think the best part of Thanksgiving dinner is leftovers. And football games. There's some great football this weekend."

"Ruby hates football," Max had said with a smirk.

"I don't hate football," Ruby replied. "I just prefer other sports."

"I'm playing club rugby," Chip said.

"Now, that's a tough sport," Glen said, getting up for cranberry sauce. "I had a friend who started a practice in orthopedics in some little college town in Ohio; he told me he spent a third of his time taking care of the rugby players. He said there was a broken nose almost every weekend."

Chip bowed his head modestly over the crusts on his plate. "I've broken my nose twice," he said.

"Dude," said Alex. "How much did it bleed?"

"A lot."

His nose did not look in the least broken. He was handsome in the fashion of Disney princes, with regular features and broad shoulders. He had lovely manners. "Thank you so much, Mrs. Latham," he said as he was leaving after lunch, Sarah and Rachel standing at the curb giddy at the thought of a newcomer in their circle. "You knew if anyone was going to do it, it would be Pearl here," Rachel had said when Ruby announced that Chip would be stopping by on his way to school from the Cape.

"That boy's hair is completely wasted on a man," Alice says now.

"Shh. We're both getting really loud." And we start to laugh, loudly.

Somewhere in the house we hear a door open, and both of us sit up, Alice smoothing out her sweater, me putting down the wineglass. Alice envisions Liam tumbling down the stairs, screaming for Mama, waking my mother and Stan. I envision my mother coming downstairs and telling us that we are keeping her and Stan awake. If Glen comes down, I will mollify him with a slice of pumpkin pie.

But it's Ruby who slips into the den and stares down at the two of us. She's wearing a tiny corduroy skirt with tights and lace-up boots, and as she eyes us she reaches up and lets her hair fall down. "Can I have some wine?" she asks, and I raise my brows as Alice says, "Come on, give the girl a glass. This time next year she'll be going to keg parties."

"Thank you so much. That's so helpful. Would you like me to tell you what Liam will be doing in fifteen years?"

"Didn't you already tell me that he would have thrown me over for some floozy?"

Ruby has returned from the kitchen with a wineglass, using the hem of her sweater to wipe it out just as her father always does. "Did you actually just use the word *floozy*?" she says, sitting cross-legged next to Alice.

Ruby is too critical to idolize anyone, but she is devoted to Alice. She notes it aloud whenever a book Alice has edited gets a good review or is on the bestseller list, and once a year she takes the train alone to New York City and goes with Alice to art museums, the theater, and restaurants. Judging by the companionable way in which they clink glasses, I suspect that this isn't the first time they've shared a bottle of wine. Ruby believes Alice is who I would have been had I chosen a more interesting life. A more interesting life that would not have included Ruby: There's the problem with her analysis.

"So?" Ruby asks, not even bothering to include me in her gaze.

"So how did your friends like him?" Alice replies, knowing how much that matters.

"Loved him. Loved. Him. Or the girls did. You know the boys. They were territorial. But I think after a while they thought he was okay. He and Eric seemed to get along pretty well. Sarah and Rachel thought he was gorgeous."

"And he likes you," says Alice.

"He made a point of saying that."

"Your grandmother thought he was so polite," I say. "She said she hasn't heard anyone use 'sir' and 'ma'am' for a long time."

"Oh, he brought you something, Mommy. It's on the kitchen table. It's olive oil. Some really good olive oil."

"He didn't need to do that. He didn't even stay over. Although I don't know where we would have put him if he had."

"He could sleep in Ruby's bed," Alice says.

"Stop!" Ruby cries.

"With me," Alice adds.

"Even worse!"

"It's been so long," Alice says.

"Oh please, stop right now—so much too much information," Ruby says.

"I agree," I say.

"He's exactly the kind of guy you would have liked in college," Alice says to me.

"Really?" Ruby says.

"He has great hair," says Alice.

"Doesn't he? Amazing hair." Ruby falls back on the pillows. "Why are you lying on the floor?"

We both laugh. "We always sat on the floor in college," Alice says.

"We had no chairs," I say.

"We had those desk chairs, but they were so uncomfortable."

Ruby rolls over onto her stomach and looks at Alice. A look of chagrin crosses her face, and she puts her head in her hands. Her hands are so pretty, with long fingers and buffed nails. She has stopped wearing polish and jewelry, only a friendship bracelet made of silken string. Rachel and Sarah have them, too, and they're not supposed to remove them until they fall off, although Sarah has to slide hers off during swim meets.

"He's so boring!" Ruby wails.

"Shh. You'll wake the house," I say, but Alice starts to cackle loudly.

"He is really boring," Alice says.

"He's a nice guy," I say indulgently.

"Boring," says Alice.

"Boring!" shouts Ruby.

"There are worse things than boring," I say.

"There's married," Alice says.

"That's enough, Al."

"How did I not realize how boring he was during the summer?" Ruby cries.

"Was every other girl there interested in him?" says Alice.

"Yes."

"Bingo!"

"I'm not that shallow," Ruby says. "I think it was because he was really well-read. He's read Aeschylus and Joseph Conrad and Eudora Welty. He's the one who told me to read John Ashbery."

"Okay, honey, no one understands John Ashbery," says Alice. "And smart is not always interesting. And well-read is not always smart. I can tell you this authoritatively."

We hear footfalls on the stairs. "You see," I say to Ruby. "You're too loud."

She giggles and rolls onto Alice. "It's not my fault," she says in a stage whisper. "It's her fault." The wine seems already to be making Ruby a little silly. "Did you eat tonight?" I whisper back to her.

"Leftovers at Sarah's. Ask Nancy if you don't believe me. God."

"Don't be such a bitch," Alice says, shoving her.

Max is standing in the doorway, blinking, in his boxer shorts and a T-shirt that says GENIUS on the front. "That's my T-shirt," Ruby says.

"Aunt Alice, Liam took his diaper off and peed on the futon."

"Oh, honey, I'm so sorry," Alice says, struggling to her feet.

"No, it's cool, it's cool. He just got a little corner of it; the rest is on the floor."

"Oh, no."

"Don't get up. I just want to know where his diapers are. I tried to put the old one on, but it won't stick anymore. Like, those tape things."

"I thought he was toilet trained," I say.

"Sometimes he has an accident at night," Alice says.

"Just tell me where the diapers are," Max says.

The two of them go upstairs. Ruby is still lying on the floor, staring at the ceiling. "I'm star-crossed," she says.

"Don't be so dramatic," I say.

"Can I sleep here?"

"It's the only place you *can* sleep. The blankets are folded on the chest in the corner."

"I mean on the floor. I'm comfortable."

"Suit yourself."

I go into the kitchen to turn out the lights. It smells of turkey. On the table is a large bottle of very, very good olive oil.

The lamps in the windows of the dining room and living room

are on, too. There must be a moon; I can see the tree branches in bas relief against the sky, a few hardy leaves holding on as November rattles to a close. On Monday José will come and remove the cornstalks and the pumpkins, and next week I will begin to put up the greenery and the garlands.

Across the street I see movement, and I wonder whether a deer is crossing to our backyard, to crop the top from the faded butterfly bushes against the side of the garage. As I turn out the last lamp, I see a man rising from a seated position on the steps to the Jacksons' front door. I step back unconsciously. "Your call," Rickie had said the last time he brought me home, bringing up the idea of outdoor lighting again. There have been two robberies in town in the past few months, although nothing much was taken—some spare cash, a little jewelry. But by the time I go to the window again no one is there. I can tell by a change in the darkness and the shadows that Alice has put out the reading lamp in Ruby's room. The street outside is empty, a long tunnel of trees embracing across the dark strip of the asphalt. The house is quiet, and very full, and Ruby is asleep on the den floor, and I go upstairs to bed.

The four panes of light on the bedroom ceiling have shifted over the course of the fall, moved closer to the edge of the room. Today their color has changed as well, materialized as a faint silver-blue. For a moment, I look through half-open eyes. No alarm, no announcer telling me that the president is at Camp David, the budget still under discussion, a Nobel laureate dead. I have read the eerie light correctly, and the lawn outside the kitchen window is deep in snow. I start the coffee earlier than usual.

It's Christmas morning, and we are becalmed. What could be nicer? Snowfall is one of the best things that can happen to a family. The centrifugal force of daily life that flings us in different directions will be stilled. Glen says Ruby's car is not stable in really bad weather. But in really bad weather the phone always rings just after dawn, the telephone tree sending its tendrils through town to say there will be no school. Then there is no need for Ruby to drive at all.

There have already been two snow days this December, winter

hard upon Thanksgiving. Last week I canceled the appointment with the woman who was expecting me to drape her banisters in blue spruce and holly and turn her mantelpieces into the sort of celebration of the holidays that, in years past, were done by families instead of landscapers. "Don't you have four-wheel drive?" she asked peevishly when I called. Most of Glen's patients canceled. Alex did not have basketball practice. The literary magazine sat fallow for a day as the school building, empty and echoing, lay beneath the drifts in a whistling wind. The girls came over to bake Christmas cookies. The boys hovered, picking at dough as Sarah slapped their grubby hands. Even Max joined in that day, putting the eyes and smiles on gingerbread men, relieved not to go to school. His spirits have lifted as the winter break approaches: two whole weeks at home. Or perhaps it is that his sessions with Dr. Vagelos are having an effect.

He and Alex and Ruby are still asleep. Once they would tumble downstairs on Christmas morning even before dawn broke; now they are content to amble into the living room for presents after nine. I let Ginger out of her kennel and she stands at the back door, calculating: How short a distance can she go in order to keep her paws warm and dry? She whines slightly and then goes to a wet space on the driveway asphalt where the snow never sticks. She sniffs at the garage door and whines, then scratches at it.

"Come on, Ging," I call quietly, the sound lost in the soft hillocks of snow.

Max had an appointment with Dr. Vagelos on the snowy day last week, and he insisted on trudging through the streets to get there. "He's a good guy," Max said when he got home, and, more important, he sat at the kitchen table with me for twenty minutes, sipping at hot chocolate, listening to me fill the silence with chatter, occasionally smiling. But I've noticed that he runs down after a therapy session, is good for a day or two, and then slowly sinks beneath the weight of his torpor and sadness. A half-dozen times this term he has missed school, claiming a sore throat or an upset stomach and sleeping the day away. Thanksgiving cheered him, because he never needed to leave the house. In years past, I would have been delighted to see any of the children devote themselves to their grandparents, to hear Max's laugh as he wrestled with Liam on the floor. "Feel free to invite any of your friends over," I had said brightly to all three, but Ruby knew what I meant. "Mom, he doesn't have any friends right now," she said, and I held up my hand to ward off the blow. "It'll get better," she said, and she put her arms around me.

Just before the Christmas break, we had teacher conferences. Because Max had forgotten to sign us up, and Alex had signed us up late, we started with Ruby. Her homeroom teacher had a sheaf of notes from her colleagues, but they all amounted to the same thing: exemplary student, participates in class, has her work done.

"I do find her a little abstracted these days," she said, "but I find most of the seniors abstracted. I've learned to make allowances."

"So nothing we should worry about?" Glen had said.

"Ruby is the least of my worries," the teacher said with a smile.

And the least of ours. Alex, too, is abstracted. "If it doesn't include a ball, he's not interested," said the homeroom teacher, who also teaches both boys math. "I'm trying to create word problems for Alex and Ben that incorporate sports."

"Batting averages?" asks Glen.

"That's a little elementary for what we're working on."

For Max, we met with the school counselor. His teachers, she said, were still worried, although they appreciated that he was seeing a psychologist. "He just doesn't seem engaged," she added kindly. Max the Mute has become Nowhere Man. Once he came close to a fistfight with one of Alex's soccer teammates who called him that.

"You guys need to just tell him to get right," Alex said one night at dinner when he thought his brother was out of earshot, and Max came barreling back down the stairs, his face fierce, and shouted, "How do you know what right is, you jerk-off?" and then barreled back up before we could even spit out our objections.

I plug in the Christmas tree and watch the white lights send sparks across the surface of the silver balls. I have a half-dozen clients now who hire me to decorate their trees; I have one who has three trees, one in the two-story living room, one in the wood-paneled den, one in the cavernous kitchen. I went into this business because I loved the slow and gradual nature of it, the undeniable logic of the natural world. Now much of what I do is simply show, an attempt to present a gaudy mask to others. There is nothing more joyless than decorating the Christmas tree of someone you barely know.

Two Swedish coffee cakes have risen overnight atop the refrigerator. Along with meat loaf, this is the only recipe my mother has bequeathed to me. Her people were Scandinavian, although she is vague about exactly where they came from. "Ancestor worship," she called it when Ruby did a genealogy project.

We use the living room for Christmas morning. Once it was littered with boxes—dolls, games, bicycles. There was a feeding frenzy at sunup. Now I sit at the kitchen table, the dog at my feet, trying to figure out when to put the coffee cakes into the oven so they will be warm when the kids finally rise. I hear a noise from outside, a bump, a thump, and Ginger raises her head, sniffs the air, growls unconvincingly, and lies flat again. In the living room there is a very expensive drum set for Max, with a card saying it will be accompanied by the renovation of the room above the garage. Ruby has two round-trip tickets to London in her stocking. Alex has a soccer ball in a Lucite case signed by the Olympic team, and the best lacrosse stick available. I miss the toys.

"You could have slept in," says Glen when he comes down at seven-thirty in old khakis, a sweatshirt, and bare feet.

"I got up as soon as it was light for old times' sake."

He gets himself a cup of coffee and puts his cold feet on my insteps. "That's mean," I say drowsily, but I don't pull away. He kisses me. Because of the weather his father has decided not to come for Christmas dinner. I think we're both relieved. Glen's father makes Ruby and Max uneasy. "Nobody ever got rich from writing," he will say to her, and "You playing any sports?" he will ask Max. Only Alex suits. "Sit down and tell the old man your stats," he will say, and Alex will obediently recite goals, assists, free throws. Glen played high school sports, but I've gotten the impression that he was somehow never good enough. His brother Doug was quarterback but broke his arm halfway through his senior season. "That's when he put on the pounds," his father likes to say, although Doug has always looked fine to me.

The baking smell fills the house, and the blue light from outside, the silence of streets becalmed by both the holiday and the weather, makes it feel like a warm, safe cave. Sometimes I feel as Max does: Why would I ever want to leave? As I'm glazing the coffee cakes the children drift down together, Ruby dwarfed by an enormous flannel nightgown, the boys in sweatpants and T-shirts. Ruby screams, then cries at her European trip and says I must join her, which is exactly what I had hoped, although I ask if she doesn't want Sarah instead. Alex turns the soccer ball around and around and reads off the names and repeats, "Where did you guys get this?"

"Santa Claus found it," Glen says.

Only Max is silent as he circles the drum set. But as I put breakfast on the kitchen table I suddenly hear a long roll, a clash of cymbals, and then a riff that seems to go on for several minutes. I'm afraid to look, afraid to hope, afraid to see that his hands are going but his face remains lifeless.

"He's going to wake the whole block," Glen says.

"I don't give a damn," I say. I peek around the corner and he is not smiling, exactly, but his body is alive. The drums were expensive, and I would have paid double just for that.

"Snow!" Alex says when they all sit down, in that delayed reaction that seems to reflect the ability of the young to concentrate on only one thing at a time.

Ruby goes to the door and bends forward to peer out of its panes. She meshes her fingers together behind her back and rocks back and forth. I can tell she wants to put everything right before she flies away, Ruby does. She wants to feel at peace with Kiernan again, to make certain Rachel will not follow her worst impulses, to heal the rift between her brothers. She has given each of the boys a poem for Christmas, and the one for Max begins, "I miss you, mousie. Come back home." Mousie and Bear—that's what she called her brothers when she was very young. When I'd asked why, years ago, she made that exasperated click of the tongue, the one most girls don't learn until adolescence, and said, "Mommy, you know."

I didn't. I don't. She does.

"Do you guys want to go sledding?" she asks without turning around.

The house has a special kind of silence in snow, as though all of our modern conveniences have been made obsolete by the primacy of the weather, as though the phones will be useless, the furnace a mere conceit of warmth, the cars an empty gesture. But to my mind the silence is enormous at the moment because I'm waiting to hear the answer from the two boys, whether Max will join Alex and Ruby, and whether Alex will join Max.

"I'm psyched," Alex says.

"Whatever," says Max.

There's the usual scramble for snow pants and gloves. No matter how many I buy, there are never enough. Mummies in down and wool, the three of them trudge down the street to the hill at its end, two Flexible Flyers, one toboggan. Glen wiggles his eyebrows at me, and we go back upstairs to our room. At midday there are no light squares on the ceiling. I worry about Max while we're having sex, which seems terrible but inevitable. Then toward the end I forget about Max, which seems terrible in a different way.

"I'm hungry again," Glen says after. He showers, and so do I. Without talking about it, we decided several years ago that our children could smell sex on us, and that we preferred that they didn't. They have their illusions about us, just as we have ours about them.

I'm hungry again, too, and I polish off part of the second coffee cake. I call my mother to thank her for the recipe, but I get the machine. Perhaps they're playing Yuletide golf in the bright white of a Florida afternoon.

Ginger barks sharply once, then again, and there is the sound of a muffled roar from the front lawn. Outside, José is running the snow blower up our front path. He's wearing a knit cap pulled down low so that it is almost impossible to see his eyes. He goes around to start on the driveway, and I pull on boots and a coat and go outside with cake on a paper plate, and a thermos of coffee. Light and sweet is how the guys like it. At least I know that much.

"I'm surprised to see you," I say when he turns the machine off.

"John send me. I got no work today, only tomorrow."

"Merry Christmas. *Feliz Navidad*." I am embarrassed by the latter, and thrust the plate at him. Laboriously, he takes off his thick gloves and takes it in his hands. He can't hold the thermos at the same time. "Come inside," I finally say.

"No, missus, I will be making a mess. John is coming back soon, and I will go with him and have this then. Thank you. *Gracias*." I have forced the poor man to be bilingual.

"When are you going home?" I say.

"Maybe not this time," he says mournfully. "Things are not so good. Lots of things."

"I'm sorry. Is there some way I can help?"

He looks at the cake, and for some reason I'm sure he is hungry. "Eat," I say, but he shakes his head.

"Maybe I could get some pay now for the summer? The Greyhound is a lot of money, and we have some problems with the little girl, Graciella. She has a problem with her"—he moves his hand in a circle around his throat, seaching for the word—"her glands."

"Tonsils?'

"Yes," he says. "Maybe I could get some pay now, then I work?"

I'm embarrassed by my indecision. It would take so little to give this man a few hundred dollars. I'm certain he would work it off when the weather turns warm. But I think of Luis, of how I'd thought he was a good man, too. I think of Rickie's warning about advances, about how the men are always asking him for a hundred because they've gotten in the hole playing cards or borrowing from a co-worker. Last summer he announced to the crew that there would be no pay without work. "No exceptions," he said.

"I have to think about it, José," I say, turning the thermos in my hands. "We usually don't do that."

"I know," he says, resigned already. "That's okay. I ask, but I know."

"You sure you don't want to come in?"

"No, missus. I do the back part, the driveway. John will come back."

"Are you having a special dinner?" I cannot stop myself—my need to know that this isn't a terrible life, that I'm not responsible for a terrible life.

"The guys bring something from the Chalet," he says. The

Chalet is the ski resort where they work in wintertime. "Last year very good."

"Rickie has something for you all," I say.

"He give it yesterday. Thank you, missus." Fifty dollars for each man. Rickie is always worried they will spend it in the bar out on the highway, the one with the neon sign that says STEAK CHOPS BEER. Nancy says sometimes the kids go there, and no one has ever seen a steak or a chop. "Nachos from the microwave," she told me. I wonder if Mexicans think we're crazy to eat nachos.

An hour later, when I'm in the kitchen fixing lunch, José knocks at the back door. He hands me a package—brown paper, red ribbon—and at first I think it is from him and am even more embarassed. But apparently it was leaning against our front door. There is no card, no writing on the outside.

That night, after we've had our roast beef and potatoes and Christmas cookies, recorded carols blending into a pleasing and familiar background noise, while Glen and Alex are watching football in the den, when Max has gone into the living room to bang away at his new drums—"Not after nine o'clock," calls Glen, and I think, Oh, let him go until ten; please, let him go forever—I show the package to Ruby. It is a photograph of her. She's outside somewhere, and her hands are aloft, almost ceremonial, as though she is conducting, or conducting a religious service. The sun is behind her, so that the edges of her hair are a haze, almost a halo. It's the sort of photograph, of joy and life and beauty, that any mother would love to have of her daughter, and if things were different I would find a nail right now and hang it on the wall.

But I knew when I opened it that there was something wrong with it, something sad and scary, so I waited until the last few minutes of the day, so as not to spoil the happiness of Christmas, the camaraderie and pink cheeks of sledding, the easy and uncomplicated dinner conversation, the drowsy uninflected evening. Ruby holds it for a long time, her face expressionless, so different from the face in the photograph. She looks almost plain in the light from the chandelier above the table, the demitasse of light. She looks almost old.

I expect her to erupt, but she doesn't. Perhaps it's the aftertaste of the day, but she just sighs. Finally she says, "I don't even know when he took this."

"Maybe last year?" I ask.

She points to a sliver of shirt at the bottom of the photo, barely visible. "I bought that at the thrift store in September. It's a pretty recent picture." She squints. "I think I'm outside of Sarah's. He has that really good zoom lens. He must have used that."

"He's just lost, sweetie." Even as I say the words they sound glib, empty.

Ruby shakes her head. "Mommy, the thing you do, trying to make everyone happy? Sometimes it makes nobody happy. You're always making excuses for him, like you're trying to make up for something, like you're trying to make it up to poor Kiernan that his life sucks. And that makes me feel bad, and it makes him feel entitled."

"He doesn't come to the house anymore."

"Oh, Mom, of course he does. You just don't see him. That ring has been under my pillow again twice."

"Why didn't you say anything?"

"What, so you could say, 'He's such a sweet guy, he was so nice to Max'?"

"Oh, honey. I'm so sorry."

I look at the photograph again. I see something I haven't noticed before: With what looks like India ink, Kiernan has drawn the ring of hearts on Ruby's finger. Silently, I point to the place, leaving a smudge on the glass.

"Of course," says Ruby.

"I'll talk to him. Your father will talk to him."

"You know, in the beginning I kind of liked it, I have to admit. It was kind of flattering. Then it was annoying. Now it's creepy, like he can't stop himself. He's always been like that, like he couldn't do anything halfway. It's one of the reasons I broke up with him. It was just so exhausting."

"I'm so sorry. I didn't get it, not really."

"Why would you? For a long time, I was happy. Why would you worry when I was happy? When we're happy, all you see is the happiness."

"I think it's just the opposite. I always think that when you're unhappy all I see is the unhappiness."

"That, too," Ruby says. She stands and looks down at the photograph. "What are you going to do with that thing?"

"I hadn't even thought about it."

"Just get it away from me," she says, and goes upstairs.

"No way," says Max from inside his room, the door closed. "No fucking way," he adds, muttering. I can scarcely hear him over the music, but I choose to ignore it. I have just asked if he wants to go with us to Nancy and Bill's house for New Year's Eve. Their children will be there, although as the evening staggers toward midnight they'll leave, Fred with his girlfriend, Sarah with Eric and Ruby and Rachel and the rest, Bob to a pool party someone has organized at the Holiday Inn for the younger teenagers, to keep them out of trouble. There's no curfew for New Year's Eve yet, but if there are many more car crashes on the winding roads around here it's only a matter of time. "Safety at any price," the head of the council has said to the local paper.

"Maybe we should stay home," I say to Glen.

"We're going out," he says as he threads his belt through the loops. "We're not going to keep catering to his moods."

"I don't think that's the word I would use to describe what's going on with him," I say.

"I don't care what word we use. We're going to the party."

After Max asks, "How late can I play my drums?" I give up and let him stay home alone. If he's on the drums, at least he won't be in his room, where I open the windows to the sharp winter air and exorcise the yeasty smell of unwashed teenage boy. There is a faint grubby impression of his body on the sheets, like the Shroud of Turin. Twice a week I gather clothes from the floor into the laundry basket and send them down the chute to the mudroom, where Ginger will snuffle through them happily. She loves Alex's sports uniforms, too, of which there are many. No. 18 in soccer, No. 21 in basketball, number still to be determined in lacrosse. Alex has gone on a ski trip, organized hastily, with the family of his friend Colin from camp. I suspect that one of Colin's school friends has canceled at the last minute, but his mother sounds nice on the phone, and says all the right things about parental oversight on the trip.

By evening's end, I am beginning to think that Max has the right idea. Each year Glen and I talk of staying home on New Year's Eve, watching an old movie, having a glass of Chardonnay and a sandwich and going to sleep at 10 P.M. But someone always has a party, and it seems churlish to say no. Nancy has sworn that she has planned a quieter version of the usual cocktail-dress-and-canapés event, but there are forty people, and chafing dishes, and endless champagne.

"Half of the people I asked are in the Caribbean," she says, popping another cork in the kitchen.

"I wish I were in the Caribbean," I say. My skin is pasty, and I have the ghost of a head cold.

Sarah has already chosen a college, the one with the new athletic center and the winning swim team. She is standing at the buffet table with an enormous pile of crab cakes on her plate. Eric is sitting in one of the dining-room chairs pushed back against the wall, frowning. Ruby has a hip pressed up against the piano, talking to Nancy's colleague from the university, the one who teaches philosophy. "My father was a philosophy major," I hear Ruby say as she catches my eye across the room and raises a glass. She's wearing a black lace dress that comes to mid-thigh. Her shoes have been abandoned by the back door. Her toenails are painted orange. I smile and lift my glass in return, amazed that I am the mother of this beautiful girl. Here's to her.

When I was Ruby's age, New Year's Eve was always anticipated, always disappointing. I remember the first New Year's I spent with Alice's family, and how she had convinced me that I would meet someone, someone older, someone wonderful. Instead, a twenty-two-year-old with beer breath had tried to push me into a closet, I had gotten Stroganoff sauce on a pink silk dress, and I had had two glasses of champagne atop four White Russians and been noisily, messily sick in Alice's bathroom.

Perhaps because of that, Alice always calls me on New Year's Eve. Her greeting never varies: "Every time I puke after a party I think of you, babe."

"When's the last time you puked after a party?"

A thoughtful silence, then: "I think I was pregnant. Does that count?"

"No. Are you going out tonight?"

"How soon they forget. Have you ever heard of anyone being able to get a babysitter on New Year's Eve?"

We've never needed one. In our circles, the children were all of an age; we brought them with us, tucked them into one another's cribs, lifted their boneless little bodies into the cars after the ball dropped in Times Square. They slept effortlessly, utterly, never awakened by the shouts, the laughter, the garbled chorus of "Auld Lang Syne." Nancy once showed me a newspaper story about a toddler who had suffocated under the coats at a party. "I've had my moments, but I think I would notice a two-year-old before I tossed my coat on the bed," she had said.

We once put coats over little Declan Donahue as Ruby and Kiernan bounced to old soul music in the living room and the twins slept on a sofa. But Declan's face, slack in sleep, had remained uncovered and elevated on the pillows, so that he looked like an enormous wooly bear of a man with the head of a seraph. That was the night Kiernan's father had kissed me in the bathroom, his hand sliding up inside my satin blouse. I vowed the next morning, while opening a bottle of Tylenol, to avoid being alone with him in the future. I wished more than once that I had kept that vow.

New Year's Eve: always disappointing, now simply dispiriting. Our children still have the slightly glassy expectant look of people determined to somehow wrest a very good time from the frigid night. After they leave, the party loses its gaiety, and suddenly there is merely a kitchen full of scraped plates and several dozen adults talking of how their tolerance for alcohol has diminished with age. "I'm in bed by ten every night," one woman says, to a thundering silence, because of course all of us are in bed by ten every night, every night but this one. Glen and Bill have a hurried conversation just after midnight, talking in the kitchen about whether the philosopher is too drunk to drive. But by the time they come into the living room to find Nancy and ask her what to do, the man has already sped away. "Were his headlights on?" Glen asks.

"Why in God's name do I do this?" Nancy says, hugging me hard at the door.

"It was a great party," I say. "There's no one I would rather spend the evening with."

"Tell me in the morning, when I can understand what you're saying. Let's have a wonderful year together. Let's live through the nightmare of sending those girls to college."

"Oh, God, don't even mention that."

"Okay, Nance, this is getting maudlin," says Bill.

"If we can't be maudlin on New Year's Eve, when the hell can we be maudlin?" Nancy cries, her arm still draped around my shoulder.

"Are you drunk?" I say to Glen as we walk home hand in hand.

"Yes, I am," he says flatly. "I'm not proud of it."

"We're too old for this. I had three Cosmopolitans, two glasses of red wine, and two glasses of champagne."

"Wow! That's a lot to drink."

Ahead, our house is lit up, the kitchen and the mudroom windows bright against the black outside. This says nothing about what is happening within. Our children have been known to go up to bed with the television and all the downstairs lights still on. Inside, I look around for clues. There is no sign of Ruby, of her little red Chinese purse on the table, of her towering purple heels in the middle of the kitchen floor. Ruby leaves a trail of herself downstairs after a party: shoes, jewelry, sometimes a box of Band-Aids for blisters. Upstairs, Max's door is shut, with no telltale line of light along its bottom sill.

"Don't turn off the lamps," I say as I take a sleeping pill.

Glen frowns. He wants to tell me that I shouldn't take a sleeping pill when I've had alcohol, but he knows I know. And I know he knows to leave the lamps on. I say this every time we get home and one of the children is still out. This is what it is like to be married: conversations in which no one actually speaks.

I carry my shoes up the stairs. There is no sound from Max's room. Ruby's light is on, and several rejected party dresses are on the floor, along with a tangle of underwear and fishnet stockings. Someday she will have forgotten about this and will be telling her own daughter that her room is a sty. Or she will insist that I was too indulgent and should have demanded that she be tidier.

"Is he asleep?" Glen whispers under the duvet, pushing up my nightgown. Glen believes in sex on New Year's Eve. Afterward, I find my nightgown wadded up at the foot of the bed. Glen puts on a T-shirt and a pair of boxer shorts, and begins to snore, and I match my breathing to his, and I immediately fall down the chute of sleep.

I half wake when I hear a noise from downstairs, and I look at the digital clock: 3:43, it says. I wait to hear Ruby on the stairs, but instead it sounds as though something drops below. Glen coughs, rolls over. For a few moments, I hear nothing. My head is muddled and now I'm not certain I heard anything at all, that it was not the closing salvos of a dream or a side effect of the sleeping pill. One night several years ago, I went downstairs because I smelled chocolate-chip cookies baking, but the kitchen was dark and smelled only of lemon oil and Ginger, who had whined softly from inside her kennel. Glen says the sleeping pills can do this.

Then I hear scuffling, and voices, and something else drops, and Glen opens his eyes. "How many times have I told them?" he hisses. So many times: We don't care how late you stay up, or whether you have your friends in, as long as you don't keep us awake.

Another sound, perhaps someone sitting down hard in a chair. "They've probably had a lot to drink," I say. "At least they're not driving around." I hear something fall with a dull thump.

Glen stands and pulls on a pair of pants. "I hate it when they make me go down there," he says.

"I'll go," I say, remembering that night I found Rachel soiled and sad on the den couch, but Glen is already starting down the stairs. I lose the sounds of his bare feet in the other noises of the house—the groan and whine of the old radiator below our window, the scratching at the siding from the tree that needs pruning, the window rattling at the end of the hall. There's more noise from below, louder, and I wonder if it is the sound of adolescent exodus, if Glen has thrown everyone out, and in the morning our daughter will be resentful, her lips set in the line that indicates we have disappointed her again. She was beautiful that evening in her black lace, her pale skin a half-moon in the boat neck. I am thinking about how she looked as sleep pulls me back under.

When I wake again, I'm not sure why. For a moment I thought someone was cooking in the kitchen, just as I had that other time, except that it was not cookies but something else. I roll onto my back and feel a piercing pain in the hollow between my neck and my skull and try to remember how much I had to drink. The bare trees outside are making shadows in the window-shaped light on the ceiling, twig fingers in black and gray, and I wonder if there's a storm coming up, and if Ruby's friends have made it home. I hear Glen coming back up the stairs but slowly, with a heavy tread, and I look toward the door. There is only a faint light in the hall, the one from Ruby's room, and he stands in the doorway, and I see that it's not him at all. Too gangly, too slender, too unkempt.

"Maxie?" I whisper softly, afraid that he will be frightened by the sound, that he will assume that I am asleep. And in one motion he moves to the bed and strikes me, hard, in the shoulder, and I cry out and roll onto the floor between the bed and the wall. I whimper, and hear breathing, and a long time seems to pass. Then I hear feet on the stairs again, this time going down, fast.

"Maxie," I repeat.

I'm facing the wall, and I don't know if I can move. There's a burning in my chest and a taste in my mouth like when I used to hide pennies under my tongue when I was little. I think I hear more noise downstairs, but I'm not sure because my heart is so loud in my ears.

I know I've lost time, because when next I hear sound, more faintly this time, it's light outside. I don't open my eyes, I'm afraid to, but there is the faint gray, the vibrating test signal, that daylight makes inside your lids when they are closed. I imagine I have had a terrible dream, but the pain is still there, and now my lips seemed to be gummed with something thick and viscous. I open my eyes slightly and see red-brown shadows all around me on the molding and the outlet and the old Oriental rug, and I close my eyes again.

The last time I wake I can hear people in the house, and I wonder if I have imagined the whole night, if Glen was right and a sleeping pill and some glasses of champagne have given me a brief vision of hell, if everyone is downstairs making breakfast and wondering when I will finally get up. "I will never do that again," I'll tell Glen when I finally go downstairs. Or maybe I won't give him the satisfaction. But then I hear footfalls on the stairs, and I lie very still, my face pressed into the edge of the rug.

"Jesus Christ," someone says, quite close by, "they're all dead?"

"Every last one," says a different voice.

I am staring into the sun. I can see its round edges faintly behind a quivering nimbus of light. It drills down into my head, and I remember that when I was young, at the lake in Michigan, one of my friends said that if you looked directly into the sun you would go blind. My mother said that wasn't true, but then she asked why in the world I would want to look into the sun in the first place.

"Mary Beth!" says a very loud voice I don't recognize. "Mary Beth, can you hear me?"

I don't want to take any chances going blind. I close my eyes and go back to sleep.

Once, when Ruby was six or seven, we were driving in the car with all three of the children in the back, sleeping. The boys were slumped in their car seats, and she was in a booster between them, her head down so that her chin was tucked into the hollow of her throat. "They're all out like a light," I had said to Glen with a smile.

Afterward, I realized that we were having a humdrum discussion, about whether we should visit some old friends who had invited us to the beach, whether we should put an addition on the house, whether it was too soon for me to go back to work. I searched my memory for whether we had mentioned that the old friends had come close to divorce because of his affair, whether we had discussed how little money we had for the addition, whether we had begun bickering because Glen didn't want me to go back to work and I wanted to get out of the house so badly. There was none of that. Our voices must have been background music, murmurs in two octaves, one bass, one alto.

But it still came as a surprise when Ruby suddenly leaned forward between our two seats and yelled, "I'm awake!," jolting the boys upright momentarily.

"*Shhhhhh!*" I had hissed.

"I'm awake," Ruby whispered gleefully. "I was just pretending to be asleep so I could listen to what you were talking about."

That is what I am doing right now. At first I kept still, kept my eyes closed, because through a muzzy haze of strange sleep I couldn't tell where I was. Then I realized by the smells and sounds that I was in a hospital. Occasionally, someone would call my name and I would lie still, listening to the beep of a monitor.

I can't seem to pierce the shroud of thick insensibility, to move past it, but once I tried very hard to concentrate and heard voices in muted conversation. My mother and Alice, then, a little later, Alice and Nancy. When Alice began to cry, a hiccuping noise not that far removed from how she laughs, a thought crossed my mind, but I put it aside and went under again.

"She's agitated," someone had said as the monitor began to quicken its high-pitched backbeat. For a moment I was reminded of something, and for a moment I had it: the time in the other hospital, with the monitor on my belly, when the nurse had said, looking at the machine printout, "You're having a contraction." And I wanted to scream "I know I'm having a contraction! I can feel it tearing me apart." The memory made my heart beat faster, and the beeps got faster, and someone took my wrist, and I went under again.

Now I am awake, trying to keep my mind as still as my body. My eyes are slightly slitted, so that I can see who is in the room but they can't see me. There was a time when Max believed that if he closed his eyes he was invisible. "I can still see you," Alex would say, looking at him. "No, you can't," Max would reply, squeezing his lids tight.

My shoulder hurts, and an IV line is pulling at the soft skin inside my elbow. There is a chair in the corner, and in it is my mother. She has magazines on her lap, but she's looking out a small window. The green paint on the wall is somehow reflected on her face, as though she's sitting on the edge of a lit swimming pool in the evening hours. It makes her look ill. She looks tired and grim, too, but she looks that way most of the time, has looked that way for most of my life. My mother never smiles in photographs. She says she doesn't like her teeth, which look ordinary to me. At our graduations, our weddings—she is the solemn woman next to the bride, the groom. I used to wonder whether there were smiling pictures taken before her husband died, or before she was married, but I've never seen any of those pictures. She begins when we do, except for her wedding portrait. There is a hint of happiness in her eyes there, but no smile.

She looks at me, then narrows her own eyes as though she's imitating me. She comes to the side of the bed and takes my hand. "It's time to wake up now, Mary Beth," she says. For a moment my lids flutter, and then I look up.

"Good," she says.

I put my other hand to my throat and cough. My shoulder throbs, and I wince. "They had you on a respirator the first day, when they thought it was worse," she says. "That's why your throat hurts. It will go away soon."

"Is she talking?" says a nurse from the doorway, and my mother holds up her hand without turning. "I'll let you know when to come back," she says in the voice she once used for failing students. The nurse withdraws.

"Where is Alex?" my mother asks. Her voice is loud, and I wonder if they all think I've lost my hearing. My vision is blurred. Maybe I have lost all my senses and just don't know it.

"Alex?" It is a sandpaper whisper, and my throat burns.

"Mary Beth, you have to focus now. This is very important. Do you have any idea where Alex is, where he might have gone? Any idea at all? Can you give me any clue?"

I close my eyes and try to think. I have it. I have it. Thinking with this brain is like breathing through a head cold, like looking at things underwater. My thoughts shimmer. My mind squints.

"Colorado," I whisper.

"Colorado?" She sounds as though I am speaking another language.

"Skiing. Colin from camp. On the fridge."

And then something extraordinary happens. My mother begins to cry. Her mouth is held so tight that the skin around her lips turns ghost-white, and the muscles of her face move spasmodically. But tears are running down her face and into the lines around her mouth. The last time I had seen her cry was at my wedding, and then I had assumed they were happy tears. These have something of joy about them, too, which I can't understand.

"Alex is skiing? In Colorado? With someone named Colin from camp?"

I blink my eyes. I think it will hurt to nod. "Yes," I hiss.

"When is he coming home?"

I close my eyes again. I hear my mother on the phone. She is telling someone to go to the ice box. "The ice box!" she barks. "The refrigerator!" You're not allowed to use a cell phone in the hospital. There were big signs when I was waiting for Max's arm to be repaired. I had had to go outside into the parking lot to call Glen. It was so hot on the asphalt that day. My hands were slick and I dropped the phone. When I drove Max home, he said the air-conditioning in the car was too cold. Glen said it was the anesthetic. I made Max a sandwich, but he fell asleep before he could eat it. Glen said it was the anesthetic. I wonder if I had anesthetic. I go under again.

I wake up. A nurse puts a thermometer under my tongue. "My

name is Brittany, Mrs. Latham," she says softly. I think I have seen her trying on a dress at Molly's Closet. When she leaves, I see Alice sitting in the chair. She's asleep, her mouth ajar. She'll be upset to realize that she drooled on her chin. She has a manuscript in her lap. I think my mother has gone to look for an ice box, but I can't remember exactly why.

I watch Alice for what feels like a long time. Nancy comes in and puts a hand on Alice's shoulder and shakes her, roughly, it seems to me. Alice starts up. "I'll take over now," Nancy says. Neither of them looks at me. When they finally do Alice cries out, then starts to cry again.

I think I remember something. "Where is Alex?" I say. My voice is a little louder.

"What?" Nancy says, almost shouts.

"Where is Alex?"

"Colorado," Alice says. "He's coming home tomorrow. He'll be here tomorrow." She's sobbing. I can scarcely understand her. Nancy leaves and comes back with my mother.

"I think you should both wait outside for a few minutes," my mother says.

Alice starts to say something, and so do I, and everyone is quiet, and I can hear the monitor, and my thoughts are not quite so fuzzy anymore, and I wish that I could go back to sleep for just a little while. I think I remember something else.

"They're all dead," I say, and I sound just like my mother—flat, cold. And then I repeat it and it doesn't sound like words at all but like a terrible song, like something from an opera. I say it one more time, and then there is a loud sound in the room, but I hear it as though my ears are plugged up. It sounds like the sound I made in the hospital when they were all yelling at me, all yelling, "Push! Now! Harder." That sound was bad, but then it was over. This time it won't stop. People are running in the halls.

Alice wails, and Nancy puts her arms around her. A nurse comes in. I feel something dripping off my chin. "A moment, please," my mother says to the nurse, pressing a tissue to my face, and I understand that she is the perfect person for this moment, that she is the perfect person to tell someone news so bad that no one else can even form the words. I wonder if she was always this way, or if she learned to be this way when someone told her terrible things. The noise gets smaller and smaller, as though it is moving away from me.

"Shh, shh, Mary Beth," my mother says, sitting on the edge of the bed, putting her face so near to mine that I can smell the shampoo she uses. "Alex is coming home tomorrow. Alex is coming home tomorrow. Do you understand?" She looks fuzzy, and when I nod her face seems to shimmer in the fluorescent light. I realize my mouth is open, and I close it. She puts her face next to mine. I feel her cheek, wet. I want everything to be still.

"Max and Ruby and Glen," she whispers.

"Someone," I finally say, and she nods.

"They don't know who." And suddenly I remember. I remember that I thought it was Max, Max who came into my room, who hit me, who hurt me. And I hear that sound again, louder this time, and my throat burns and my shoulder aches and the lights in the room are all like suns and I am so, so ashamed that I thought my poor sad boy could have hurt any of us. My mother holds me tightly.

"Alex," I say when I can speak again.

"The police thought it was him. Because he was gone. Because they couldn't find him. No one knew he was away."

"Alex?" I say again.

"I didn't believe it. I couldn't believe it. I told them they were wrong."

"Does she need a sedative?" says the young nurse from the

doorway. What is her name again? I can't remember. The monitor is making so much noise. I can't breathe. It's like a head cold.

The difference between the doctor and the nurse is that the doctor has a white coat. It's just like Glen's. It must have come from the same place. The doctor is a woman. She tells the nurses what to do, but I can't really hear her. That sound is in my ears. The sun dims. My mother's mouth moves, but there are no words. I think that when Alex comes home I will make him chocolate pudding. Chocolate pudding is his favorite. The sound stops, and I am gone again.

Ginger is wandering around the kitchen of the guesthouse at Olivia and Ted's, looking for a corner in which to settle. Three, four times she makes the small circle and finally decides that the best place to lie is directly in front of the stove. I don't have it in me to try to move her, although this makes it difficult to reach the burners. My left arm is a damaged wing, floppy and unreliable. A physical therapist comes three times a week and makes me squeeze a tennis ball. "Much better, Mrs. Latham," she says, looking at my arm, avoiding my eyes. My mind tells my body to do things, and it stubbornly refuses, as though it is still half-asleep. Since I left the hospital three weeks ago, my mind has slowly become accustomed to demands that are ignored by my body.

Ginger whimpers and I give her a piece of carrot. She chews noisily and whimpers again.

I am making vegetable soup. It's a good recipe, and it freezes well. I will put it in ice-cube trays. Then when I want lunch, or

Alex wants lunch, or both of us want dinner, I can take out a few cubes and heat it back up. It's very good soup. Glen always loved it this time of year. "Soup!" he would say, as though a bowl of wet-hot was the greatest gift a person could give. Alex says he likes it, too, but I can't remember if this is true. He mainly eats at Olivia's house now, with Ben and Ben's brothers. When he is here he stands with his plate in his hand, leaning against the kitchen counter. I think it's because the table is tiny, only big enough for two. When we sit at it together, across from each other, it tells a story neither of us wants to believe.

I take out the ice-cube trays. There are only two of them. I have made a lot of soup. There's no more room in the freezer. There is the lasagna I made last week, and the lamb stew, and the four loaves of bread, one with cheese. This is what I've always done. I've always had food in the freezer so there would be a good, hot meal for dinner, even when I am out of the house.

I don't go out of the guesthouse much. I mainly stay here, inside. It's a nice place, small and cozy, decorated the way Olivia does things. Warm. Homey. Pretty. It's the kind of place that makes you feel safe. Sometimes I walk around the edge of the woods with Ginger, but she always wants to go back inside, and so do I. There's old snow on the ground, and dark pits in the snow, grimy pits of cinders and mud and sad tattered grass. The pits are my footprints. The snow has a glossy veneer of ice, and Ginger leaves no prints because she is too light to break through. For the first two weeks she ate nothing at all, not even her favorites—slices of apple, pork-chop bones. "Come on, you know you want this," Alex would say, sitting cross-legged on the floor with some scrap of meat or cheese on his palm. She would put her head on her front paws and look up at him, her brow twitching.

She will be ten years old in May. We used to work out how old the kids would be when Ginger was five, when Ginger was ten. We never went any higher than that. We didn't want to think about how old they would be when Ginger was put to sleep.

I was the one who went to sleep, sleep so deep that the police officers thought I was dead while they walked around my house. One of them took Ginger out to his car and put her in the back, behind the metal grille. Then they let her out because she threw herself so hard against the grille that she broke two of her incisors and ripped out a dewclaw. Olivia took her to the vet while I was in the hospital, and the vet pulled the two teeth and bandaged her paw. She still limps a bit, and I wonder if it's more memory than injury.

Ginger saved my life. Our next-door neighbor woke on New Year's Day and saw the back door open, waving wildly in a cold sleety wind, and when he went over to shut it—"Hello?" I imagine him calling, although I never heard him. "Glen? Mary Beth? Everything okay?"—he heard Ginger keening inside her kennel. He called the police. That's what I'm told. Everything about that night is what I'm told. All I heard were the sounds of my kids' friends hanging out in the den and making too much noise. All I heard was my husband going downstairs to reprimand them and send them home. Or that's what I thought I heard. Nancy says the newspapers wrote that I slept through it all, which is more or less true. I can imagine myself reading that about someone else and disbelieving it. That's what people do: They imagine themselves in your place, and they know that they would be different, better. They scare themselves a little with borrowed tragedy, and then they retreat to the safety of their own safe place, or what they think is their own safe place.

When I start to imagine myself in my place, I take another pill. The way it makes me feel reminds me of how I saw the world, and how the world saw me, when my wedding veil was over my face, before Glen lifted it. The blusher, they call that piece of the veil that covers your face and gives everything around a soft white-wash. Sometime soon I am going to stop taking the pills. But not at night. I can't imagine how I will ever sleep again otherwise. I take the sleeping pill, and then I pick up a book, turning the pages in the exact rhythm of someone who is reading. I have no idea what has happened on the page, and suddenly I am asleep for five or six hours. Alex doesn't know it, but there is a baby monitor under his bed. The receiver is under my pillow, turned up as high as it will go, so that any sound would wake me from my drugged sleep. Before I take the pill, I listen for a half hour. I watch the clock. There's never any sound.

Ginger rearranges herself against the stove and drops her head heavily on the floor. I stir the soup and then move into the little living room and sit down on the sofa. My mind whirrs and stops, whirrs and stops, like a broken clock. I lose time all the time now, the way I did that night, the way I did in the hospital. But I'm awake when it happens. I look across the room at the beveled frame of a mirror or the oval doorknob and I'm in a waking dream, except that there's nothing in it, no people, no feeling. From time to time I hear a familiar voice, and when I do I shiver and the waking dream is over and I find something to do, even if it's only to stir the soup again. Sometimes when I move I realize that my face is wet. I wipe it with a paper towel. I can't think of it as crying. The good thing about living in this new place, where I still don't know how to shift the oven racks or set the thermostat exactly right, is that I don't feel like this is my life. It's some suspended animation, between what was and something else, something I can't think about. I don't think of what comes next, except that there is a recipe for chili in a cookbook on the shelf here that I might try. Chili, tomorrow. Or maybe even today.

It's not even noon yet. I wonder how I will fill the rest of the day, and I think that maybe I will put Ginger in the car and drive around the mountain roads, passing some of the houses where I have planted things in the past. You can do things in a car that you can't really do anywhere else. Scream. Curse. Talk to yourself, or to people who aren't there. No one can hear you in a car, although at traffic lights it's important to stop so that the person in the next lane won't look over and think you're crazy. "Poor Mary Beth Latham," the person might tell everyone, at school, at the club. "I saw her talking to herself at the corner of Main Street and Valley Road."

The first time I went out in the car, I made sure to get back by three-thirty so I could be home when Alex came in. I heard the doors of Olivia's Suburban slam, and I arranged myself in the kitchen, by the little table but not at it, and I told my brain to give my face a smile, and it did, although when I told it to put my left hand on the back of one of the little ladder-back chairs it refused. Ginger whined, and after ten minutes Alex had not come, and I ran up the hill in a pair of thin driving shoes that were sodden by the time I got to the back door of Olivia's house.

"What?" Olivia said when she saw my face and heard the dog barking shrilly.

"I heard your car," I said, "but Alex hasn't come home. Do you know where he is?"

"Basketball," she said, very low and slow, her hand still on my arm, her eyes locked on mine as she pulled me into the house. "They have basketball this afternoon." Her precise English voice is so calm that I understand, and believe. In the hospital and then afterward, when she had stayed with me, I noticed for the first time that Alice's voice is glissando: up the scale, down the scale. It made my head hurt and my heart beat faster. "When is Aunt Alice going home?" Alex had asked one night as we ate sandwiches again for dinner, and I said without thinking, "Tomorrow." Liam was living with his Trinidadian nanny, but he cried each night when the sun went down. "I'll be back soon, babe," Alice had said as she kissed me.

Olivia's voice is as measured and restful as Olivia herself. She saved my life, too. She gave us both a place to stay. When Alex came back from Colorado, with a toffee-colored tan, when I was still in the hospital, she put him in Ben's room, and for the first three nights she slept on an inflatable mattress in the hallway just outside the door. "He says he doesn't want to talk about it," Ben had told her. We don't talk about it. Alex goes to school. I cook his meals. Together, the week after I left the hospital, we went to the memorial service. I held Alex's hand tight throughout it. It felt life-less in mine. That's mostly what I remember. Sarah spoke, and Ezra, and Nancy and Bill together, and Glen's brother Doug, and the high school choir sang. I think it was "You've Got a Friend," although I am not certain. I took a lot of pills that day. But I remember Alex's hand, and the big bouquets of amaryllis and evergreens on the stage at the community center, and the photographs of Glen and Ruby and Max on easels. There was a picture in the center of all five of us together in London. Max was looking to the side. Ruby's hair was in her face. "Is that the best one?" Glen had asked when I chose it for our Christmas card. "Everyone's moving in every one of them," I'd replied. "This is the one with the fewest people moving."

Ruby's friend Jacqui, the girl she roomed with at the summer writing program, read a poem of Ruby's I had never heard before:

How can I ask for more
Than this minute, when the stars lie bright against the velvet
Without the curtain of cloud

And the earth beneath smells ripe and full
Of both of us, lying here,
Looking toward heaven.

I remember I wept then, and Alex's hand became rigid in mine, and he had a hard and angry frown, the face that men make when they're trying not to break. Glen's father had the same look. Behind him Stan sat with his arm around my mother and heaved into an enormous handkerchief, and my mother patted his big, meaty leg as though it were a baby that required comfort.

I never spoke to Jacqui after she read at the service. Somewhere on the little desk in the living room of this little house, in the big pile of papers, there is a lovely letter from her, and a note from that boy Chip that Ruby met at the college writing program, and the girl Max liked at camp. The pile was much much bigger in the beginning, but Nancy went through it every day after work for a week, and took out the religious tracts about a better place and life everlasting, and the messages from inmates who wondered if I wanted to correspond, and the letters, in their unmistakable spiky block print, from the schizophrenics who needed me to understand that my family was being held prisoner in a nuclear facility in the desert. "There are so many pathetic crazy people in the world," Nancy had said through clenched teeth, and for a moment I thought she meant me.

She never saw the letter from Deborah Donahue or I'm sure she would have thrown it away, perhaps even burned it. "You killed my son," Kiernan's mother wrote, in a block print not unlike those of the crazy people. We'd always been in unlikely sympathy with each other, Deborah and I. There was a year there, when the kids were small, when even our menstrual cycles were in sync, and we made a pact not to go to each other's house at those times because we were both so out of sorts that we would certainly quarrel. Now we are both bereaved mothers who had seen disaster creeping up and had somehow convinced ourselves that it was an optical illusion.

Kiernan's father came to the memorial service. He tried to hug me afterward, but I turned away from him. I do remember that. There was a large ring of public avoidance around him, as though he had a contagious disease, or gave off a force field. "I can't believe he had the unmitigated gall to come to this," Nancy had said, loud enough for him to hear.

"It's fine," I whispered, and moved away. What did it matter to me? What did anything matter to me? Except Alex. This is what I have to keep reminding myself. In the hospital, my mother had heard one of the nurses whispering that my whole family was gone. "She has a son," my mother said coldly. "She has a son."

I have a son. He will be hungry. Because of the hospital, and our shut-up house, and the police, and the questions, people had not come to us with casseroles and cakes the way they do after someone has died. When I look in the packed freezer, I realize I am making my own funeral meats.

I carry most of the pot of soup up to Olivia's house, and she answers the door and says, "I've just put the kettle on." Ginger comes in, too, and lies between the two of us beneath the kitchen table. I don't think Ginger should be left alone. The house is so quiet between our sentences that I can hear the grandfather clock in the hall tick, but Olivia doesn't always try to fill the silence. She is a good listener, except that I have nothing to say, or nothing I can say aloud. When the ticking becomes too sharp, I go back down the hill with no memory of what we've talked about. I sit on the sofa again, Ginger's head on one of my insteps. I finger the long scar on my shoulder and think, Glen is gone, Ruby is gone, Max is gone. It's the way I used to memorize poetry when I was younger. It's like I am trying to teach it to myself so I will understand.

So this is what it is like not to be medicated, or, at least, medicated less: The light feels like shards of glass, the glass in the windows looks like mirrors, the mirrors reflect back a gray woman with black eyes. I'm wearing the same dress I wore to the memorial service, and as I zip it awkwardly, trying to snake my good arm up the middle of my back, I tell myself that I will throw the dress away in the morning. "Give it to Goodwill," I know my mother will say, but I think its fabric now holds its history, so that it would be like donating a sweater full of moths or a chest of drawers with woodworm.

I pull into the lot in front of the lawyer's office, and as I do men in dark suits emerge from a line of cars. The slam of metal doors is my welcome. They converge on me, and I think they look like pallbearers: Glen's father; his brother Doug; my brother, Richard; Nancy's husband, Bill. The men are here to mourn the way that feels most useful to them, by taking care of business. One by one, they kiss my cheek. They have come together in a caravan from

Nancy's husband's insurance office, and I wonder if their cars had the lights on like a funeral procession as they came over the back roads.

My brother moves in to take my hand and we walk, entwined, into the large, glistening lobby. He announces us. Glen's father smoothes back his hair with the flat of his hand. His jacket is open, and I'm certain his suit would not button if he tried. I think it's the same suit he wore eleven years ago, when his wife died of breast cancer. Even then he didn't cry. "They did everything they could," he repeated to the mourners, and "She fought it to the very end." The widows have been bringing him pots of stew and plates of cookies ever since, but he still lives alone and runs the roofing company with Glen's brother Peter, still climbs the ladder and straddles the eaves. Peter's wife buys his clothes and arranges for his cleaning woman and does his grocery shopping, so that his life is not so different than it was when his wife was alive. I used to say that to Glen all the time, but now I'm ashamed, because now I know that there is something about having another person in the house, even if you barely speak to them, barely notice them, that is far far different from being in the house alone.

"How are you doing, Dad?" I say, and he coughs, to hide his bloodshot eyes, and because I hardly ever call him this, and the kindness makes him feel exposed.

"Okay for an old man," he says, as usual, but he squeezes my shoulder.

Glen says that when he was little he thought his father was a giant, and he's still a big man, aging the way big men do, with a hard medicine ball of a belly and a thick neck thrust forward like a raptor's. He insisted on coming. So did my brother, although the way he keeps putting his hand to his heart, to the breast pocket where he keeps his phone, tells me his office is buzzing him inces- santly. I like and admire my brother, but in that way you do someone you see twice a year at parties. He feels the same about me. We would do anything for each other but are grateful that we have never really had to.

"How's Alex?" asks my father-in-law in the elevator. "Is he getting much playing time?"

"He's only a freshman, Pop," says Doug.

"For a freshman, he gets a lot of playing time," says Bill. "Unless he gets injured, he can probably wind up playing in college. Not Division 1, but one of the smaller places."

"I don't know," my father-in-law says. "They got monsters playing college ball now. Freaks of nature. You have to see how big he gets."

My brother sees the look on my face and squeezes my hand. Without the pills the squeeze feels hard, more like he is trying to bring me to my senses than to comfort me. Maybe he's afraid that I'll scream if I hear another word about whether Alex can play college basketball. Maybe he's simply concerned that I am going to scream. Even those who know me best look at me now as though they are afraid. They are afraid of me, afraid that if I broke down under this great weight it would be a horrible thing to see. They can't know that I spend all my time and energy now making certain that that doesn't happen, for Alex's sake. "She has a son," my mother told the nurses.

I remember the lawyer's office from the signing of our wills, five or six years ago. His name is Reinhold. It seems amazing to me that I have been able to recall that, even though it is written on a file I am holding in my lap. I can't remember his first name, but it doesn't matter. "Hello, Mr. Reinhold," I say, and he says, "Please, call me Larry." "Larry," I repeat dutifully. He comes around the desk, leans in, murmurs, "Mary Beth, I'm so sorry." I wave a hand in the air to stop him from saying more. People don't understand words—how empty, how useless, how awful they can be. Words don't soothe; they only set us apart. Please, I want to say, be quiet, so I can be ordinary again, so we can act as though this is business as usual, so I can go back to the sofa in Olivia's guesthouse and make my mind blank.

People's looks are just as bad. When I go out, which is still not often, their looks are like words, too. Once their eyes would move over me unthinkingly, an offhand observation of a look—glib, empty, the equivalent of "Have a nice day." Now they stammer as they try not to stare: smooth, smooth, stop, back, stop, back, stutter, slide down. It's like a dance move: Oh my God, oh my God, do you know who that is, that poor woman. Even the receptionist out front did it. I am like a burn victim, except that they are all imagining my scars. And I am feeling them, feeling the skin gone, the nerves exposed. I have to get back to the house.

Our lawyer has decorated his office as though he is a British barrister: mahogany desk and credenza, red leather chairs, hunting prints. I think Glen and I joked about it after we left the last time, but for a moment I hear Glen's chuckle and I make my mind blank again. Some straight chairs are brought in from the conference room to accommodate all the men. The medications must stay in your system. I will have to concentrate very hard to follow the conversation.

"Do any of you happen to be attorneys?" Larry Reinhold asks.

"We're businessmen," says my father-in-law.

It's all quite simple, really. There's no need for these men to be here in the first place. Perhaps they felt done out of some ceremonial role when I decided, in the hospital, that I would have the bodies cremated quickly. The bodies, I said to myself over and over again as though it would make me believe it. "I wanted to say goodbye," said my father-in-law, whose wife had appeared in her open casket in her Easter suit from the year before, her usual lipstick—Coral Reef, I think it was called—on her thin lips.

I had already said goodbye. I said goodbye to Max when we were leaving for the New Year's Eve party at Nancy and Bill's. Max had been behind the door of his room, and I could hear him shuffling around, waiting for us to go, and I tell myself now that it is all right that I didn't push my way in, nuzzle his neck, tidy his hair, drive him wild with my affectionate meddlings. I said goodbye to Ruby as she put on her coat over her dress to leave for some other, younger, better party. I said goodbye as I held her close, her hair tumbled over my face, and I tell myself now that it is all right that I didn't remind her to be careful, to come home early, force her to turn on me with her impatient face and shut off my nervous burbles. I said goodbye to Glen as he rose in a temper, his spot in the bed warm beside me as I fell back to sleep, and I tell myself now that it is all right that I didn't say to him, one last time, the way I did when we were young, with my heart and not simply my lips, "I love you."

"Would you like to see them?" they had asked me in the hospital, and suddenly, with terror and revulsion, I had known that they were there, in the same building, waiting to be claimed, waiting for someone to make some decision. I suddenly understood that, if I stumbled into the hall and then the elevator and rode down to the bowels of the building, I could find their bodies—not them, just some terrible battered empty facsimile. "No," I said. "No." For a moment I thought that terrible noise would begin again, now that I knew that the noise came from inside myself.

"Are you certain?" Nancy said. "It might help." Help what, I thought even through the haze. Help to kill them forever, to turn my laughing, loving family into a silent parade of the sightless and the still?

"Stop," I'd said, and Alice had looked at Nancy with horror and what looked like hatred and said, "Just leave her alone. Leave her alone."

"It's a simple 'I love you' will," Larry the lawyer says. What a lovely legal term. I love you, I love you. It means that if I died everything we had belonged to Glen, and if he died everything belonged to me. I love you I love you I love you. The sentence is running through my mind, a continuous loop, like one of those digital signs. I love you. Glen wrote it every year when he sent roses on my birthday, on the little card the florist gave him: I love you. Larry's mouth moves. Bill's mouth moves. I love you I love you. I've missed something. I'm not sure what. I try to pay attention again, but I can't seem to do it. I love you, I love you, where am I?

"... guardian," Larry says.

"Obviously, that's not an issue," Bill says.

I remembered how, years ago, we had argued over who to appoint legal guardian of our children. I wanted to talk about Deborah and Kevin. But Glen wouldn't hear of it even before Declan drowned. In my will now, my brother, Richard, and his wife would get Alex if anything happened to me. I look over at my brother, and he runs his hand over the back of my chair. I will change that as soon as I have a chance to think about it. Olivia, I think, or maybe Alice.

Glen was so careful, so responsible. The insurance on the house means there is no mortgage left to pay. The value of his practice means that there are three potential buyers already. And Glen's life insurance means that I now have a great deal of money. Bill knows all this, since he is our insurance agent. "So she's set for life?" my father-in-law asks, and I know that this will be one of the things he will say: Glen made sure his wife was set for life. A kind of lottery.

Everything's done. The will will be probated. The insurance

money will be paid into our investment account. The investment account will be transferred to my name alone. Glen's practice will be sold. "Highest bidder, correct?" says Bill, but I speak.

"I want to interview them," I say suddenly. I'm surprised to hear myself.

"The potential buyers?" says Larry Reinhold.

"We can take care of that for you," Bill says. Everyone wants to do things for me. I wonder what they think I will find to do when everything is done for me. Make soup. Drive aimlessly. Page through cookbooks. Sleep. The ghost of Mary Beth Latham will move, senseless, through her own existence, waiting for something to do, waiting for someone to call. Waiting, and listening, for three familiar voices.

"I want to interview them," I repeat. "I don't want Glen's patients to wind up with someone they won't like. He wouldn't want that." It is something I can do, I think. I love you, I think. I almost say it aloud.

No one responds. Finally Larry makes a note, and nods. "I can arrange that. Probably here, don't you think, not in the office itself? Anything else?"

"What about a lawsuit?" my father-in-law says. "Can we sue that son of a bitch? Can we sue his mother and father for their, their, you know—"

"Negligence," Doug says. "Is that doable?"

It took them three days to find Kiernan. The local police were out of their depth, if you were being kind, or incompetent, if you are talking to Glen's father. They spent a full day looking for Alex after they found bloody clothes in a pile on the floor of his room and his bed still made. They visited the homes of the kids' friends, they interviewed the neighbors, they made a mess of the house and any evidence to be found there. And three days later, when the story, and the screwups, and the fact that Alex had been thousands of miles away while they combed the forest for him were all over the newspapers, the state police took over. They went up into the room above the garage, and there was Kiernan, hanging from a rafter with a gaudy blue-and-gold nylon rope around his neck, a rope I had bought to tie some plywood to the roof of my car for a landscaping project I could no longer remember. The only reason I remember the rope was because it was in the school colors.

Apparently, he'd been living above our garage on and off for months, while his mother thought he was spending the weekend with his father, while his father thought he was with her, while both of them thought he was at the home of a new school friend, although he hadn't made any friends because he had barely attended the new school. When someone called to say he'd missed class, he'd erase the message; when the letters arrived, he destroyed them. How cold he must have been as winter closed in, in that uninsulated room, huddled in his old sleeping bag, the one he'd used all those nights when he and Ruby watched the heavens. He'd been telling the truth at Halloween, when he said he was working on a project. It covered the bare walls of the garage room: dozens and dozens of photographs he had taken of the members of our family—at the dinner table, in the yard, on Main Street, outside the high school. Ruby dominated, of course, but we were all there, and once he had pasted them up he spraypainted over the wall of black-and-white images the words HAPPY FAMILIES over and over in red. The police didn't get the reference to *Anna Karenina,* but I did. Ruby and Kiernan had read the novel in AP English, and Ruby had been disdainful of Anna for leaving her son behind and choosing Vronsky instead. Kiernan had said she couldn't help it, it was love that made her do it, love that made her leap in front of that speeding train, it was love that made people do things they wouldn't do otherwise.

I heard Alice and Nancy talking about it, and about the fact that a gallery in New York had asked to remove the walls of the garage and exhibit the whole thing. "People have no shame," Nancy had said, and Alice said, "Did you see the picture of it?" and Nancy said, "Don't tell me it's really amazing, because if I hear that one more time I will hit someone."

I think I was supposed to be sleeping when they had that conversation, when they were discussing the "various scenarios" of what happened that evening in terms of timing and intent. But when I imagined those red letters obliterating our faces, our eyes, our lives, the only scenario that really made sense to me was the one I found hardest to believe. He just wanted to wipe us all out.

"No lawsuit," I say, and I think Larry Reinhold looks relieved. Perhaps he knows what I know: that either I am a woman who was blind to the mania of a young man who was a fixture in her own household or I am a woman who knew exactly what he was capable of and embraced him nonetheless.

"We're not talking money here," my father-in-law continues. "We're talking responsibility. If he was still alive, he'd be convicted and he'd rot in jail. Now it's like nobody has to take responsibility." I remember what Glen once said of his father, "Everything has to be somebody's fault. If lightning strikes your house, it has to be because you put the lightning rod in the wrong place."

"No," I repeat. "End of discussion." I want to go home. I want my pills. I can't breathe. There is a moth hole in my dress.

I've already risen to my feet to shake Larry's hand by the time my father-in-law says, "What about me? Can I sue the bastards?" I'm on my way to the door as Doug says, "Pop, this is not the place."

"What the hell do you mean? It's a lawyer's office."

"Pop, come on."

I felt obliged to invite them all to lunch. I'll finally have a chance to empty out the freezer. The lasagna, the whole-wheat rolls. We sit in the living room with plates balanced on our laps. Ginger barks when the strange men enter the house, then moves around the room, her nose raised and searching blindly. My brother gives her a piece of bread. "Richard, don't," I say reflexively. "She'll get fat."

"Alex might feel different about a lawsuit," Glen's father says.

"Pop, enough," says Doug.

"Where is he?" my father-in-law says.

"He's at school. Then he has basketball until six. Do you want to join us for dinner? You'd be welcome." I feel as though I am saying lines from a play. I can't wait for them to leave. When they're gone, I can sit in a chair. Just sit.

"We got six hours in the car," he says, cleaning his plate with a piece of bread. "I got a job starting first thing in the morning. Maybe we'll go over and watch him play ball."

As they start to leave, I pull my brother-in-law into the bedroom. "You make sure he doesn't say a word to Alex, you hear me? I'm trying to keep him on an even keel, and I don't want your father upsetting him."

"I'm on it, MB," Doug says. He's the only one who calls me that, and I've always found it endearing. In some ways, he is more like my brother than my real brother, who is more like my doctor. My brother was on the phone to the nurses' station, overseeing my medication and my care, the whole time I was in the hospital. He stayed on the line with me the third night, when they wanted to discharge me but I was afraid to leave. "It feels like when I put my feet on the floor I'm stepping into an empty space," I'd said, working hard to string the words together. "It's like, just like when we went to the lake and I fell in that deep spot and went down and Daddy had to pull me out. It feels just like that."

There had been silence, and then my brother said, "That was me, not Dad." I don't know what to believe anymore. "I'm going to get them to change your medication," Richard had said.

"I don't know how the hell you're holding it together," my brother-in-law says, and I almost laugh at the idea. "I just can't get my mind around it—you know what I mean?" he continues. "You know, sometimes we'd go a month, two months without talking. But I always knew Glen had my back. It's like I lost a piece of myself." He looks up, then away again. "I can't believe I'm saying this to you, of all people. And you know what kills me? I remember meeting that kid here two summers ago. What was it, Memorial Day weekend? He seemed like a nice kid. We all thought he seemed like a nice kid. The papers said he dropped acid or PCP or something. I never would have figured him for a druggie."

Apparently, that is one of the various scenarios. Kiernan was bipolar and wasn't medicated, was medicated and had stopped taking his medicine, was addicted to drugs, was addicted to alcohol. Was addicted to us. What difference does it make now?

"Who knows?" I say wearily.

"Douglas!" barks my father-in-law from the front door. Cold air shoots through the little house. Ginger pushes her muzzle into my hand and licks my fingers, greasy with the bit of butter I put on the bread to try to get it down.

I know I'm supposed to hate Kiernan, but I can't manage that, any more than I can manage to believe that I will never see Ruby again, or Max, or Glen. Maybe it will all come later—the realization, the rage. I remember how we put in a security system to keep intruders out of the house, and how we only used it when we went on vacations. It didn't matter: Our intruder had a place at our table, knew where we hid the Easter eggs and where we'd buried the pet guinea pigs, was so familiar that when I saw him in the bedroom doorway that last time I thought he was my own son, come to kill me.

Ginger jumps up on the counter and eats a piece of bread. A big piece, mine, with only a small corner nibbled. She runs into the bedroom, crawls beneath the dust ruffle, assuming I'll try to pry open her stubborn jaws, but I let her go. Let her get fat. I clean the kitchen, lie down on the couch. Ginger stays under the bed. It must be like a cave. For a moment, I wish I could go under there. It reminds me of when I wanted to get into Ruby's crib when she was an infant so that I could see what she was seeing. "Okay, that's nuts, Mary Beth," Glen had said.

The phone rings. It's Olivia's cell. "Can I have Chinese with Ben?" Alex asks. The insurance, the house, the will—it's all done, and everything seems softer and smoother because of the pills. Let him eat there. It must be noisy and bright and uncomplicated there.

"Grandpop came to practice," says Alex. "He says if I grow enough I might be able to play college ball. He and Coach have the same tattoo."

"Semper fi," I say.

"Grandpop says it means 'stay strong.' "

"More or less," I say. "It means 'always faithful.' " And, as the words leave my mouth, I put my fist to my lips. There is something about the phrase, about what it means to me now, that makes me feel as though I am going to begin to scream. I understand that I will have to be faithful forever myself—to memory, to history, to a life that has ceased to exist except in my mind.

"Ben's mom says she'll send me home with a flashlight," Alex says. "She says she'll stand in the door and watch."

There is a long silence while I try to push back the wave of my feelings. My knuckles press on my front teeth. Always faithful. Always. My God, always is such a long, long time.

"Mom?" Alex says. "You there?"

"I'll stand at the door and wait, too," I say, but he is already gone, and soon so am I. Sleep, sleep. It is the only time I feel safe. What an irony. Sleep. I love you, I think as I drift away.

I have a new phone. The old one is somewhere in my old house. I haven't been there, or even driven by it. "Have you figured out what you're going to do with the house?" my father-in-law always says when he calls. "Not yet," I say. "You're going to have a hard time selling it," he says. "I know," I say.

I have a new phone number, too. Somehow reporters discovered the old one, before they lost interest in me. Alice says we were lucky: In early January a senator was arrested for sexual misconduct in a restroom, and an earthquake took down a section of a small town south of San Francisco. A day after that, a terrorist cell was uncovered in Detroit. The police chief had told reporters that my house looked like the scene of a terrorist attack, and I suppose he was right. But instead of religious or political zeal, the attack on us was fueled by something more potent—love, rage, despair, all those things that the adult world decries and can't understand because it has ceased to feel them. If only Kiernan could have lived long enough to learn how to feel less.

My phone rings, and the man's voice on the other end is slightly familiar; at first I think it's one of the reporters, who has gotten interested in us again. There's a buzz on the line, and a sound like the one a needle used to make skittering across an album on a turntable. Then the noise clears and I hear, "Mrs. Latham? It's Dr. Vagelos."

I'm standing in the kitchen at the table. It's March, and the roof is dripping loudly into the gravel gully around the foundation.

"Yes?" I say.

"I wanted to talk to you about your son."

I can hear the water hitting the stones. *Ping. Ping.* The smallest sounds are loud to me now. Last year Max started to read all these comic books about the apocalypse, the end of the world. "Disaster porn," Ruby had said dismissively. Now I understand the point. The visions of cities being leveled are only attempts by human beings to come up with an alternative universe in which they are not sentenced to grieve alone. I know how disaster really comes, not with a mushroom cloud but with a whimper, a handful of matted tissues, the loud, incessant plink of water on gravel.

"He's dead," I blurt out. And for some reason saying it aloud makes it more real than it has ever been before, more real than when the death certificates came in the mail, more real than when the lawyer made me sign the papers for the insurance and the estate, more real than when the square boxes heavy with ashes arrived from the funeral home and I put them on the top shelf of the closet in the bedroom. For a moment I lose all the air in my body, and then I put the phone down on the table and walk out the back door onto the grass. I don't know how much time passes, but when I step back inside there is no one on the phone. Then it rings again, and I hear Dr. Vagelos's voice, softer now.

"I'm so sorry," he says without preamble, and I remember that

I thought I saw him at the memorial service. Dark hair, dark frames on his glasses. His glasses. That was how I remembered who he was. If it was him. There were so many faces that day. Patients, classmates, neighbors, clients, friends. So many.

"Thank you," I say, as always.

"I'm actually calling about Alex."

"Alex?"

"He came by to see me yesterday. He wants to work with me. It's a little unusual, treating brothers, but I do it from time to time, especially if they're twins. I'd like to help him out if it's all right with you."

"Alex? Alex wants to talk to you?"

"If that's all right with you."

"He didn't say anything to me."

"I thought that might be the case. I get the impression that he's concerned about worrying you. I know you know this already, but he's in a tough position. People use the term 'survivor's guilt' casually, but it's a real phenomenon. I think he feels the need to talk to somebody who's outside his usual circle." As he speaks I can see the doctor in my mind, see him and the photograph of him and his brother. I assumed his brother was alive, but maybe I was wrong about that. I don't want to ask him. I've discovered death is the thing people don't want to discuss.

In the silence he adds, "If you're uncomfortable with me because of Max, I can recommend someone else." And for a moment I feel such love for this man, who has spoken my son's name. No one does this; no one says their names. And because I am as guilty as the rest, I repeat it back: "Max."

"I miss seeing Max," Dr. Vagelos says, and with a great effort I say, "I do, too."

I sit for a long time at the table, and then I walk up the hill to

Olivia's house. I've begun to think about looking for a place to rent, although Olivia and Ted have said over and over that we can stay in the guesthouse indefinitely, that Ben loves having Alex nearby, that Ben's grades have improved in the past two months because the two of them do homework together, that the younger boys feel as though they have another older brother.

"I need to talk to you," I say when she opens the back door.

I tell her about the phone call from Dr. Vagelos. She looks down at her hands, flat on the table, and then says, "Don't you think it's a good idea? I think it's a good idea."

"Do you think he's struggling? Are you worried about how he's behaving around you and the boys?"

"Not really," she says. "He's quieter than he once was, but I think it would be strange if he wasn't. Ben says he seems sad sometimes. He says sometimes Alex starts to talk about Max, and then stops, as though he still doesn't know how to do it, or what to say. But they're boys. They don't pour their hearts out, do they? I wish he could. And if he actually took the time to go on his own to see this man and ask to work with him, I think that's all to the good. He needs to vent. I assume he doesn't feel there's anywhere to do that except perhaps this doctor's office."

"Has he ever really let go with Ben? I mean, they're best friends." And even as I say it, I realize that I have not spoken with Alice or Nancy or Olivia herself about any of this, that my greatest care has been to keep the agony and the anger I feel away from the light, for fear that if it can be clearly seen it will be insupportable. As though she can hear my thoughts, Olivia replies, in a soft voice, "I'm sure sometimes it seems easier, or at least simpler, not to talk about it."

"Even with me."

"Especially with you." Her blue eyes sparkle in her bright white kitchen, and I realize that she is on the verge of tears. I think of the circle that has grown up around us, our families, our friends, and how we have all taken a vow of silence that is eating us alive.

I nod and stand, walk down the hill, and get my purse and keys. I put Ginger in the back of the car, and begin to drive. I drive fast, slow down, speed up again, past hills and valleys, past narrow gravel one-lane roads and town intersections. I am aimless, with no destination. I find myself at the weekend house where we put in all those large trees, and I let Ginger out. She sniffs suspiciously at the unfamiliar ground, then squats and jumps back into the car. I can tell by the suggestion of green shoots at the end of a few branches that the trees all took, all except one close to the drive that looks like a gray skeleton. It will need to be pulled up and replaced, and I wonder who will do it. The idea that someday I would be standing here, with Rickie and a backhoe and a plan for the future, for the future of something as simple as a tree, seems unthinkable. I can see that woman, in her Capri khakis and her gardening clogs, with her hands on her hips. Yet somehow she is not me.

And yet I have suddenly decided to try to pretend to be her for just this afternoon, for the sake of my son. I park on Main Street and walk past Molly's Closet, the three flowery dresses on the mannequins in the window a harbinger of a spring that seems unlikely as the cold weather drags into March. I go into the drugstore, and the pharmacist, who is on the phone, waves while I look at things I do not really see and will not buy. I choose some shampoo that I realize is the same shampoo I already have in the bathroom. I look up at the second-story window to the room where Max took his drum lessons, but there's no sign of movement there.

My phone rings. It's Alice. "Hey, honey," she says softly. It's been a while since she asked my advice about Liam, and I miss it. I decide to tell her so.

"You have so much on your plate," she says.

"I have nothing on my plate. I've just spent an hour doing—

what were those things you told me about in church, where you walked around and looked at those plaques of Jesus making it up the hill? They had numbers, and prayers, or something?"

"The Stations of the Cross? I haven't thought of the stations of the cross in years. The only one I can remember is when Veronica wipes his face."

"Who's Veronica?"

"I have no idea. You don't mean the real Stations of the Cross, do you?"

"No, I'm on Main Street, doing the stations of the cross of Center Valley. I feel like I have to try to act like a normal person. It's been two months already."

"Oh, honey," says Alice. "Two months is no time at all."

"Alex wants to see a shrink. Do you think that's a good thing? Olivia thinks it's a good thing."

"I think it's a good thing."

"I guess I do, too. How's Liam?"

"He's in love with the preschool teacher. Just like you warned me."

I fall silent. What else did I warn Alice about? Improperly fastened car seats? Little plastic toy pieces? Those are the kinds of things people warned me about. They didn't warn me about strange noises in the middle of the night, about the room above the garage.

"Mary Beth?" Alice says.

"Sorry, sorry, I'm distracted. I have to go. I'm going to go to the hardware store. I need a hammer."

I buy a hammer.

It's the middle of the day, and there are few people on Main Street. The wind is still harsh, and the jaundiced clouds suggest rain. But naturally I run into one of the people I feel least inclined to see, Rachel's mother, Sandy. I have to call Alice back and tell her that there was a special cross awaiting me. There are people who want all the trappings of tragedy without any of the pain, and I know Sandy is one of them, and that she's told anyone who will ask, and even some who don't, that we are close close friends and that she's devastated by what happened. Her hug lasts too long, and her eyes fill too quickly. "I think of you constantly," she says.

"Thank you," I say.

"This has been terrible for Rachel," she says. "She feels responsible. She and Sarah feel responsible."

"That's ridiculous."

"You can't help your feelings. Your feelings are your feelings." She sounds as though she is reading aloud from a self-help book. I have a whole shelf of them now: *Working Your Way Through Grief, How It Feels to Lose a Child, The Legacy of Violence, Prayer and Healing.* People sent them to me. Stan's daughter sent one called *Making a New Life.* I can't find it, and I suspect that my mother threw it away after she threw it at the wall. When I got married, I got a silver chafing dish with a Sterno candle underneath, and when Ruby was born I got a black velvet dress with a delicate lace collar in an infant size. These books are every bit as useless. When I go home, I think, I'm going to put them all in the recycling bin.

"Tell Rachel I send my love."

"She wants to see you. This has been terrible for her. She misses you all so much." She leans in close, conspiratorial. "She's going to a psychiatrist. I had no choice."

I nod.

"She's lost ten pounds since it happened," Sandy continues in a confidential way, and she can't stop herself from sounding pleased.

Our conversation runs down quickly. I can't blame Sandy for that. Small talk feels too small, big talk too enormous. I already know this from shameful experience. I've thought often in the past two months of the couple in town whose son died of leukemia.

The first time I saw his mother afterward I said the right things, even remembered that he played guitar and wrote songs. But the second time, after her bereavement was a little shopworn, I couldn't figure out how to move forward. I saw her on the sidewalk and arranged my face just so—not smiling, not sad, just attentive. We stood on the street and worked to reach across the divide, and the working made it impossible to bridge it. Her survival seemed not only incredible but somehow unseemly. "How is she making it through the day?" we would ask ourselves, smug in the knowledge that our children would be dirtying the kitchen and leaving towels on the bathroom floor that very night. One of the worst aspects of living now on the far shore is that across the chasm I can see my glib unknowing former self. I despise that woman, her foolish little worries and her cheap sympathies. She knew nothing. But I can't truly wish on her what I know now.

I stop at the florist and buy an orchid plant for Olivia, and the florist tells me she has heard from several people that they hope I will be back in the landscaping business soon. I drive past the deserted motel outside town and suspect that that won't happen. The police spent two days questioning all the Mexican guys, and when the questioning was done my men left the state and then left the country, which they had all entered illegally. I knew they were illegal, of course. I just never asked. I wonder if José is living with his two little daughters now, if the younger one has managed to get her tonsils removed. The ramshackle windows in the motel are broken out, and someone has dumped some old tires to one side of the parking lot. In the paper the other day, it said the town was thinking of demanding that the owner repair the place or tear it down.

Maybe that's what someone will do with my house, too. If they raze it, rip off the dormers and the roof, reduce the garage to a pile of old planks, will it be as though New Year's Eve never happened?

I know that Nancy arranged for a cleaning crew, that the couch in the living room where the police found Ruby lying is gone, that the carpet in our bedroom was disposed of, and the carpet in the den, too. But I know those things only by hearing other people discuss them. This is what I wonder: Did they turn out the lights? If I had driven by afterward, would I have seen the yellow glow in the winter night, seen the lamps burning to welcome me home? If I lived across the street, would I have watched the lights go out over time, one by one, until the dark house disappeared in the dark night?

Nancy went into our old house and packed a duffel bag with Alex's clothes and his uniforms and his balls and bats. She brought over his soccer ball, too, the signed one in the Lucite case, but it's on the top shelf of his closet, behind a box packed with his swim trunks and his camp polo shirts.

The high school glows in the night, not yellow but the harsh white of fluorescence, light that deters rather than welcomes. A row of cars makes a wall between its low-slung beige walls and the road. One of the juniors took the curve I'm on too sharply four days ago and was airlifted to the hospital with a broken back. It's one more way in which what happened to our family has started to fade in the town consciousness.

I pull up next to Olivia's car. She's half turned toward the back-seat. I can tell she is reprimanding one of the little boys. She doesn't raise her voice; she has a clipped tone that I suspect is more effective than my shrill rants ever were. She sees me, stops, and then smiles. Little Luke follows her eyes, looks at me, and then frowns dramatically, his lower lip out, his brow furrowed. It's become clear that he resents all the attention his mother gives me.

Alex and Ben run out to the car together, their winter jackets unzipped, their backpacks bouncing off their right shoulders, their faces crimson from exertion and sweat. I hear Alex laugh, and I re-

alize that it's the first time I have heard that sound for months, perhaps since Christmas Day. He has a deep laugh now, not a man's
laugh but moving toward it. I see him run toward Olivia's car, and
suddenly I realize why I drove here without even knowing it.
Among Ben's family Alex is comfortable, easy, insulated from rage
and grief and bitterness and brokenness and horror and silence.
Among Ben's family he can pretend to forget what happened, pretend that everything is nice and normal, that life is simple and safe.
He could so easily become their family's Kiernan, a boy seeking a
temporary place in a happier kitchen.

Olivia gets out of the car and says, "Alex, love, look who's
here." I get out, too, and look at my son. His face is expressionless.

"What's wrong?" he says, and it's all I can do not to say what's
in my mind, not to say, What more could be wrong?

"Nothing," I say. "I just thought we could go out for pizza. Ben
can come if you want."

Alex looks at Ben, then back at me. Olivia says warmly, "I'm
keeping Ben with us. You take Alex. Are you going to drive him
to school tomorrow?" And in that moment, when I know that she
sees and understands it all, Olivia becomes not just my savior but
my friend. To cap it off, she winks at me.

"I have to pee very much!" yells Luke from inside the car.

"I have a lot of homework," Alex says as we pull away.

"We'll make it fast," I say. My voice sounds false to me, and I realize it is my company voice, the one I used with Sandy, and with
the man in the hardware store who told me which sort of hammer
to buy. "We'll make it fast," I say again, and this time I sound more
like me.

"Cool," Alex says.

"How was practice?"

"The new coach is really mean."

"Really?"

"Nobody likes him. Like, he's really sarcastic? He goes to me, 'Latham, the ball belongs to the whole team, not just you.' Like I'm a ball hog? And I wasn't hogging the ball."

I haven't met the new coach, but I love him for his gift of meanness. I love him for not being kind and gentle to Alex, for not reminding him and all the others that Alex is indelibly marked as wounded. I will go to the next game and I will say, "Hi, I'm Alex's mother."

"I talked to Dr. Vagelos today about meeting with you," I say as we come down a steep hill. Alex rummages through his backpack as I decide what to say next. And I wonder if he is as careful with me as I am with him.

I do not say, What made you go to see him? I do not say, Why didn't you tell me? I do not say, Why can't you talk to me? I do not say, What does it feel like, to be you, to have them all gone? I know what it feels like to be fatherless, with a mother who never speaks of it. It feels bad. It feels so bad.

I say, "That sounds good to me."

"Cool," Alex says. After a few minutes he says, "I really feel like pizza."

"Anchovies?" I want to say. It is an old family joke. "Not if you value your life," I can hear Ruby replying. She taught both the boys to say it, too.

In silence, we drive as the night fills the car.

Alice is coming to visit for two days. "There's a crafts fair!" she says, as though she were describing a Broadway opening or a royal visit. As her car comes down the drive Ginger barks, and I look up the slope toward Olivia's house. I imagine that Olivia has pulled the flowered curtains in her bedroom gently back to watch Alice arrive. Alice is bad at keeping secrets, and she will surely tell me if Olivia called to say it might be a good weekend to stay with me. This is another thing I've come to expect but cannot like: the idea that people are talking about me, taking my emotional temperature. My father-in-law calls, and then the next day Glen's brother Doug does, too, and I imagine the conversation that took place between them: She sounded down, she's not getting out much, she needs to get to work, to get a house, to get out of the house. At least Nancy refuses to hide behind pleasantries: The last time we spoke, she said, "I was looking for you at the basketball game. Where were you?"

Where was I? Was that the night I was watching the movie on television, or the night I cleaned the bathroom? Or was it a more ordinary night, a night when I had a cup of tea and steered my mind through a treacherous maze, past the sight of Ruby behind the wheel of her Volvo smiling up at me, past Max pounding away at his drums with his hair marking time, past Glen bending to pet the dog and then laying his arm along the back of the couch behind me. My memories are booby-trapped. A week ago, I was in the supermarket and found myself in front of the freezer case, staring at boxes of veggie burgers, the kind I had to track down for Ruby when she stopped eating meat in eighth grade. I abandoned the cart, and the shopping trip, and drove home, shaking. Yesterday I found a black dress sock among my T-shirts, one lone sock of the sort my husband wore all his grown-up life, and I held it to my face, then left it on the edge of the bathroom sink, then hid it under the vanity so that Alex would not see it, then took it from beneath the sink and put it back in the drawer where I first found it. The photographs and family mementoes are still in the other house, the haunted house, the abandoned house. And yet I am ambushed still, by frozen food, by misplaced socks.

"I brought bagels!" Alice says, holding the paper bag aloft.

"You brought enough bagels for an army," I say.

"Mary Beth, I know you're going to kill me for saying this, but you just sounded like your mother," she says, and I swat her arm, and she hugs me. When I smile, it is like the front door to our old house, all disused rusty hinges. But I try.

Alex and Ben have gone away for a weekend basketball workshop. "I have to go," Alex had said when he handed me the consent form and saw the look on my face. I drove over to the high school to watch the team get on the bus. I handed Alex his duffel bag and a box of chocolate-chip cookies. "They're still warm," I'd said. As the doors to the bus closed with a hiss, I saw the cookies being passed from seat to seat. Alex was talking to someone across the aisle as the bus pulled out. I waved goodbye to no one.

"Can you join us for dinner?" Olivia had said as we walked back to our cars.

"I think I'll just stay in tonight," I said, as though that was not what I did every night.

"Let's go out to dinner!" Alice says, and I understand that this is the visit designed to reintroduce me to the outside world—the happy visit, the small-talk visit. Even Alice is afraid to hear what I am thinking. I don't blame her; I am afraid to think what I am thinking. We drive to a steak house where Nancy and I have had dinner several times, and Alice talks about a book on Thomas Jefferson that she is editing, and a controversy about a water-treatment plant in her neighborhood, and the price of real estate in New York, and I let her words roll over me, my face arranged as though I am listening. There is a trick to this, but I have learned it: uh-huh, uh-huh, nod, uh-huh, uh-huh, nod.

"Is that not good?" she finally asks, looking at my steak.

"I had a big lunch," I say.

"Doggie bag?" says the waitress.

"We actually have a dog to bring it to," says Alice.

Ginger gets half, and we put the other half in the refrigerator. "For later," says Alice. What that means is that in four days, which seems the proper length of time, I will throw it away. Alice bends to look inside the fridge. "What is that?" she says, pointing.

"It's a turkey. Rickie brought it over the other day. One of the guys I work with."

"The big guy?"

I nod.

"A whole turkey?"

"And a cordless drill," I add. He had appeared at the door in a down jacket and a baseball cap, his brawny arms full. He had grown a beard, and there were crumbs in it. I offered him coffee, but he couldn't stay, or said he couldn't. A turkey and a power tool: I pictured him racking his brain. I'd kissed his cheek.

"I'm exhausted," I say to Alice, and I am. It is exhausting to pretend to be a different person for this length of time. Or not a different person—the same old person, who seems like someone I knew a long time ago. Mostly I only have to do it in small doses—ten minutes here, an hour there. The rest of the time, I busy myself with small repetitive tasks. I have thought about learning how to knit, but I picture Alex leaving for school in misshapen sweaters and stuffing them guiltily to the back of his locker. Maybe I will make an afghan. Someone once said that no one really wants an afghan. It was me, before, that other me.

"It's not even nine o'clock," Alice says. She sits on the couch, and I sit next to her, both of us facing forward. We have used up all our small talk. We must look like two people waiting on a bench for a bus. Two strangers.

"I don't know how to do this in person," she finally says. "Somehow it's easier to talk on the phone." Her voice sounds husky, and when I look she is crying. She sobs, and I rub her back.

"Oh, my God," she finally cries. "This is just unforgivable. Why am I the one sitting here crying while you comfort me? I'm ashamed of myself." Ginger sniffs at her face, whines slightly. Ginger is distressed by tears. This helps me to stop, sometimes.

"It's all right, Al."

"What's all right? That I'm completely useless to you? That I spent the entire evening trying to act as though nothing had happened in the past six months except that an apartment in my building sold for two million dollars? That you're my best friend and I can't even find a way to talk to you?"

"It goes both ways," I say. I know this is true. How many times in the past three months have I been reminded of Ruby's two selves, the careful courteous young woman who spoke so sweetly to strangers and the person she let loose at home, where she was safe, where she could be spiky and harsh and uncertain and at sea? I have two selves now, too, the one that goes out in the world and says what sound like the right things and nods and listens and even sometimes smiles, and the real woman, who watches her in wonder, who is nothing but a wound, a wound that will not stop throbbing except when it is anesthetized. I know what the world wants: It wants me to heal. But to heal I would have to forget, and if I forget my family truly dies.

I manage to bury her, that wounded woman. I try to push her down. But last night when I came back from the high school, knowing that Alex was gone until Sunday night, she had taken over the house, her self-possessed twin banished to the closet with my wool coat and scarf. The quiet was like a hand over my mouth and nose, and I felt that I would suffocate. I was afraid I would start to scream, and I went into Alex's room, which faces away from Olivia's house, so that no one would hear me. I sat down on my son's borrowed bed, and realized that it was uncomfortable, that the mattress sagged in the middle, and I filled the room with wailing. For some reason, I found myself repeating aloud the words "No more. No more." It was not so much that I wanted to die; it was just that I could not bear the incessant feeling of being alive. And then it occurred to me that I was already dead, that what was left behind was a carapace, like the shells of cicadas we found a few summers ago. I had been full, of creating children, of taking care, of tasks and plans and a big bright future, and now all that was left was a translucent skin of what had once been my life.

"Can we talk? Really talk?" Alice says, mopping at her eyes with the side of her sleeve the way she had in college.

"About what?"

"About everything. About them. About how you're feeling. About what it's like."

I sit for a moment and truly think about what she has said instead of pretending I am thinking. I owe Alice more than the Mary Beth I have designed for public consumption, but I can't show her that other, hidden woman. She is too terrible, as though I have been throttled and cut up, too, as though the real me is maimed and torn and murdered. I can't show Alice the body. She is not as tough as she thinks she is. She has a hidden woman, too, a softer, less certain self.

"I can't really do that yet," I finally say. I think perhaps I will never be able to do it, not in the way Alice means. Why should I share what no one wants to know? Why should I listen to the words of those who know nothing? I can predict what they will say:

It will get easier.

Lie.

You can handle this.

Lie.

Time heals.

Lie. Time just passes. Slowly.

"I'm afraid for you," Alice says. "I feel like I'm failing you. When we were young, I was so good at this."

"Don't mope!" I say. "That's what you always said."

"Hey, I got you to go to a lot of parties and bars you didn't want to go to by saying that. I got you to go to that party where you met Glen."

"I remember," I say. "Remember when you thought you might want to become a therapist?"

"Wow!" says Alice. "I'd almost forgotten about that."

"And how you volunteered on that help line, talking to people about their problems?"

Alice winces. "And after two weeks," I add, "you came back to the room and said, 'I quit. I'm only interested in the problems of people I actually know.' "

"That's true. But now . . ." Alice says, her voice starting to quiver.

"I know. I know." I hug her, hard. "Did Olivia call you and tell you to come today?"

"Olivia? No. Alex did. He said you'd be alone for the weekend. I was going to come anyhow, soon, but he told me this weekend would be good because he was going away."

I sit back. "He keeps surprising me," I say. "First the therapist, then you."

"I don't think me sitting here crying is what he had in mind," Alice says, blowing her nose. "At least you have him. Oh, God, that's a stupid thing to say, isn't it?"

"No," I say, "it's the truth." But I don't have him in the way Alice means. When he comes home, he goes into his room and shuts the door. The music comes on, and I am reminded of Max, except that, as always, Alex has reversed things. He is contented out in the world, but when he comes back here—to this little house, to his makeshift home, to the kitchen table with just two chairs— his loss is a terrible, palpable thing. He puts it in a box of a bedroom, holds it prisoner.

"I really am tired," I say. "Do you mind staying in Alex's room? I changed the sheets." I know that Alice wants to share a room with me, the way we did when we were young, but that would mean she would sleep on Glen's side of the bed. And I can't bear that.

The next morning, we go to the crafts fair. Alice buys Liam a felt jester's hat with bells. She buys a silk blouse made out of pieces of old kimonos, and earrings for her assistant's birthday. I wander past pieces of pottery, copper wind chimes, tapestry scarves, and stop in front of a booth with framed samplers, a display of axioms: "A Daughter Is a Lifelong Friend." "There's a Special Place in Heaven for the Mothers of Little Boys." "Live Laugh Love." A woman is sitting in a lawn chair, cross-stitching a piece that says "More Today Than Yesterday." "Can I help you?" she asks. "No," I reply.

"You didn't get anything?" Alice says at the car. I should have bought something, anything, to soothe her.

When we get home we have bagels with smoked salmon and even capers, which Alice has brought in a little jar, and we walk up to the house so that Alice can see Olivia. "She's great," she says as we walk down the hill again. "She's been a good friend," I say, and when I see Alice's face I say, "Al, you've been wonderful. You've been there from the very beginning."

"I feel like I haven't done enough."

"There's not that much anyone can do," I say.

Ginger follows behind us. "Let's walk in the woods," says Alice. A deer trail leads from the back of the guesthouse deep into the thick pines. Alex says there is a stream farther in, but I have never gone that far. When I walk too far, even with the dog with me, I begin to feel afraid. I'm not afraid of those things people might imagine, of sudden sounds, the appearance of a stranger. It is that with each step I feel that I am walking into another world, the world of Mary Beth without Glen, Mary Beth without Ruby and Max. That's why I couldn't buy anything at the fair, none of the mohair throws or wooden salad bowls or even a string of glass beads. If I acquire anything, it means I am building an afterlife.

"Let's go back," I say to Alice.

Nancy has invited me for lunch with the two girls, with Sarah and Rachel. There are daffodils in a vase on the round table in one corner of her kitchen. Sarah has baked a quiche, and Rachel made Waldorf salad. There is a women's-magazine quality to the event: Have a Girls' Lunch with the Girls in Your Life! But sometimes I feel as though everything in my life now is a how-to article: How to raise an only child. How to tell if you're using too much medication. How to get out of bed in the morning.

"The girls need to talk to you," Nancy had said when she called. That's why I am going, for the girls.

Basketball season has given way to lacrosse, winter to spring. It has been nearly four months since I was at Nancy's house for the New Year's party. I wonder if Nancy has even thought about how difficult it is for me to be here, to walk through a door that is the last place I held Ruby in my arms. She and I haven't seen each other very much since the weeks right after I left the hospital.

Nancy had been fierce and focused when ferocity and focus were required. She had bullied the nursing staff and called the school and harassed the police and taken care of Ruby's friends, who poured into her house. They sat on the den floor and watched the recordings of school events and looked at old yearbooks and told one another stories. Sarah taped the stories, and wrote them all down and sent them to me in a big box. I haven't read them yet. I have so many boxes that I don't want to open.

But Nancy seems unable to soften with the passage of time, to offer solace or simply silence, as Alice does on the phone and Olivia has in her kitchen. She barks questions at me, or instructions: I need to see a grief counselor, to walk through the old house, to demand the police report. "I would want to see the photographs," she has said sternly. "I would want to know." She thinks the facts are important, the precise choreography of that night. Maybe it's because she's a biologist. Maybe it's a scientific approach.

I know as much as I need to know. My daughter was strangled. My son was stabbed several times. My husband was stabbed twice, in the back and in the neck. The chief of police told me this when he came to see me. "That was a wise decision you made, to have your mother do the identifications," he said, as though I would know exactly what he meant.

Perhaps it will please Nancy to hear that I've been looking at rental houses. The agent took me to see one, and when I walked outside I was looking into Kiernan's old backyard. There was a slight dip to one side that I knew had once been the pool. The deck was still there, the deck where Deborah and I had spent so many afternoons holding each other upright against the turgid drift of daily mothering, the deck where my husband tried to breathe life back into little Declan after pulling him from the clear blue water. "Not this one," I had called over my shoulder to the agent as I walked through the rental house and back to the car.

Rachel and Sarah come downstairs as soon as I ring the bell. I hug them both tightly, as though I were trying to absorb them into my body. Both of them are still wearing their friendship bracelets. Rachel is indeed thinner. Sarah looks exhausted and has cut her hair. It's not becoming. Both of their eyes gleam with tears as soon as they see me. "You look good," Rachel says. I look down. I'm wearing a gray sweater and black pants. Both are baggy, and too warm for the weather. I'm cold all the time, and I suspect I've lost a lot of weight. There is no scale in Olivia's guest cottage.

"I love seeing you guys," I say as Nancy stands in the kitchen, watching.

"Let's sit," she says.

I tell them I'm looking for a house to rent, and tell them about some of the terrible places I've seen, trying to make it all sound amusing, and ordinary: the house so close to the road that the high beams of passing cars would scour the living-room wall; the one that smelled like cats; the one that had a sink in the bedroom and no closet; the one that had an indoor pool, so that even the kitchen smelled like chlorine. "I know those people," Sarah said. "Their son was on the swim team when I was a freshman. Even they couldn't stand the smell."

I send love to Nancy from Alice and from my mother, although I am making this up: I can tell that Alice doesn't like Nancy, not after the days in the hospital, and my mother isn't in the habit of sending love to anyone. I ask about the basketball coach, whose meanness has now become legendary. I coax the girls into discussing those things they won't talk about because they worry that they will make me sad: their college plans, the prom, the summer. All the things that Ruby will never do. The college counselor had called me to tell me she was preparing to contact all the schools and rescind Ruby's applications. I had been asleep when the phone rang, and I had taken some pills, and I shrieked at her, "Don't you dare! Don't you dare!" Now I receive the acceptance letters. "Please send your deposit by May 1 in order to hold your place," they all say. I've put them in the drawer, beneath my night-gowns. Ruby could have gone anywhere.

Instead, they'll plant a tree in the senior courtyard of the high school, a flowering pear that will have a spring snowfall of tiny white blossoms every April. They'll put a page in the yearbook, al-though I suspect they had a hard time finding a really good picture of Ruby that had not been taken by Kiernan. On the bottom of the page will be the quote from "Thanatopsis" that Ruby loved and that I will always hear in Glen's voice. The entire poem was on the back of the program for the memorial service, and days later I noticed that the last two words were "pleasant dreams." Sometimes I say that to Alex at night, before he disappears into his room. I don't dream at all because of the medication. I am so glad not to dream.

Sarah clears the plates. There's carrot cake for dessert. Suddenly we're all very quiet, and I realize that no one else is at home. I hear something fall heavily in the next room, as though there is some-one clumsy I can't see, and a sharp sword of panic pierces my side. Then the cat enters the kitchen and I know I've simply heard him leap to the floor from the furniture. My hand goes to the ropy scar in my shoulder where the knife went in.

Sarah and Rachel look at each other, and then Sarah inhales, hard. "Rachel and I think there are some things we need to tell you," she says.

"About Kiernan," says Rachel, holding the patterned blue-and-yellow napkin to her mouth.

"I think I know."

"No, you don't. Not really," says Rachel. "He was following her everywhere. We were all like, Ruby, it's stalking, what he's doing. We even told her she should go to the police. We told her she needed to go to you and Dr. Latham."

"He left things in her car," Sarah says. "We would get to the car and there would be flowers or a book of poems. Once she yelled 'Kiernan! Stop!' as loud as she could. But we never saw him."

"And he would call her a million times a day. She couldn't leave her phone on. She would go to get her messages, and her mailbox would be full. He was totally obsessed. And sometimes, when we did see him, he seemed—I don't know, he seemed pretty off."

"We knew he couldn't be going to that new school," Sarah says. "He was around too much. But she wouldn't do anything. I think she felt like it was her fault. Like she had made him crazy or something."

"We told her she should call Kiernan's mother, but she said she couldn't."

"She said she didn't want you or Dr. Latham to do it, either."

"We tried to get her to tell you that somebody needed to do something," Rachel says.

"We told her over and over again to tell you how bad things were getting," Sarah says.

"Nobody knew he was in the garage," Rachel adds.

"We would have said something to you if we'd known he was in the garage."

"Ruby would have freaked if she knew," Rachel says. Suddenly it's quiet again. The cat rubs against my ankles.

"We just wanted you to know that we tried to tell her," Sarah says. "We really tried."

"She just wouldn't. You know how Ruby was when she didn't

want to do something. We just wish now that we'd said something to you, even if she got mad at us for doing it."

"So why didn't you two tell me?" I say softly. "The two of you were at the house all the time. Why didn't you just pull me aside and tell me what was going on so I could have done something about it? I wouldn't have told Ruby."

"We wanted to, we almost did one day, but we didn't know how Ruby would feel about it," Sarah says. "We didn't want to go behind her back. She told us how happy you were that Kiernan was nice to Max. And we were worried about Max, too."

"But that really wasn't the issue," I say. "The issue was that all this was going on and the grown-ups should have known. Her father and I should have known about it."

"She said you did know," Sarah says.

For a moment I am speechless, and then I realize that, as always, Ruby was right. I'd seen the ring, seen the photograph on Christmas Day. I had heard Kiernan scream out his love as he sobbed on our lawn after the prom. I knew about it all, and I had done nothing. I had searched for the line between my daughter's care and her ability to care for herself, and I had figured it all wrong.

Rachel bursts into tears. "I hate this!" she wails. "I miss Ruby so much. Everything is ruined. Everything!"

Sarah puts her arms around Rachel and begins to cry, too. "We knew how much you loved Kiernan," she stammers.

"But you know I loved Ruby more," I say.

"We all loved Ruby so so much," Rachel cries. "We're so sorry. It's all our fault."

"Oh, honey, no. It's not your fault."

"It is!" Rachel wails.

"That's enough," Nancy says in a low voice. "Sarah, take her upstairs."

Rachel whispers, "I want to stay."

"Right now," Nancy barks, and Sarah gets up and her chair falls over and I jump slightly again. I put my face in my hands.

"I'm sorry," I say. "I'm not used to talking about this. I'm sorry. I'll go upstairs in a few minutes. I'm so sorry they think they were at fault."

"You should be." And Nancy's voice is so harsh, so venomous, that I look up. She is in a rage, her face mottled and clenched. The last time I saw her like this was when she was passed over for the promotion at work that she had thought was a certainty.

"You obviously have something you want to get off your chest," I say.

"Me? Me? What about you? At what point in this whole conversation are you going to acknowledge Kevin Donahue?"

I know my face has gone red, but I refuse to drop my eyes from hers.

"I talked to Deborah," Nancy continues. "She thinks you're responsible for Kiernan's death. She thinks you set in motion the entire chain of events. She thinks you had an affair with her husband and that that's when her family fell apart."

I listen for any sound from upstairs, but there is none. "Could we continue this conversation someplace where the girls won't overhear it?" I say coolly. I'm stunned and very angry, and the fissure in my shoulder aches with adrenaline and emotion and perhaps some primitive muscle memory, as though Kiernan is once again slicing at me with one of my own carving knives.

"How do you know they don't already know? How do you know Ruby didn't know back then? And what about Kiernan? Maybe he knew, too. How do you know Deborah didn't tell Kiernan, and Kiernan didn't tell Ruby?"

Nancy doesn't really know, and neither did Deborah. At least that's what I tell myself. I don't know for sure. All I know is that one evening I was finishing up the foundation plantings at a house where Kevin was building a stone wall. After the coffee shop he owned had foundered under the weight of Declan's death, he opened a framing shop, then closed it and went into patio construction in a small way. "He's always got some surefire project," Glen had said harshly. Kevin and I had both been working in a cul de sac of new construction, chatting during lunch breaks, talking about the work as we stood side by side, and when the sun fell that evening, a bloody disk beneath a striation of gray clouds, Kevin came into the bare garage where both of us left our tools, its walls still smelling of fresh wood.

I can still evoke the feeling after all this time. He leaned in to kiss me and pulled me into the whole length of him, and there was that burst of sensation that you forget until it is improbably and unexpectedly resurrected—nothing more or less than heat and need and drive. It only lasts for a minute or two, and then is swiftly replaced by the awkward and embarrassing logistics: buttons, bare floors. I remember a Sheetrock nail beneath one thigh that branded me with a livid red circle. But that was later. In that instant, at the outset, there is only ever one sensation: yes. Yes. Yes. Now.

There were three times that week—two in the garage, one upstairs. Maybe my marriage had grown stale. Maybe I had begun to notice gray hair amid the brown. Maybe Ruby's flowering made me conscious of my own fading. Maybe I was living out every cliché about women that I had ever heard or read. But at the time it felt as though none of it had anything to do with my husband, my family, my everyday self. For a moment I felt sharply, strongly, undeniably something that I had long missed, and then when it was done I felt only chagrin and disgust. All I know is that when Kevin called me at home and wanted to meet somewhere more romantic, as he put it, I never allowed myself to be alone with him again. For a month or two he called and called, just as his son would later do with my daughter, and I left his messages unanswered. At a party he tried to corner me in a guest bedroom, and I pushed past him with an embarrassed laugh. And it would not be deceptive or delusionary to say that within a year I had learned not to think of what happened, to unmake its place in my life.

"She was my best friend!" I imagined Deborah shrieking as she threw him out. But that's just my imagination. Kevin was so unfaithful and unwise that the last straw could well have been someone else—that girl who worked at the quarry where he bought stone, the teacher at the middle school who cut a broad swath through the fathers before she moved on. But it's possible that he had told her about me. That foolish man, with his bright blue eyes and his seductive grin, might have thought he was doing it out of expiation, but if he did it it was because he knew it was the perfect form of torture.

Deborah crossed Main Street the next time she saw me, so I knew something was wrong. Then she simply faded from my life. But she couldn't keep Kiernan away.

"I don't want the Donahues here anymore," Glen had said one morning from behind the shield of the newspaper, and I said nothing. I told myself it was because of the scene Deborah had caused in their yard when she finally threw Kevin out, not because of anything she had told Glen, not because of the angry red circle burned into the back of my leg. It had left no scar.

I say quietly now, leaning toward Nancy, "Let me ask you a question, Nance. Are you angry because you think I did what you're accusing me of? Or are you really angry because you think I did it and I didn't tell you about it?"

I stand and put my napkin back on the table. She had loved me when we shared the same life—husband, children, safety, security, control. She always hated uncertainty. A scientist, after all. I was a universe gone awry.

"How do you know that Glen wasn't unfaithful?" I ask. "Or Bill, for that matter?"

She inhales loudly. "Glen? Glen cheated on you?"

"Not that I know of, but what do I know? What do you? I thought Kiernan was a great kid. I thought Ruby was going to college in September. How do you know, Nance? How do you know what's right in front of you when you're looking the other way?"

"If you know anything about my husband or my children, maybe you should come right out and say it."

"I don't, and you are missing the point. The point is that I don't know anything, but that doesn't mean there's nothing to know. The point is that we're all icebergs. Ninety percent is under the surface. Thanks for lunch. Tell the girls I said goodbye, and that I'm sorry I upset them." At the door I am tempted to turn back, to say "fair-weather friend." But I can't manage it.

I drive without knowing where I'm going, drive while I cry and then stop crying and feel something worse than tears, something finished and dead and done.

Once Ruby and I were sitting in the yard, watching the monarchs swarm the bee balm. It must have been early September, one of those slow late-summer days when school had just begun yet everything felt tentative—the textbook unopened, the sweaters still packed into their plastic beneath the bed. Ruby loved to tell me things I didn't know, and that afternoon, as we sipped lemonade and scuffed our bare feet through the shaggy grass, she had told me about the butterfly effect, how the beating of their wings in Mexico could cause a breeze in our backyard.

"That's kind of terrifying," I replied. But even as I spoke I realized that that was what we had all believed from the moment we had children. The breast-fed baby became the confident adult. The toddler who listened to a bedtime story went on to a doctorate. We flapped our wings in our kitchens, and a wind blew through their futures.

"It is terrifying," Ruby had said, but with gusto. "But it makes you think before you act." That was how she spoke then, as though life could be analyzed and therefore lived not simply well but according to plan. And I remember knowing at that moment that someday, when her first child had colic or her second clung to his thumb and his blanket into preschool, she would turn to me and tell me that she had had no idea what life truly asked of us.

My ghost daughter talks of butterflies, her legs graceful beneath thrift-store dresses. My ghost son slouches past me, his hair untidy. My ghost husband lies with me at night, so that half of the bed is still made each morning, the pillows still plumped. Did I arrive at this half-life because three times I was unfaithful, which for a mother is not simply betrayal of a man but of a family and a vocation? Did I trade my ordinary, average, perfect life for hasty couplings on a cement floor?

Did Ruby know it, or sense it, and stop eating to stifle her horror, her fear, her own sexual yearnings? Did she turn to Kiernan for solace, or to somehow make amends? Did Kiernan believe his parents had divorced because of me? Did he turn our own family into a lifeboat despite or because of that? Did he go mad when Ruby deserted him and left him alone in open water? Did he put his hands around her throat and snuff her voice because he'd heard it raised against him? Did he intend to leave the house afterward, Ruby crumpled in one corner of the couch, when he was surprised by Max, coming in from the den where he had dozed off? Did he take the knife from the kitchen block then and stab Max with wild and panicked strokes, then sit and marvel at how far he had gone in so short a time? How long did he wait there, bloodying the kitchen chair where he had sat through so many meals, before Glen came down the stairs and he stabbed him in the back? Was it then that he decided to go upstairs and kill Alex and me, too, to obliterate the happy family that had been the last thing he saw each night as he slept above the garage, close enough to hear the bursts of laughter, see the lamplight, smell the cooking? Or had he planned to do that from the very beginning, to wipe those smiles off all our faces?

I wonder what he thought when he realized that Alex was not at home. I wonder if he felt a sense of defeat, or frustration or perhaps even relief, as he left his own bloodstained jeans and T-shirt in the center of the bedroom floor and put on clean clothes from Alex's drawer. And then there was only me. I wonder if he thought he had put the blade through my heart, or if, finally, I was the one he couldn't bear to kill. I even wonder if he meant to leave me alive as retribution. I wonder how much that happened was the drugs he had apparently been taking, how much the drinking no one had acknowledged, how much the erosion of his self from isolation and grief, how much an illness that seemed ominous only in retrospect.

I wonder how much was me.

I drive so fast that my tires lift off the road on the curves, then so slowly that the teenager in a car behind me sounds the horn until I pull over. The dead place is still inside me because Nancy has said aloud only what has been a whisper ever since I half woke in the hospital. Now it is screaming, the voice that says my children and my husband are dead because I was not careful enough, attentive enough, good enough, awake enough. Not enough.

When I pull into the driveway of the guesthouse I'm breathing hard, and I put my head on the steering wheel, and then I look up to make certain Alex is not watching from the window. Sometimes I live so much in my mind that I forget what is right before my eyes.

Soccer, basketball, now lacrosse. Alex has the perfect schedule for a boy who doesn't want to think too much. He is busy almost every waking hour. I don't see him much, my boy. Or I see him, I am near him, but I don't talk to him. Sometimes when we are in the car I try:

How was school?

Fine.

How was the algebra test?

Hard.

How was practice?

Good.

The headphones go on, the music plays. We both lapse into a reverie. In the rearview mirror I see a flash of something, and for a moment I think it is Max's hair.

The headphones come off. "There's a dance Friday," he says. That's what passes for conversation. I am lost without the familiar sibling conversational badminton. Ruby talks to Max. Max talks to

Alex. Glen and I listen. This was how it went, night after night, year after year. I remember my mother and me, after Richard left for college, bent over our meat loaf in a thick cloud of silence, broken mainly by the click of forks on Melmac.

Alex and I have little opportunity to talk. For the last two months of school he has early practice Tuesdays and Thursdays, after-school practice every day until 6:00, Dr. Vagelos Wednesdays from 6:30 until 7:30, four hours of homework each night, a game every Saturday. I pick him up from lacrosse practice, I go to every game, I sit in the next room while he studies. "Mom, chill," he says sometimes, as though he can read my anxious mind. Last week he brought me a form: Eligible sophomores will take driver's ed. I keep forgetting to sign it. I try to drive him everywhere myself. I have never said it or even let the thought take full form in my mind, but I know it is so that if there is an accident we will be together. I try to spend Sundays alone with him, but he sleeps until noon, and he likes to watch TV and to talk on the phone to a girl named Elizabeth. "What's Elizabeth like?" I ask. "She's pretty cool," Alex says. I see her one day as Alex is getting into the car after practice. She is tall and narrow, with long light hair and enormous eyes. Their joined hands make me nervous. "We need to get home," I call more sharply than I mean to from the car window.

For several weeks I kept him close and away from Ben's house, telling myself that sooner or later he would have to become accustomed to our amputated family. I know Olivia understood. She stops by from time to time during the day, but she never stays long, as though she has an intuition for the limits of my social skills. Last week she came over to the guesthouse when everyone was at school to ask me if I would stay with her sons the weekend she and Ted were going to New York for a business conference. My eyes filled at the idea that she would trust me with their safety. I knew there were those in town who said I had been careless, that

I should have set the alarm or gone downstairs or even called the police. I wondered how many parents now came awake at any sound from downstairs.

"I can't think who else I could ask," Olivia had said. "I mean, four of them. Even I find it overwhelming. I pictured posting it on the board at the university and having all the students burst out laughing at the thought. Or demanding huge sums to do it."

"I'm demanding huge sums," I had said.

"I will gladly pay."

"You've already done so much for us. I swear that we'll have found our own place by summer. It's just grim, what's out there for rent. I probably should buy something." I don't want to buy something for the same reason I don't want to go to any of the dozen therapists whose names have been recommended to me. The point of that is to move on. I don't want to move on. I want to go back.

"You can stay here as long as you like," she said. "My boys love it. Ted loves it. We all do."

I'm staying in their guest room Friday and Saturday night while they are in New York. It's one of those smallish rooms in which all the bits and pieces that didn't land elsewhere have come to rest: an old pine dresser, a chair upholstered in poppy-colored linen, a log-cabin quilt. As a result, it is the nicest room in the house. As I'm drifting off to sleep the first night, Luke, who is five now, appears in the doorway, a black silhouette backlit by the hall light. I shiver and then try to smile.

"I had a bad dream," he says, edging closer and frowning at me.

"What was it, honey?"

"There were monsters."

"Get in," I say, flipping back the quilt and moving over. Olivia says occasionally Luke wets the bed. I hope it won't be tonight. I'm sorry now that I took half a sleeping pill, even though it doesn't do much anymore. What if the monsters return? I have to learn to sleep again without medication. I remember the last time I did. It was in another world, another life.

Luke turns onto his side and puts his thumb in his mouth, speaking around it. "What?" I say.

He doesn't remove the thumb, but he says very loudly, "I have a penis."

I nod, and as I watch, his eyes close, and he is asleep, as though he's the one who is drugged. And then I am asleep too. I wake just before dawn, moonlight still bright through the open curtains. It paints Luke's smooth brow silver.

Here is one of the worst things about having someone you love die: It happens again every single morning. The soft web of sleep begins to clear and then, in an instant, your mind asks and answers a dreadful question. Instead of doing battle with this, I have now decided to yield to it in this last hour of the night, when I am always awake and always newly bereaved. Luke makes it easier, the soft clicking sound as he works his thumb, pinker and more swollen than its partner. First I mourn people who had disappeared long ago: little Max squatting in the tall grass at the back of the yard to watch the crickets, Ruby at five lifting her dress over her head with sheer ebullience. Then I mourn imaginary people: Max the New York comic-book artist, Ruby the professor of poetry at a small college. I invent my own children. Sometimes Max and Alex and Ruby are all together, strung in a line across the street, pulling their sleds toward the hill, the sun so bright on the silver of the snow that it makes a burst of light and I am dazzled and they disappear. Luke is in Glen's place in the bed, and I reach out a hand and touch his hair lightly.

At six-thirty, his eyes open. "I like pancakes," he says. At seven he asks to call his mother, and at eight I let him do so. "I told Alex's mommy that I have a penis," I hear him say to her.

"You have my permission to banish him to his own room," Olivia tells me tartly.

"Are you ready for tonight?" I ask.

Ted is the director of research and development for a big pharmaceutical company, and there is a black-tie dinner tonight. We went to Molly's Closet together to shop for a dress. Molly had watched me pull into the space in front of her window, and her smile was fixed and ready when we entered. I sat on the bench outside the fitting room and tried to think of nothing. But each time I looked I saw Ruby's feet, her baby toe curved, beneath one of the curtains. Olivia had emerged in an ice-blue silk dress—"the goddess look," Molly said—with a jeweled clip in her hair. And from behind me I heard clearly a single word, said with the high clear sound of a Christmas bell: "Perfection!" I couldn't turn, afraid both of the possibility that Ruby would be standing there, winding her hair up, her eyes alight with approval, and the possibility that there would be no one there at all, just another empty space. I stared straight ahead, sightless.

Looking at me, Olivia had said sadly, "No good?" And with an effort I had focused, looked her up and down, and said without thinking, "It's perfection. Perfection."

"Give my love to, to—your boy," Molly said to me. I was quiet in the car.

"Sorry," I'd finally said. "I'm distracted. I've got so much to do. My mother is coming in three weeks for the high school graduation, and my father-in-law, and who knows who else. It could turn out to be a houseful. It'll be fine. I certainly shouldn't complain to you, of all people. I'm sure you'd love to see your parents more often." There is a large photograph on the piano in Olivia's living room, two handsome people in sweaters and hats, laughing at the camera.

"They're both gone, actually," Olivia had replied in an offhand tone that I suspected she'd used for just this subject many times in the past. "They were in a motor crash, a long time ago, when I was at Oxford. That was how I met Ted. He was there doing the Rhodes, and we met at a pub, and I thought, Ah, so you want to whisk me far, far away from here? Yes, please."

"Oh, my God. I can't believe I'm just hearing about this."

"Everyone has something, don't you think? It's just that it doesn't come up in the usual way. You don't chat up some nice woman at a drinks party and suddenly say, 'Oh, so your parents are dead. Mine, too.' Bit of a bitch, isn't it?"

"I don't even need to tell anyone," I said. "Everyone already knows. Did you hear Molly hesitate as we were leaving? As though if she had said children, plural, by mistake I would have fallen apart."

"It was a bit like that for me in the beginning. My parents were rather well known, and it was a horrid accident. But then people forget. Everyone has something."

My mother had said something similar when she was leaving the last time to return to Florida. "This happens to everyone, this losing people," she said as she stood in the hallway with her suitcase, a valedictory she had clearly been rehearsing. "It just usually happens in stages, not all at once. You've had the worst that anyone could have, Mary Beth. But you still have to figure out how to get on with your life."

"I don't know what my life is now," I had said.

"You have a child. That's what matters."

"I like cartoons," says Luke, sitting cross-legged on the floor in the den on Sunday morning. I wonder if he ever asks for anything, or if he always just says what he likes and expects it to follow. He has slept in my bed again. "You're not my mother," he said before he fell asleep. "I know," I replied.

Andrew and Aidan emerge from their rooms. "Can we call our mom and dad?" Aidan says.

"Yes," I say.

"Shut up about your penis," Andrew says to Luke.

"I'm telling Dad you said shut up," Aidan says.

"You're mean," Luke says, to one or the other.

"Boys," I say darkly, and I feel joyous for just a moment at the familiar bickering, and then I feel terrible because of the joy, and then I make bacon. When Alex and Ben come wandering out, they organize a game of Frisbee on the lawn, and Luke runs back and forth, back and forth, the disk sailing over his head until finally he collapses in tears and I settle him with some cartoons and a cookie. The bigger boys come in to play Battleship. "Hit and sunk!" I hear for what seems like hours, and then I make them all gather at the big pine table to do some homework. "Andrew keeps putting his foot on my foot," Aidan says.

"Mummy!" screams Luke as we hear a car.

Ted walks us down to the guesthouse. Alex goes inside, and we stand at the door as a sharp sudden wind starts to whip around us. "Maybe we'll have a storm tonight," I say, looking up at the clouds sailing swiftly past.

"I can't thank you enough," Ted says.

"It was nothing," I say, and I realize that it's almost true. It was not so terrible, being with other people for two entire days. Or perhaps it was because the people were children, who didn't think to worry, fuss, wonder how I was feeling, persuade me to share. They wanted me only to provide meals, mediate quarrels, keep order. "Really, they were great," I add.

"Yeah, and a whole hell of a lot of work. Believe me, I know. But I really mean thanks for what you've done for Olivia. Getting to be friends with you has made a real difference for her. It hasn't been easy, living in a strange place, not really knowing anyone, having so many kids so close together. She's been kind of lonely. And now, not so much. She really values your friendship."

"And I value hers. I mean that."

"Well, good. You can take her shopping anytime. That was some dress the two of you picked out for her."

"It was perfection," I say.

We're in Times Square walking north, Alice, Alex, and I. We're dwarfed by sports stars and musicians and actors, great flat giants hovering over the three of us on enormous billboards as we thread our way among street vendors and tourists taking one another's pictures on the sidewalks. A man hands Alex a flyer for a strip club, and I try to take it from his hand. "Lady, lady," Alex says, "be cool." Earlier I had tried to take his arm as we left the subway for the street. "Okay, no," he said flatly, jamming his fists into his pockets. He has grown another inch or two, and now he is not a boy who has lost his baby fat but a half-man, bearded, basso, a different species from my own.

"Are you sad about how grown-up he's gotten?" Alice had asked when I mentioned it the night before, her fingers idly playing with Liam's too-long hair. There are so many ways in which she is trying to keep him a baby, from the matted curls to the onesie pajamas.

"No, not really," I replied. I am sad that Max will never grow up, that Ruby will never grow older. But I don't say that. It's nice that Alice still asks me the old commonplace questions.

Alex wants to go to a Times Square store that sells sports gear, then through Central Park to the Museum of Natural History. Alice has gotten Alex tickets to a Yankees game and to a concert at a downtown club. She's been so thoughtful; a graduate student at Columbia who lives in a studio apartment in her building is going to take Alex to both, so that she and I can have time for ourselves. The student's name is Nate, and apparently he loves baseball and music in equal measures. He is getting his doctorate in anthropology.

"Nate's coming up to meet you," Alice had said to us when we first arrived, and she buried her face in Liam's hair.

"Nate is great!" Liam yelled.

Our ride to New York had been an unexpected interlude. The farther the car traveled from the guesthouse, and our old house, and our town, and all the people in it, the calmer I felt. My shoulders seemed to soften with every mile. When we pulled into a rest stop—coffee for me, two burgers, fries, and a Coke for Alex—I felt a little as though we were just like everyone else. Twice I had thought about canceling this trip, not sure I could bear the drive, the distance, the feigned normalcy.

"Have a nice day," said the girl behind the counter, looking Alex up and down.

"You, too," I replied.

Liam was right: Nate was great. He engaged Alex in a long arcane conversation about the Knicks and how a variety of injuries had affected their last season. It is the kind of conversation Alex used to have with his father. "They've got no defense," Glen would say, and Alex would sigh. I wish I could remember more of those conversations, but I never paid any attention. Sometimes now Alex has them on the phone with my father-in-law.

"Nate, will you read to me?" Liam had asked, standing between Nate's knees, his small hands braced on Nate's thighs. "I can read to you," Alex had said kindly, but Liam stared up at Nate's face and shook his head. I watched as Nate lifted Liam onto one knee and continued to talk to Alex, segueing into baseball, while Liam leaned against him and sucked his thumb. Alice brought Liam a sippy cup of milk, Alex a Coke, and Nate a beer.

"I can play baseball," Liam said, interrupting.

"You sit and listen," Alice said, offering me a glass of wine. Nate looked up at her and smiled, and she smiled back. She went into the kitchen to get cheese, and I followed and grabbed her arm at the sink.

"I'm in shock," I said.

"What?"

"Don't play dumb with me. How old is he, and how long have you been seeing him?"

"Seeing him? Are you my mother?"

"Okay, fine. How long have you been sleeping with him?"

"You're being really loud," Alice whispered.

"Fine," I whispered back. "Answer my question."

And with a sweet smile Alice replied, "He's thirty-four, and I met him in February."

"How?"

"He lives in the building. He asked me to dinner. He wouldn't take no for an answer. I told him I was almost ten years older than he is. I told him I had a child. I was as mean to him as I know how to be."

"That's mean," I said.

"It didn't make any difference. He outlasted me."

"And you didn't tell me."

"I thought you would think I was nuts."

I put my arms around her, and I thought that was only partly true. She hadn't told me because it was happy news at a terrible time. And then, because it seemed to me that all I truly heard now of any conversation was what went unsaid, I told her that.

"That's true," she said. "I couldn't picture myself calling you and saying, 'Oh, honey, guess what? I've got a boyfriend.' "

"Is he a boyfriend?"

"He introduced me to his mother."

"Wow!"

"And here's the best thing—she had him late in life. So she's nowhere near my age. Not even close."

"Does she know about Liam?"

"She brought him a stuffed monkey."

"She's a better woman than I would be."

"Me, too. I keep trying to imagine Liam with a girlfriend who is ten years older than he is. Nate says he thinks his mother worried that he was gay when he moved to New York, so she's just relieved that I'm female."

"Where's he from?"

"Nova Scotia."

"Maybe he's using you for a green card," I said darkly.

"I don't care," she said, and I hugged her again. I will have to learn to be generous about this, about other people's happiness. Rachel and Sarah. Olivia and Alice. Even Alex. There will come a time when good things will happen to him, and I will have to make certain to welcome his triumphs and his joys, and to make sure they're not always shadowed by his father, his brother, his sister.

"Nate is great," Alex had said that morning, reading the account of the game in the morning paper. "He knows a lot about the museum. He can't go with us because he has to teach some class, but he told me what to see."

When we reach the Natural History museum, Alex pulls a

piece of folded lined paper from his back pocket. It is Nate's list. Ocean life, it says. Space center. We spend four hours wandering from marvel to marvel. Only once am I undone by memory and sensation, and that's when I enter the butterfly exhibit and watch them fan the air with stained-glass wings. I lean my head against a cool wall and breathe deeply, then move on. "Mom, check this out," Alex says, standing with his head thrown back beneath the blue whale tethered to a beveled ceiling, and for a moment he is a boy again, a boy without cares. I think about how much Max and Ruby and Glen would enjoy this and wish we had all done it together years ago.

We take the subway back to Alice's neighborhood in Brooklyn. Across the subway car from us sit a man in a turban, a woman covered with tattoos, a woman in a black suit reading an anthology of poetry, and a teenage boy about Alex's age, doing what looks like math homework in a spiral notebook. I feel anonymous, and glad to be so. At a row of brick houses with worn stoops Alex says, "It's so cool to live here, isn't it?" A small white truck is trolling the block, the man at the wheel calling something I can't catch in a singsong voice. "The knife sharpener," Alice says. "You can bring your knives out to the truck."

"That is so cool," Alex says, with no hint of what I feel—the sharpened knives, a frisson of fear.

In an Italian restaurant he finishes a plate of gnocchi, some veal, an ice-cream dessert striped like a flag. I let him have an inch worth of red wine in his glass. He and Alice discuss the space show at the museum and a book she is editing on life on Mars. "That is a cool job," Alex says. I am an ordinary woman with her son and an old friend eating dinner. It's the first time I have felt ordinary in so long—free of public scrutiny, and sympathy, and judgment, too. I know there is judgment. The mother of one of the boys on the basketball team took the coach aside and said her son found it upsetting to play on the same team as Alex. The coach said he would be sorry to lose him. The kid said his mother was psycho. The mother backed down. I should stare at her at the games with a defiant gaze, but instead my eyes drop when she looks over at me. No one judges me as harshly as I judge myself. No one wants me hidden away as much as I want to hide. It's as though I'm one of those burn victims, with a face so scarred and stripped that other people have to look, then look away.

In the window of a thrift shop Alex sees an old army jacket, and we make him try it on, and only the sleeves are a little long. Alice rolls them up once. "I wonder who Steiner was," Alex says, looking at the name stamped above the heart. "You should buy it," I say, and we do.

Alex is sleeping in Liam's room, on a couch where the nanny sleeps when Alice has to work late, and as we have another drink just before midnight I hear him on the baby monitor. "Dude, the giant squid," I hear, but I can't make out the rest.

"He can't be talking to Liam, can he?" I ask.

"If Liam were awake, he wouldn't be letting Alex get a word in edgewise. I think Liam is a little jealous that we went out without him, and that Nate is paying attention to Alex. Which reminds me—I need to ask you an enormous favor."

"Shoot."

"Can I make you Liam's legal guardian if anything happens to me?"

"Nothing's going to happen to you."

"Nothing's going to happen to me," she agrees. "But I need to know that there's someone backstopping me. My parents are just too old. My father just turned seventy-seven."

"What about your brothers?"

"Okay, babe, let's recap: John is married to a crazy person; Jim is married to a woman who didn't want to have her own kids, much less mine; Tommy isn't married, because that would demand a commitment; and Teddy is a closet case. I love them all. But daddy material? No way."

"I'm not trying to get out of this. I just want to be able to stand up in court and say, 'Yes, Your Honor, I know she has four brothers, but she didn't think a single one of them would make a competent parent. Except maybe the closet case.' "

"Is that a yes?"

"Of course it is. You would do the same for me. You came close to having to."

"Stop."

"It's true."

On the monitor we hear Alex say something else. It sounds like "up and down the stairs." Or maybe it was "all around, and scared."

"Alex seems pretty good," Alice says.

"He does. He did decide to go to the therapist. Maybe that's helping."

"He's always had a really even keel."

"I know. He's the only one I can imagine getting through this. Ruby or, God forbid, Max? I can't imagine it."

Alice rubs at her eyes. "Glen is the one I think about sometimes. If anything had happened to you, I don't think he could have survived." Her lip trembles.

"You've made it through this whole visit without crying," I say. "Don't mess it up now." I do my crying privately. Early in the morning, I had gone out to walk along the promenade that skirts the river. I walked for nearly two hours, first with no companions except a pair of police officers and a man asleep on a bench, then surrounded by runners who had the sure, smooth pace of those following a familiar route. When I wept, they scarcely looked at me. Perhaps, with everyone living so close together, city dwellers expect to have a walk-on role in other people's dramas and tragedies.

I hear Alex laugh, speak, choke up, laugh again.

"Maybe he's talking in his sleep," I say. I'm glad there is a receiver for the baby monitor in the living room, where I've insisted on sleeping. I worry that Alex may have a nightmare in the unfamiliar place. He mutters more as I doze.

But when I wake at five and tiptoe in, Alex looks like he is sleeping the sleep of the teenage boy, so deep it cannot be shaken even by Liam, who has climbed into bed with Alex and has thrown one chubby leg over Alex's long scarred one. I go back into the living room, and think about Glen, and how he would have liked the space show, and how he would have sneaked away to the gift shop to buy me a keepsake. Alex's keepsake will be his new jacket. "That jacket is totally great," I hear Ruby saying. "Hands off, dude," Alex says to Max, and Max makes a face, as though he is thinking, That jacket's not for you, dude, it's for me. I will sneak it out of your closet the first chance I get.

Nate and Alex exchange a complex power handshake as we prepare to leave the next morning. Liam looks confused, then distressed. "Mama!" he says. "I want to go to the park."

"Do not screw this up," I whisper as I hug Alice.

"I hear you," she says.

In the car Alex puts on his headphones, and I listen to a public-radio program. A resonant voice describes colony-collapse disorder. "All over the country, beekeepers are opening their hives to discover that all their bees are dead," the reporter says. An interview with a monosyllabic writer follows, and my mind wanders. I wonder if Alice will call to ask my advice, slowly, tentatively, about getting married. I wonder if I will ask her advice someday, about being the only parent of an only child. I look over at Alex. What

I can hear of his music, from deep inside the headphones, is tuneless and metallic, like the buzzing of bees.

"I hope Ginger is all right," I say when he takes the headphones off for a moment.

"She's fine. I called Ben yesterday. Luke is hanging out with her."

"Did you have a good time?"

"Mom, I kept thinking, Why am I going away when I could just hang out with my friends? But I had a really great time. Much better than I expected."

"Me, too. So I have a great idea—what about living there?"

"I was thinking that. Nate told me there are so many good colleges in New York. Even if I couldn't get into Columbia, there are other places where you can go and still be in the city. He said there are even some Division 3 schools where maybe I could play. I'm really going to think about it."

I look out the windshield. The yellow line is rushing up at me. "I was thinking sooner," I say. I pause. "There's no reason we couldn't move to Brooklyn. There are lots of good private schools. That's what Alice said. Everybody says they're really hard to get into, but with what a great athlete you are I bet they'd be glad to have you."

Alex is silent. His headphones rest in his lap. "Who are you?" I hear The Who singing faintly, but it sounds like just waah-waah.

"I mean, you really liked the city, right? There would be so much to do, and you don't have to drive; you can just take the subway, go to the movies with your friends. Alice says—"

"I'm not moving," Alex says flatly. "I'm not leaving my friends and my school. I'm not moving." He has turned toward me, and his voice is rising. I put out my hand as though we're going to brake suddenly. "I'm not moving," he yells.

"All right, sorry, I hear you. Calm down."

He's breathing hard, the way he does on the soccer field.

"I just thought it might be a good change for us," I say softly.

"I'm not moving."

"I heard you."

We drive in silence for what seems like a long time. I can't find another decent radio station. He puts on his headphones. I've spoiled it. I don't know what to do, or what to do next. The memorial service, the will, the insurance: No one tells you what to do after, when things are supposed to go back to normal. I suppose what comes next is pretend-normal. I feel exhausted thinking about it.

We stop to eat. In the bright light of a diner, I see that Alex needs a shave. This is an astonishing thought. From time to time he runs a razor over his face, but it has been more a declaration of maturity than an actual need. "What about this summer?" I ask brightly, as though nothing has happened.

"Mom, camp. I go to camp every summer."

"You want to go again?"

"Mom, you signed me up last year. I get to be a junior counselor."

He's right. I signed them all up. Max was going to be the drummer in his camp's rock band. Ruby was going to take advanced poetry composition. Glen and I talked about taking a vacation, perhaps in Nantucket or Martha's Vineyard. I'm interviewing the last doctor interested in Glen's practice first thing in the morning. The sign outside will be changed, the name embroidered on the white coat will be different. Someone else will win the writing prize at graduation. Someone else will play computer chess with Ezra. The surface of the ocean of daily life will close over the three of them and the water will look smooth again. They will live only in a tableau that plays ceaselessly in my mind.

"Sorry, sorry, I don't know where my head was," I say, pushing my plate aside.

"We're not moving, right?" Alex says when we're back in the car.

"Not if you don't want to."

"Is Aunt Alice going to marry Nate?" he asks.

"Too soon to tell," I say.

"She should," he says, and puts the headphones back on.

"Ruby Lee Latham," it says in overwrought calligraphy. The diploma is in a leather folder propped on the bookshelf in the small hallway. When I pass it, I touch it. It reminds me of Alice again, of going to church with Alice and her family and how all of them reflexively put two fingers in the deep marble bowl of water at the head of the aisle. My hand does the same with the diploma. It feels warm to me.

Everything happens all at once at the high school now, now that the school year is winding down again. They plant the tree and read three of Ruby's poems, the ones I've heard before. The literary magazine is dedicated to her, the yearbook to Ruby and Max, which is a comfort, because otherwise it is as though Max has disappeared into the past the same way he disappeared into his room, into his head, into his unhappiness. Sarah and Rachel and Eric and a boy named Gregory I have never met come over on their way to the prom. Sarah is wearing a yellow dress, Rachel something strapless and peach-colored. "That dress was made for you," I say to Rachel, and she glows, and Gregory puts his arm around her waist and smiles. He has brought Rachel a wrist corsage of roses and ferns. Rachel and Sarah have brought me a big bouquet of daisies. I put them in a pitcher in the middle of the table. They're such nice girls. I hope they don't think I slept with Kiernan's father. My face burns at the thought. I take their picture.

"I've heard so many great things about you, Mrs. Latham," says Gregory, and I wonder whether losing Ruby has brought Rachel to this—to a nice boy, a kind boy, a boy who brings flowers and looks at her as though she deserves them.

"Is Alex here?" Rachel asks. She leans close. "We really like his girlfriend."

Nancy is the first person I see on the football field when I arrive for graduation. She kisses my cheek and my mother's, shakes my father-in-law's hand. Then she looks at me and says, "This must be such a hard day for you."

"It's a big day for Sarah," I say, looking toward the long long line of students in blue caps and gowns. They are taking one another's pictures, talking about plans for the parties, laughing and waving to their families. The principal had asked if I wanted to accept Ruby's diploma onstage, but I told him I was afraid it would attract too much attention, distract from the happiness of the day. The sun is strong, the sky white-blue, and for just a moment I feel dizzy, but I blink and look back at Nancy and smile. I hope the smile doesn't look as false as it feels. I'm wearing a bright red dress, and I don't care what anyone says or thinks about that. It is a Ruby color, a Ruby dress.

Alex is already here, sitting with a group of his teammates, ready to cheer for the graduating seniors from the soccer, basketball, and lacrosse teams. He is standing, scanning the crowd, and then he comes over and hugs us all. As he strides back to the bleachers, my mother touches my arm. "We should sit down," she says.

I press my hands together tightly in my lap as the alphabetical procession unfolds. Finally, "Ruby Lee Latham," the principal says, after Kimora Kim and Robert Landman. There is a rumble, like the sound of a plane, or a train, a rumble as the entire audience rises. The applause is like my heart beating in my ears, but magnified a million times, as though my heart might explode. I look up from my chair, and it is as though I am sitting at the bottom of a deep well, with walls of people all around me, and I drop my head into my hands. The clapping goes on for a long time. "Stand up, Mary Beth," my mother says, her hand on my shoulder, but I can't.

"Max Evan Latham," I whisper as the applause dies down and the principal goes on to Christine Lessig, whose name has been called right after Ruby's since they were in first grade together. Her parents are sitting at the end of our row, and I lean forward to nod, and they nod back, her mother's face wet and shining.

"Well, that's over," says my mother when we get back to the guesthouse, and my father-in-law makes them both old-fashioneds from mixers he brought in a big brown bag. "Jesus Christ, I'm starving," he says, as he hands my mother the drink. Alex comes out of the smaller bedroom in a T-shirt and shorts. "What's for lunch?" he says. "He's always hungry," says my mother. "He's a growing boy," says Glen's father.

"Fried chicken and mac and cheese," I say.

"You are the world's best mom," says Alex.

("It's true," Ruby and Max say in unison behind him. Glen just smiles.)

Glen's father drives my mother to the airport in the evening, then continues on across the interstate. "Anything you need, Mary Beth," he says. "I know," I say. He wants us to come for Thanksgiving. I say I can't plan that far ahead. My mind goes blank at the thought.

It's the same when I leave Alex at camp: I'm not sure what to do afterward. He and Ben are in different cabins, the junior assistants to college students from Australia and the Czech Republic. Their beds are set a little apart from those of the nine-year-old campers they will oversee. Alex is helping with the junior soccer league and basketball drills. He has an official polo shirt. The word LATHAM is embroidered across his heart under the camp insignia.

"I wonder if you can keep those," I say, and Alex gives me a look. "Because they're totally lame?" he says.

I walk up a steep hill to the camp office. The director comes out and shakes my hand and says some familiar words about taking special care of Alex. I tell him that I know no phone calls are permitted, but that I hope he will make an exception. He says that Alex is welcome to call home.

In the parking lot, a blond woman so thin her skin is translucent approaches me slowly. "Alex's mom? I'm Colin's mom," she says, and we both try to smile. The skin around her eyes is the gray-blue of a threatening sky.

"I never called to thank you," I say.

"For what?"

"For taking him skiing. For getting him on a plane home so quickly. For having your husband fly back with him."

"We all felt terrible about what happened. We tried to do our best to help. The hardest part—" She stops.

"Not being able to tell him?"

"That was it. Knowing, and knowing we had to pretend. Your mother said we should just tell him you were in the hospital. I don't know if he knew we were hiding the truth or not."

"I'm just grateful for what you did. I'm embarrassed that I didn't call or write and thank you."

"Don't think twice. I didn't. I was a little preoccupied myself." She shrugs, and her hand goes to her heart. "A touch of breast cancer." Another woman showing one face to the world and living a different life within. I put my hand out to hers.

"Oh, God, I'm so sorry."

"They say it'll be fine. But it's hard on the kids. Colin, especially. He and Alex are so close, and then this." She shrugs again. It looks like a habitual gesture, almost a tic. "Shit happens," she says, and we both smile ruefully.

"Mom." I hear a cry from across the playing fields, and I turn. "Mom?" yells Alex. "You're still here?"

I stop at a nursery to buy some perennials and some zinnias. I think perhaps I will plant the perennials around the back door of the guesthouse. I am making a to-do list—not things I need to get done but things I need to do to fill the time. Few of my customers have called. Some of the ones with sprawling grounds, with trees that need pruning and large beds that need mulch, have heard that I no longer have the staff required. Rickie is working for the university as assistant facilities director. John is doing all the landscaping for the county. "You know if you need me I can help you out in a heartbeat, Mary Beth," he said when we ran into each other at the garden center. But I'm mainly doing smaller gardens for some of the people who first employed me when Latham Landscaping was just me, two college kids, and an answering machine. Mrs. Feeney, a woman in her nineties who has had me plant annuals and window boxes for her for years, had said to me when she called to make arrangements, "I don't take the local paper anymore. It's too depressing. But I gather that was you, wasn't it, at New Year's?"

"Yes, it was."

"I was sorry to hear it," she said. "You're in my prayers. Can you do the same for me that you did last year?"

"Of course," I said. It was a relief to speak to someone so matter-of-fact. Probably by the time you're over ninety you've witnessed, perhaps experienced, every sort of tragedy imaginable, loved people who died in wars and people who died in automobile accidents and people who just died suddenly and senselessly, went out like a used-up lightbulb. She liked impatiens, Mrs. Feeney, and dahlias and petunias, all the bright-colored old-fashioned flowers that weren't too finicky and lasted only through summer. I'd tried to interest her in hydrangeas once, but she just shook her head.

I expected to miss my work more, but I don't. It was the kind of job you have because you have children, that gives you room for supermarket shopping, soccer games and after-school pickups, and gives you something to tell people at parties. I love to make things grow, to deadhead the foxglove and watch it improbably have a second flowering, to dig up a big bristly clump of old day lilies in the fall and break it up into five or six smaller plants and then have each of them burst into bloom the following summer. But I realize now that I don't really care for landscaping plans, terrace beds, drystone pathways, pergolas—all the things people want to make their gardens into what magazines now call "outdoor rooms." My idea of an outdoor room is a screened porch with a picnic table.

I stop at a diner just across the state line and sit at the counter with the newspaper. There are two horrible murders in it. There is one nearly every week. I didn't really notice before. I have a cheese omelet and coffee. I eat half of the omelet. "Was everything okay?" says the young waitress, worried that the cook has messed up and so messed up her tip. "Can I box that up for you?" Yes. No. I leave a ten on a six-dollar check so her mind will be at ease. I've started to buy a few clothes in smaller sizes. "You look fantastic!" Rachel's mother, Sandy, said last week when I ran into her at the drugstore. She doesn't. Sandy has decided to go blond, and with her dark eyes and brows she looks as though she's wearing a wig. She kept talking for nearly twenty minutes, and I sensed that she was lonely, that perhaps at the very last minute she's realized that with Rachel at college she will arrive home every night to that particular tangible silence that falls like dust over a house that is uninhabited all day long. I know I will feel it when I come home this evening, although Alex has left such disorder that I'll have a day or two of laundry and stripped beds to keep the vibration of the empty rooms from buzzing in my ears. At least I have Ginger. How pathetic that sounds. Sandy should get a cat, but then I remember that Rachel is allergic, to cats and to nuts. I always had to be so careful when I cooked for her.

An hour from home, and I realize that I must have just missed some violent weather. Twice I have to navigate around trees across the road, and my tires bump over limbs and branches. The tar is shiny, the clouds low, and when I put on my headlights they reflect back harshly from the patent-leather surface of the road. Then I'm in a patch of rain so heavy that I pull over, the wipers useless against the water sloughing down the sides of the car. It drags silt across the road in a red-brown swath, and I hear a noise that sounds like gunshots but is probably the limbs of big trees snapping in a gusty wind. The radio signal is scratchy, but after a few minutes the announcer says that there is a storm warning, and that we all should take shelter and stay off the roads.

"Too late," I say aloud, and put in one of the music mixes Alex has left in the car.

The storm is fierce, and no other cars pass me. After a while, like a passage in a classical concerto, the music of the storm slows, the melody of drops on metal and tar the same but more muted, less violent. I begin to drive again, and soon there's just the tapping of intermittent drops as the counterpoint to Alex's music. I hit "skip" and "scan" and finally come upon an old song that is almost all drums called "Wipeout." No words, just a maniacal beat. Then I go back over the rest of the songs, and realize that the music is Max's, although I could swear Alex was playing it this morning on the trip to camp.

The winds and rain have ripped through town, and as I crest the hill I see a blurry scrum of red lights that must be the town fire engines around an electric pole down on Main Street. It's dusky in the stormy summer afternoon, but there are no lights glowing inside the stores or restaurants, and I wonder if there will be electricity in the guesthouse when I arrive. Olivia has left a battery-powered lantern by the back door for her guests.

I come down the hill toward the turnoff for Olivia's house. Two large stands of poplars have toppled from the shallow ridge above, and the road ends in a snarled wall of limbs and leaves. The rain has stopped, and the late-day light is gilding the wet trees; I think I can see a large nest on the ground beside one of them. What a waste that would be, to build a home stick by stick, to line it with moss and lay some eggs and then watch as the whole thing fell from the sky, to become nothing but a mess of shards and twigs on the shoulder of the road.

I pull over as far as I can, but there is a steep downward pitch into heavy forest, far too steep to allow me to maneuver around the poplars. I can't take any chances. I am all Alex has. I've used some of Glen's insurance money to buy an enormous policy on my own life. "Mary Beth, if anything happened he'd have plenty of resources, between the payout on Glen and the practice and the eventual sale of the house," Nancy's husband, Bill, had said. I bought the insurance anyway.

I turn my car around and go back a mile or so up the hill, where

I know there's a small gravel road that Olivia says snakes around the crest and then drops into a gully behind her house. At its end, it joins up with the road that is blocked by the trees. I've never been down it before. "Hidden Cottage Road," it's called, and soon I know why. There's nothing on it for more than a mile, the trees so thick that they make a dark ruffled roof over the car, until after one perilous S curve the road swerves so sharply that an insensible driver would careen onto a narrow stone drive that undulates away without any discernible object. And because it's late, and I've been driving almost all day, and I can't seem to drive in the car alone without seeing faces in the rearview mirror and hearing voices from the backseat, that's exactly what I do.

I can see that the drive divides to create a large oval and then meets again in front of an old farmhouse, its white paint glowing in the silvery half-light of the stormy evening. It's all that glows; the house is dark, and, despite the shadow of curtains at the window and an ornamental milk can by the door, it has the unmistakable desolation of a house that no one lives in anymore.

In the center of the driveway oval is a concolor pine, a soft-needled variant for which I've always had a weakness. We had chosen one once as our Christmas tree, or I had and Glen went along. But the children had all complained that it was a weird tree, not what we were used to, that the color was wrong, not green enough. The next year we reverted to a Fraser fir.

This one is a stupendous Christmas tree, but one for a public place, the nave of a cathedral, a town hall. It's at least forty feet tall, trained into a perfect triangle. The only reason I have been able to see the house at all is because my car slid to one side on the gravel drive. Otherwise, the concolor shields the house from view. I try to gauge the direction and wonder if it makes the house dark in daylight, but it's set too far from it to cast a shadow over its rooms, or to fall through the roof during a bad storm.

Stuck in the ground in front of the pine is a battered sign. FOR SALE BY OWNER, it says, with a phone number below. There's no paper in my purse, so I write on my palm with a pen.

I'm sitting on the screened porch perspiring as a hummingbird makes noisy feints at a fuchsia hanging from a bracket just outside. The back of the house is shaded by a curtain of forest, the light falling harshly out of the shadows onto the path to the barn. It's early August, steamy, with a loamy smell, and the front of my T-shirt is gray with perspiration. Sanding hardwood floors is a dirty job, and I have been doing it since just after dawn.

Olivia used an expression one day that I'd never heard before. "Safe as houses," she'd said about something and, when she saw the look on my face, added, "Don't Americans use that one? It means certain, sure." She said she thought it had something to do with real estate as an investment, and I assume she was right. Ruby's English teacher had told me that Olivia's father was once the editor of the *Oxford English Dictionary*.

I liked the way the expression sounded, but I thought it meant something else, the way that a house made you feel. In the way that sinners stubbornly continue to believe in good, or agnostics glimpse God when their plane starts to bounce on a zephyr, I still somewhere inside believed a home could keep us safe.

It wasn't exactly for sale by owner. The number on the sign was that of an art historian at the university, whose mother was fading into nothing in a nursing home. "It's just too large for one person," the woman had said, as though she had to justify selling the place where she'd grown up. "You've seen it. You know."

The professor, a tiny woman in a black shift, met me at the house two days after the storm. At dusk the huge concolor had been silvery, a tree that carried its own shadows in its branches. But in full sunlight its green needles had a faint bluish sheen.

"That's some tree," I said.

"My father said it was Christmas all year round," she replied.

A living room with a fireplace, a dining room with wainscoting, a kitchen along the rear of the house that hadn't been changed for fifty years, a screened porch straight across the back to balance the open porch in front. A steep and narrow staircase led to four small-ish bedrooms, two on either side of a hall with a bath between them. The gravel drive continued down to the small barn, red faded to russet. A foursquare, old-fashioned, unimaginative house, the sort whose layout you know before you ever set foot inside.

"There's no garage," the professor said.

"That's fine," I replied.

I'd rented it for six months with an option to buy. It was the middle ground between past and future, an acknowledgment that I had to do something without doing too much, without facing a deed and a mortgage document with only my name on it. And it provided me with tasks to occupy my days. "Can I do some fixing up?" I'd asked, and the professor had looked around at the dingy walls and the chipped woodwork. "If you'd like," she said. I'd given her a check at the beginning of July, and then gone to work there every day, stripping wallpaper, applying paint, ripping up the faded greenish carpeting that ran through the house like creeping mold. Beneath the pressed vinyl in the kitchen, designed to look like no one's idea of bricks, was red linoleum with black flecks, vintage schoolroom stuff. I scrubbed it and put on a sealer.

The only sounds were nature sounds, birds and wind and the occasional shower, dropping onto the leaves with a muted *rat-tat-tat*. I talked to myself sometimes, with no one to hear, no one to care, no one to whisper that Mary Beth Latham hadn't really gotten over what happened, as though someday I would and would be cheery and bright. Twice a raccoon in the garbage can gave me a fright, and one afternoon a dark car pulled into the driveway, the first car I'd seen since the professor and I made a rental deal. I'd held my hammer so tight there was a purple dent in my hand afterward. A man was at the wheel, a man in a white sport shirt.

"Um, hello?" he'd called, looking at the hammer as he walked toward me, his face shadowed by a baseball cap. "It's me? Ed Jackson?" When he got a little closer, my heart began to slow slightly.

"Officer Jackson," I said. "I didn't recognize you right away." But I recognized his voice. I'd heard it when I was lying on the floor of my bedroom on the morning of January 1.

"You're really in the middle of nowhere out here," he said.

"It's fine," I replied.

"You putting in a security system?" I just smiled. "Everyone asks me that," I said. He'd brought me a rubber plant, one of those big smooth-leafed plants that look as though they are artificial. There was a red bow around the pot. I'd put it on the back porch, out of the way.

Sometimes Olivia would stop by after she had dropped the younger boys at day camp and clean up after me, ripping away the bright blue painter's tape, emptying the sander bag. One day she appeared suddenly from out of the woods, a fairy princess with a halo of dust motes.

"Where did you come from?" I'd called from a bedroom window.

"Just below," she called back. "I reckon it's a mile and a half through the woods. There's a clear deer trail for most of it. It took me thirty minutes, but these boys will make it twenty on the run. If the trees weren't so thick, we could put in a zip line."

"I'm there as soon as you say the word," Alice had said on the phone. "It sounds perfect."

"It's pretty ordinary, but the setting is nice," I replied.

She was at the lake in Michigan with Liam, and with Nate, too. Her brothers liked Nate and so did her mother. "My father's skeptical," she said. "He told my brother Tommy that Nate probably had the wrong idea about me because I was a single mother."

"He means Nate will think you're fast."

"Oh my God, that's exactly the word my dad used. Who says that anymore? And, by the way, did my father miss the part about the donor sperm?"

"Don't use the word 'sperm' around your father."

"Anyhow, he says Nate may be trying to take advantage of me. I told Tommy that he's taking advantage of me every chance he gets."

"And Tommy said, 'Oh jeez, Al, shut it.' "

"Exactly."

The work is close to done now. That's what I wanted, to have the house ready when Alex returned from camp. That's why I didn't buy it, so Alex can decide. "You're going to let a fifteen-year-old decide whether to buy a house?" Alice asked to the rhythmic sound of Liam beating something metal against the phone.

"It's his house, too," I said.

"I understand that, but— Honey! Honey! Don't hit me with that again, or no beach! Do you hear me? No beach, no swim-mies!" Liam wailed. "Okay, who was just giving parenting advice here?"

"I just want him to be comfortable," I said, sighing.

All morning a truck has been bringing furniture and boxes. My mother has been here for four days, glad, she says, to leave the harsh Florida sun, and she's been packing up our old house. I will never go there again. I've told her what to bring: Alex's nearly new double bed, his scarred old desk, his posters, his books. The chair that ended up in Max's room, the old oak rocker with the upholstered seat in which I nursed the two of them and Ruby, too. The upholstery is now a bright red-and-yellow plaid, but if you peeled it off you would find yellow polka dots, and beneath that rocking horses, and beneath that the ugly cracked imitation green leather that was there when I bought it at a junk shop in Chicago. Glen and I had carried it home, each of us holding one thick arm. A nameless neighbor helped Glen carry it upstairs. I had plans to strip it down to its mellow golden patina, but first there was one child, then three, and now I would never change it.

I've decided to keep the good antiques—the desk from the living room, the armoire in the kitchen, the mahogany pieces from our bedroom. The paintings will all be transplanted, although there is one beautiful landscape in watercolors that Olivia has admired and that I plan to give her. I don't believe the den is tainted, so I've told my mother to have the movers bring over all the furniture from that room. The two couches and the wing chairs, the coffee table and the big bookshelves—together they will fill the living room. Everything else in the house will go. "What about the mirrors?" my mother asked.

"Give the mirrors away," I said. I'm not sure why.

The night before, my mother and I had shared a pitcher of cold mint tea at the little table in the guesthouse, and she looked around and said, "You were lucky to have this place."

"I know."

"I wish I had." I didn't know exactly what she meant, but I let it lie. I was no longer inclined to pick at the scabs of our shared past. The boxes had come up the drive, gone down to the barn, labeled in black marker in her block print. I watched from a window as the men carried them, my whole life in cardboard, everything I'd loved and lost: G suits, M books, R sweaters. And I remembered that the same sort of boxes had been stored in the basement of the house where I grew up. The ironing board had been set up down there, and as I pressed a skirt or a shirt I would look at them, stacked to one side of the cast-iron boiler: J books, J shirts, J misc. I never thought of opening them, and I hadn't thought until now of what happened to them after my mother sold the house and moved South with Stan. Were they in some storage unit alongside boxes filled with Stan's first wife's dresses and costume jewelry? Or had my mother finally carried them to the Goodwill, or consigned some to the curb for the morning trash collection? I could ask her, I suppose, but what difference would it make? Whatever she did was fine. That's what I've learned. It's fine. Whatever you manage to do.

I look down at the cement floor of the screened porch. I've decided to paint it with three coats of red deck paint, but first I have to finish the last of the bedrooms. The downstairs is done. The walls are painted pale yellow to try to capture the sun. My body is sore every night, and I welcome the soreness. The third evening I worked here, I lay down on an old chaise in the yard to rest for a few minutes before I closed up. The gnats had worried my damp face, and I closed my eyes against them and fell asleep without medication for the first time in seven months.

I had a dream then, the first dream I'd had in all that time. That was why I wanted the pills, not so that I could sleep but so that I wouldn't dream. I was so afraid that the vague imaginings that circled me during the daytime would become sharp and vivid in the dark, in my unprotected unconscious mind. I was so afraid that I would see, moment by moment, step by step, what happened first to Ruby, then to Max, and finally to Glen.

But the dream I had was nothing like that—no loud noises, no muffled screams, no blood. It was scarcely a real dream at all. There were no improbable or unrecognizable places or people, none of the strange and nonsensical occurrences we have learned to recognize as the weird back roads of our minds. How often did we come down to the table in the morning, squinting against the light, groping for coffee, saying to one another, "I had the weirdest dream last night." Animals. Movie actors. Winged flight. Free falls. We were always sure we knew what the others' dreams meant, but we could never parse our own.

The dream I had in the yard, as the gnats gave way to mosquitoes that bit at my arms (I would discover later) and a bat flew through the open porch and the kitchen doors and into the dining room (I would discover the next day), was simple and straightforward. We were all at the kitchen table. Glen was in his seat at the head, I in mine opposite him. Ruby was at his right hand, Alex at his left, Max between Alex and me. For years we'd threatened to change this, when their arguments would escalate into pushing or slaps, but we couldn't bear to. This was where we had all always been.

The sixth chair, the chair where Kiernan always sat, was gone.

The table was set for dinner, but there was no food. We were all talking to one another and smiling, even Max. Ruby lifted her napkin and put it on her lap. Ginger was underneath the table. Glen said something to Max, and he passed the salt. When they moved their lips, I couldn't hear them.

"Where's the food?" I said, and everyone laughed, and suddenly

I was wide awake, as though I had shattered the vision by asking the question.

The dream hadn't had time to fade, and I was confused by my position, and the dark yard, and the woods, and the porch and the house. Ginger was asleep at the end of the chaise, snuffling softly. I lay there and looked up at the stars, which seemed exceptionally bright. Then I closed my eyes and tried to see them all again, gathered around the dinner table. Why had I cared about the food? Why had I spoken aloud? I closed my eyes, but the dream, bidden, refused to return. When I looked at my watch I saw that it was nearly five, and I got up and made coffee and began to sand again.

I have halved the dose of the sleeping pills now. I have the sedatives of hard work and long days, wet heat and dark nights. And Alex isn't here, so I don't have to worry about being conscious if he cries out, or of holding myself together when he walks in. Most of the time I sleep on the new mattress I had delivered, which is in the dining room until the lacquer on the bedroom floor is dry and set. "Aren't you scared out there?" Nancy had said when we saw each other at the farmers' market. I can no longer manage the empty social answer everyone wants. "What's left for me to be scared of?" I had replied softly, and walked off to weigh some peaches.

When I got into my car, she appeared at the window. "Mary Beth, I feel like we need to clear the air," she said. "Anytime," I replied.

My mother is afraid that many people will do what I first did— that they will miss the sharp curve and careen into my front yard. But in all the time I've been working here there have been only a handful of cars that have come down the road, most of them lost and therefore driving slowly, looking for direction. Even my mother has had a hard time finding me. When she arrives with the last load of furniture, she brings sandwiches and a cherry pie. Her face is filthy. She has hired a service to clean the old house thoroughly. "Inside and out," she keeps saying, and I wonder if the latter means that she has asked them to clean the garage as well. A couple with two young daughters have signed a contract to buy the house at only slightly less than the others in the neighborhood. I ordered the real-estate agent to tell anyone who wanted to look the truth about what had happened, and she complained that it drove most of the buyers away. But these two apparently were unconcerned. They told her they believed making happy memories could expunge the events of that night. I know what they mean, because I am trying hard to feel the same.

"They're measuring for carpet," my mother says disapprovingly. "And new cabinets in the kitchen."

We carry our sandwiches out to the porch and eat in silence. My mother must be tired. She is fit and thin—thinner, now, perhaps than she used to be—but she is seventy years old, and she has been working hard for days. I've searched for traces of tears on her face, but I've seen nothing, which means nothing. She's good at keeping herself to herself, so good that it is difficult for me to know how to speak to her sometimes. As I wrap up the second half of the sandwich to eat for dinner later, I say, forcing myself to look into her face, "Thank you for everything, Mom. You've been a rock through all this."

I've taken her by surprise, and she looks down. Finally she says, "I have great admiration for how you've handled yourself, Mary Beth. You've been very strong."

"Did I have a choice?"

"That's not the point. Lots of people would have fallen apart in this situation." I wonder how falling apart would feel different from this. I can't believe it would be worse.

In the silence the crickets are loud, an insistent snapping sound.

Finally I say, "You saw them." It is an imprecise, almost mysterious sentence, but as my mother looks up I realize that she not only knows what I mean; she has been waiting for this moment. She nods.

"The chief of police told me you had to identify them," I say, and she nods again.

"How did they look?"

My mother sets her mouth. "Like they were asleep," she says.

"I don't believe you."

"I'm telling you, they looked like they were asleep. There were sheets pulled up to their chins, and they looked like they were asleep."

"The police have pictures I could look at," I say.

"There are pictures in all these boxes, too," my mother says. "There's Ruby on a pony at a farm, and there's Max swimming in a lake, and there's your wedding picture, and your tenth-anniversary party. If you want to look at pictures, look at those pictures."

"I don't want to look at pictures," I say.

"Not yet," my mother says. She hands me her paper napkin to wipe my tears.

"In the beginning, all I wanted to know was what those last few minutes were like," I say. "I imagined it all the time. I was afraid to imagine it. What they were thinking. Whether it hurt. Whether Glen knew about Max and Ruby. I felt like that was the worst part. And now I feel like the worst part is just—"

"That they're gone."

"All the things they're missing. All the life they won't get to have."

"That's it," my mother says, looking me in the eye, her mouth held tight, as though she's angry. "All those unlived years." She takes my hand, and suddenly I have a vision, sharp and clear, and it is of Max and Ruby and Glen, side by side, asleep. Max's mouth is a little ajar. Ruby's hair cloaks her neck and shoulders. My mother has done it. She has made me see what she wanted me to see. The one person who understands is the one person I never expected to understand me.

Together we are quiet and still.

"I hope Alex likes this place," I finally say.

My mother looks around her. She doesn't like old houses, my mother. Sometimes I think the nicest thing Stan ever did for her was to take her to a place where everyone had skylights and double sinks and soaking tubs.

"He'll like it fine," she says. "You'll make it nice for him."

My father-in-law doesn't like old houses much, either. I had told Doug that I was thinking of buying this one, and two days later Glen's father came down the driveway in one of the roofing trucks, collapsible ladders rattling on the side racks as he lurched down toward the back. He climbed slowly from the cab—leg, leg, a heave, and the torso followed—and looked up disapprovingly as I came out the porch door.

"Slate," he said. "You know why you don't see slate much anymore? One, it's expensive. Two, it's a bitch to maintain."

"There's no sign of water damage in the attic."

"No obvious sign," he said, and took one of the ladders off the truck.

At noon he broke for lunch. Glen had once told me that his father broke for lunch at noon every day, no matter what. Saturdays, Sundays. During the high school graduation, which began at eleven, his left leg had begun to jiggle uncontrollably by twelve-thirty.

"You want the good news first?" he said, popping the cap off a beer he'd brought in a cooler. "The good news is it's hundred-year slate."

"What's the bad news?"

"The house is almost eighty years old. In twenty years, you'll need a new roof."

"I can handle that," I said.

"In twenty years, I'll need a new roof," I say to my mother.

She shrugs, goes inside, and cuts us both a slice of pie. I eat around the edges of mine. I have some tea. "Do you think there's any point in going over there one last time?" she says. "The closing date is right after Labor Day. After that, you'll never have the chance again."

"I can't do it. I just can't. I can't even drive down the street. If I pulled up in front of the house—I don't know what I'd do, but it wouldn't be good. So I guess if the question is do I think it would be helpful, the answer is no. Just the opposite. Completely the opposite."

"Done," my mother says, and I don't know if she means her slice of pie or the conversation or our old house. She taps the edge of my plate insistently and goes inside. I slide my pie onto the floor, and Ginger makes it disappear in an instant.

My mother calls from the kitchen. "Let's arrange furniture," she says.

The parents are asked to stand at the base of the hill to wait for the campers to bring their duffel bags down. "I hate this part," one of the mothers says, folding and refolding her arms across her chest. I always felt that it was a good way to avoid the crazed parental scrum, but today I'm wild to run up the long drive to cabin 14, where my junior-counselor son has been sleeping amid a dozen little boys. "He'll never want to have kids after this," a voice trills sarcastically in the back of my mind, and I realize it's Ruby's. I want to talk back to her, but there are so many people around. A tall man with colorless hair combed over an evaporating hairline shoulders his way toward me. "Alex's mom?" he says. "Colin's dad. It's good to meet you in person. I think I met your husband two summers ago." He looks up the hill. "Any sign of them?"

A trickle of small boys begins to appear. Behind them comes a pickup piled high with duffels. "Brendan! Brendan!" calls one of the mothers. A faint aurora of camera flashes lights the line of descending campers. One of the boys falls, and a man darts forward.

"You're okay," he says in an insistent voice. "You're okay." Colin's dad and I drift to the back of the crowd, trading forgotten first names. His is Jack. We agree that it seems unlikely that our boys were ever this small. Alex told me Colin wears a size 14 shoe. I look down at Jack's moccasins. Heredity.

"Were we this crazy?" I whisper, watching the parents of the younger boys.

"I wasn't. My wife was."

I look around. "Where is she?"

Jack shrugs. Perhaps it's a family trait, like shoe size. "She's at home. She wasn't feeling well."

"Oh, no," I say, and I suddenly, almost explosively find myself fighting tears. This happens to me from time to time now, usually because of someone else's misfortune. The morning I came upon a fawn with its legs smashed on the shoulder of the road—that had begun a crying jag that lasted for a long time.

"Justin!" a mother calls as the line of campers grows into a jostling crowd.

"Look," Colin's dad says, and at the top of the hill I see Alex. As he walks, a small boy runs up behind him and grabs his hand, and Alex grins, turns back to call something. "There's Colin," his father says warmly, and a giant of a boy runs to Alex's other side.

"How tall is he?"

"Six-three," Jack says. "We hope he's almost done."

"Wow!" I say.

"That's my counselor, Mommy," I hear one of the little boys cry in that high, birdlike little-boy voice. Chirping, we used to call it when Max told a story. Alex had a lower voice. "Hey, lady," he calls as he draws near. When he squeezes me, he feels like a grown-up in my arms, long-boned and strong. Every summer I'm sure he has changed, but this summer I'm certain of it.

"Where's Mom?" Colin asks sharply.

"Waiting at home," says his father. "Making you dinner." Subtext, subtext. If I had been able to do this a year ago, to hear the words that were not being spoken, would everything have been different?

My eyes fill again. "I missed you so much," I say, my mouth against Alex's shoulder.

The little boy is still stuck close to his side. "Hey, Charlie," Alex says, "this is my mom." Charlie waves. His thumb creeps toward his mouth, then goes into his pocket like a temptation placed well out of sight. Alex walks with him to the office. When he emerges, he looks grim. He and Colin give each other handshakes that turn into back slaps that turn into hard hugs. "I am definitely coming to visit, man," Colin says.

"Yeah, that's dubious, dude. You say that every year."

On the car ride home I tell Alex about the storm, how the rain had blinded me, how I careened into the house we're now renting. I explain that his grandmother came to help me, and his grandfather inspected the roof, but that I had done the painting and the floors myself, and that I suspected it had done me more good than weight lifting or jogging. "That's dubious," he says.

"So 'dubious' was this year's camp word?" I finally ask.

"I guess," he says, and then he falls asleep, slumped to one side. When he wakes up at a truck stop he says, "You know that kid Charlie? His parents sent him to camp from England. I had to sleep in his bunk the first week because he cried every night. Now he has to fly back all by himself, with some sign around his neck with, like, his name and phone number and stuff. His parents must be total assholes."

"Language," I say. There are usually two or three intensely profane days after camp before the habits of civilization are relearned. As we stand in line for hot dogs I say, "I don't think the camp should have agreed to that. That's inhuman."

"What?"

"Charlie. England."

"Totally dubious, right?"

When we turn onto the road, I begin to talk too fast—about how Ben's house is a short walk through the woods, about how I have left the room next to Alex's empty so he can use it for whatever he wants, about how well I think the chimney will draw. I'm breathless by the time we get down the drive and turn in front of the front porch. I've put rockers along it. I had placed them in a row yesterday, then realized there were five and took one out to the screened porch and put it in a corner. When I open the front door, Ginger leaps out and puts her paws on Alex's chest, licking frantically at his stubbly chin. He takes her paws in his hands and dances with her, then sits down on one of the rockers and rubs behind her ears.

"Do you like it here, good girl? Do you? Is this a good place?" Ginger rolls onto her back and pedals with her paws as he scratches her belly. "Plenty of squirrels, huh?" He looks up and shakes his head. "That's a monster tree," he says.

The phone rings once, twice, three times, but I ignore it as he circles the interior of the house, looks out the windows, opens the refrigerator. When we get to his room, which I've painted a soft gray, he asks, "Is that my bed? From the house?"

"Yeah," I say. "The movers brought it over."

He sits on the edge. There are new sheets, a new quilt. It looks like a new bed. It's nearly new.

"Cool," he says.

I have an enormous casserole in the oven, chicken tetrazzini just the way he likes it, without the mushrooms, and a big plate of brownies. He takes a shower like he does every time he comes home from camp, where, I've been told, the water is too cold, too hard, too much of a trickle, where the towels always smell of mildew and someone is always taking the decent soap. He takes a long, long shower, and I turn the oven on.

"Can Elizabeth come over?" he asks when he comes downstairs smelling of lemons.

"Of course," I say a little too heartily. Elizabeth has never come to the house before. I was formally introduced at graduation. I was happy to see that she was wearing a pretty floral dress, neither too low nor too short.

And suddenly, before I know it, Elizabeth is standing on the screened porch with her best friend, who tells me her name is Allison Holzberg, and three boys from the soccer team, who will be seniors this year, one of them Allison's boyfriend, all of them Alex's teammates. I spread quilts on the back lawn and put the food out on the kitchen counter and make a salad and open some applesauce. And in an instant, just in an instant, with the slamming of screen doors and the crunch of car wheels on gravel and the tintinnabulation of silver on china, our house is that house once more—the house where the kids come, and go, and come again. I feel something strange inside and wish I could catch it somehow and put it in a jar, like fireflies, with holes in the top so it can breathe.

"You really should have Colin come visit," I say as I pour lemonade into paper cups.

"My best friend from camp," he tells the others. "With, you know, Ben. He's dubious, dudes. Totally dubious."

All the casserole and all the brownies are eaten, even though the two girls have eaten very little of either. They help me carry the plastic plates into the kitchen. I've never done a big load of dishes here before, and I let them help me load the dishwasher because this is the first time I've used it and I'm not yet accustomed to some specific way of doing it. "Are you a sophomore, too, Allison?" I ask in my friendly-mother voice, which sounds slightly false from disuse.

"I am, Mrs. Latham," she says. "And I don't know if you re-member, but I was at your house last Halloween. Your other house. You know. The old house." Her voice is wavering, and I inject, "Tell me your costume. Then I'll remember. There were so many of you guys there."

"Annie Oakley?" she says, and suddenly I do remember her, her hair in braids, chaps hugging her legs, a huge cowboy hat.

"You were adorable," I say. But I can't bring myself to promise that there will be a party again this year. "Trick or treat," I hear Max say, and I turn back to the sink.

The boys are talking in the yard, and when we're done in the kitchen they scramble to their feet and come inside. For some rea-son, they take up more room than the size of their bodies would suggest. The girls don't displace much space; I've noticed this be-fore. But with the guys inside the room is suddenly crowded, and I notice how small it is. Alex is as tall as the older ones, although his shoulders and his waist are not as broad.

"You ready?" Alex says to Elizabeth.

"Where are you going?"

"To Tony's for ice cream."

"Ice cream?" I say. "Didn't you all have enough to eat?"

"There's never enough to eat," growls one of the boys, who the others call Moose. He's the son of the orthodontist who put in Max's palate expander. We were waiting until this year to see if it would resolve his crowding problem and make braces unnecessary.

"Plus we'll get to see everybody, hang out, whatever. Come on."

Suddenly Alex has moved up into a different teenage gene pool, the one in cars. I wish Glen were here to tell me what to do.

"Who's driving?" I ask.

"God, Mom. Come on."

"Dude, it's cool," says Terrence, who is one of the captains of the team. "It's me, Mrs. Latham. And I'm eighteen, so I've already been driving for two years. No tickets, no accidents. Swear." And suddenly they're all in the car, and I'm waving, and in an instant there is nothing but the dishwasher's hum and the spotty thump of night insects hitting the screens and the silence that presses on me like a low ceiling. I try to hold on to the moment, the feeling, the noise and life in the house, but it is gone, at least for now.

I go back into the kitchen and there is an inch of water on the old linoleum. "Oh, goddamnit!" I yell, scrabbling under the sink for the water valve. Mop, bucket, towels. In the morning, I have to call the plumber.

By eleven, I've cleaned up the mess and done all the dishes by hand. The casserole dish soaks in the sink. I throw Alex's duffel bag down to the basement; I know from past years that there will be nothing in it except clothes so filthy with mud and sweat that some of the shorts and nearly all of the socks will simply have to be pitched. I could start the wash now, but the basement is damp and dimly lit, and there are centipedes that undulate up the stone walls. Suddenly I realize I am exhausted and drained, that my body hurts as though I have been planting, exercising, running. I sit on the porch for a while, looking out at nothing. It is a moonless night, and the tree line has merged into the black night sky. I go inside and turn on the television, pick up a book, pretend to be doing something when what I am doing is listening for the sound of a car on the road, tires grabbing at the loose gravel. Midnight is Alex's curfew. I am sure he will ask to have it extended this year, but I won't agree. Ruby had midnight for the first two years of high school, then 12:30, then finally 1 A.M. senior year. The only exceptions were special occasions: birthday parties, prom. New

Year's Eve, of course. Ruby was allowed to come in late on New Year's Eve. Another mistake.

By one o'clock, I've started to do the laundry because I can't sit still and when I read I have no idea what I have just read. It sounds as though the weather is changing; there's the sharp intermittent whistling of a storm wind through the trees. I've called Alex's cell phone twice, but when I empty his duffel onto the concrete floor of the basement I find it amid a welter of T-shirts, its battery dead. I wonder if I should call Elizabeth's parents, but her last name is Jackson and I know there are at least three or four families in town by that name, and I don't know which is hers. I think of calling Olivia to get Terrence's phone number from the team list, then remember that Olivia is in London, on vacation with Ted and the boys. I could call her cell phone—it is morning in England, blessed safe morning—but I don't think she travels with the team list. I check with information and get a number for the sole Holzberg family in the area, which must be Allison's, but then I can't make myself call. I remember how this would occasionally happen, how the mother of one of Ruby's friends would phone and wake us, stammering apologies. No, I would say, Ruby was home, in bed, had been for some time. I wonder if Deborah had ever wanted to call looking for Kiernan, whether she had started to dial the old familiar number and then hung up.

At quarter to two I'm in the basement, putting the first load in the dryer, imagining Alex as the car hits a tree, as the ambulance sirens sound, when I hear a noise from above and Ginger barks. I take the stairs quickly, stumbling on the top one, and go to the door. The SUV is idling, and Alex slides from the backseat, calling something to the guys inside. I stand in the doorway with my arms crossed over my chest. With the overhead light just above me, I must look like an avenging angel.

"Where the hell have you been?" I ask.

Alex goes right into the kitchen, and I hear the water running. When he comes back into the living room, his eyes are half shadowed by his hair, but I can see that they're red. I step closer and smell beer.

"What the hell are you thinking?" I shout.

"Nobody can even find this place," he says, blinking and slurring. "Like, even at the gas station they didn't know how to get here. They never even heard of it. None of the guys ever even heard of it. Hidden Valley Road? What the hell? I bet the cops never even heard of it."

"It's Hidden Cottage Road, Alex. Hidden Cottage."

"Oh, great. I don't even know the name of my own street. That's great. I don't even know where I live."

"You're grounded," I say.

"I don't even know where my house is." He looks around and does a little two-step because swiveling his head has left him off balance. "Is this my house? I don't know. Where the hell am I?"

"Go to bed, Alex," I say. "We can talk in the morning, when you're sober."

"Where's my bed? Huh? Where's my bed?"

"Go upstairs."

He goes upstairs and shuts the door, and I hear a heavy thump and know he will be asleep atop the new comforter, the new sheets, with his clothes and his shoes on. I'm twitchy with the adrenaline buzz I've always gotten after a fight with my children. One night, after a midnight dispute with Ruby over the smell of pot in her hair, I rearranged the kitchen cabinets. Glen had come down after an hour, watched what I was doing, then gone back to bed. He could yell at the kids and be asleep again in a minute. That was what I had thought would happen on New Year's Eve.

I wish Glen were here. I want to take a pill to sleep, but now I can't, never can again. How can I allow myself to be insensible on nights like this one, insensible to what happens elsewhere? I've already done too much of that. When I packed up our things in the guesthouse, I crawled beneath the bed in which Alex slept to remove the baby monitor, but it was already gone. For months I'd been sleeping with the receiver, thinking I was hearing the sound of peaceful sleep, when I'd been hearing nothing at all.

I lie in bed. There's no light from outside on the ceiling. Once, I start to doze and am awakened by the throaty bark of some animal outside. Ginger is sleeping in Alex's room; I picture her opening her eyes, raising her head, then settling herself again. Later, I wake from a half-sleep to hear retching from the bathroom across the hall. I turn over and look at the digital clock on the floor in a corner of the half-furnished room. It's just after four, that cursed hour when night has worn itself out but morning is forever away. One of the babies always used to wake then, wanting to be nursed, but I'm not certain which one. I only remember the inexorability of the darkness. I lie still for a few minutes, then sigh and go downstairs to make coffee and nurse it on the porch as the dryer tumbles and the sun struggles to rise again. There is one last load of wash to do, all jeans, and I empty Alex's pockets, hoping I won't find a joint or a condom. It's been a long night.

But, incredibly, all his pockets are empty except for a stray M & M and a key that I don't recognize. Last of all are the jeans he wore home from camp, and in the back pocket I find his wallet. Without qualm, I open it and look inside. Seven dollars. His school ID card. A picture of Elizabeth holding some sort of certificate, smiling and squinting. Glen's college yearbook photograph, black-and-white and blurred in the fashion of the time. I'd wondered where that picture had gone. Behind it is a piece of unlined paper, folded into a small square so that when it's open the folds are furry and thin. It looks as though it may fall apart soon into a handful of tiny rectangles.

Of course I recognize Ruby's pretty, slightly mannered writing, the enormous curving tails of the *Y*s, the crossing of the *T*s extravagant. She always wrote that way when she copied the final draft of a poem, still young enough to believe that you could change your penmanship and thus change yourself. It is the poem she wrote for Alex for Christmas. I don't know where Max's wound up. Maybe it's in his wallet, too, wherever his wallet might be. Maybe someday I will open a box and find it.

Oh, bear,
I see you in your wooly coat
Moving swiftly on your big paws.
I know there is a small voice inside of you,
Asking for honey.
But when you try to speak,
They just hear a growly sound.
Only you know what you are saying.

I read it over and over. The sun rises. The porch grows warm. I fold the last of the laundry, read the poem again, refold it, and put Alex's wallet on the kitchen counter. I want to copy it, but it seems wrong somehow, and that night in bed I realize that I have committed it to memory without even trying.

I'm at the garden center loading mums into the back of the car. Mrs. Feeney likes mums. Every year, right after Labor Day, she calls and asks for mums in the planters on either side of her front and back doors. One year I found some beautiful hybrids, coppery petals with a warm brown center. The next year she said, "I want the same old yellow ones." I have gotten the same old yellow ones, and a rose of Sharon bush that I intend to plant by the door to the back porch. It will flower white in summer. Rickie and John are going to plant a weeping cherry on one side of Olivia's house, a forever thank-you to her for taking us in, giving us a temporary home. "You must stop thanking me," Olivia had said to me one day. "Do you have any notion of what a loose end I was at before I met you?" A loose end—that's what we women call it, when we are overwhelmed by the care of small children, the weight of small tasks, a life in which we fall into bed at the end of the day exhausted from being all things to all people.

I linger over the tattered half-price perennials in the back, the boxes of bulbs. Much of the land around the house is in shade, and I'm not certain how much of a garden to plant. Olivia has had the men who tend her lawn cut a path through the brambles up the hill to my house. Ben and Alex have painted Xs on the trees. Soon the terrain will be well worn. Alex hasn't exactly said that he likes the house, or even that he's willing to stay, but he has invited Elizabeth over for dinner twice since he was grounded. I told him that if they were in his room the door must remain open, but they mainly sat on the screened porch, or hiked through the woods, or watched television with me. She is polite and quiet and always jumps up to set the table. She calls him Alexander, his full name. For some reason, I like that about her. I wonder if Ruby ever passed Elizabeth in the halls of the high school, if she and Max were ever in the same class. Maybe someday I will know.

I did ask Alex if he wanted to visit the old house one last time before it was sold. I've given the lawyer power of attorney, so that I won't actually have to sign the papers or face the buyers, with their jubilant new-home smiles.

"I've been there," Alex had replied flatly. "I looked in the windows. It's, like, completely empty." But that evening after dinner, staring out the kitchen door to the yard, he suddenly asked, "Have you been over there?"

"No," I replied, knowing immediately what he meant. "I just can't. I feel like I should, but I can't."

"Nana moved all this stuff?"

I nodded. "It was an incredible thing she did for me. For us. I don't know what I would have done otherwise."

He thought, then said, "Ben's mom, maybe. Or Aunt Alice. Or maybe Sarah's mom."

"I just couldn't do it myself."

He patted my arm awkwardly, looked at me, then away again. "It's cool, Mom. You don't need to. It's just, like, a house. Like, a building, you know? It's just a house." I wonder if he knows he's fooling himself.

I buy a hundred bulbs—white and yellow tulips and blue hyacinths. I'll dig trenches and plant them in patches and hope that the squirrels don't unearth them all. I want some tuberous begonias, but there's nothing here. That's one of the only things I wanted from the other house, cuttings of shrubs and flowers. I suppose I can start from scratch. I buy two oak-leaf hydrangeas. There's a sunny spot to one side of the front porch, and I've had good luck with them in the past.

I'd walked around the property that morning, looking at it with my professional eyes, deciding how much needed to be done right away. Newts were crossing the driveway on their bowed legs, orange semicolons in the patches of sun through the trees. One looked unusually large, but as I bent over it I realized that it was a leaf, turned orange and red too early and whirled down to earth. Soon it will be fall, then winter. It will snow, and no matter what I do it will be Christmas. I'm a little better than I was six months ago, whatever that means. I manage to listen to people talk for a longer time before my mind retreats into a dark cave, manage to go longer without shutting down or seizing up, going blank or crying. The outside woman, the woman who thanks the sales clerk and loads the groceries into the car without taking notice of how few bags there are, is in control more of the time. But Christmas terrifies her—and New Year's, of course. If I were a magician, I would make November turn to January. It is as though December will undo all the small steps I've taken to try to make a life for Alex that is anything like the life he once had.

I have until January 1 to decide whether to buy the house. When the agent used that date I shivered, the shiver that my mother always used to say meant someone walking over your grave. But I won't wait. I love the hidden cottage. The isolation that everyone else finds worrisome enfolds me and makes my aloneness seem natural. Alex is good about staying home, but he and Elizabeth together, their eyes and fingers and conversation reaching toward each other, make me feel conspicuously alone. I am a widow. The first time this thought crossed my mind, it seemed preposterous. I'm still a mother, because Alex went skiing instead of staying home. But I am a widow because Glen went to see who was making all that noise downstairs.

My phone rings. It's Alice's number on the screen. I'll call her back when I'm done loading the car with plants. Alice has a new job. She's the editor of a small imprint, publishing one literary novel a month. She is delighted. I've been talking to her in a desultory way about doing some freelance copyediting. It seems that I should have something more to do than buy Mrs. Feeney's mums and cook for Alex and Elizabeth. I do attend every soccer game. Terrence finds it hard to meet my eye after unloading my drunken son from his SUV. Terrence's mother says he raved about my chicken tetrazzini. We lie to each other pleasantly in the bleachers, lie by omission. How are you? Good. The kids? Great! What if I told the truth? How are you? Barely alive. The kids? Well, I only have one left, and I have no idea how he's really doing. When I went for my physical, our doctor asked if I needed anything for anxiety. "I don't take those things anymore," I said.

"That's a good idea unless you need them," he replied.

I shut the back hatch after I load the copper sundial. Rickie has said he will pour a concrete pad to anchor it. He stops by frequently, Rickie does, always with some random offering: a wheelbarrow, a ten-pound ham, a map of the county. Last time he came by, he staked out a square for the sundial and dug a hole for its footing. I'm going to put it near the back of the backyard, where the light breaks through the leaf canopy. When I do, Alex will be sure that I have decided to buy the house, and so will I. I slide into the driver's seat, thinking about whether I should plant some bulbs around the sundial's base, when I simultaneously feel and hear the sudden explosion that means someone has hit the back of my car, hard. I haven't put on my seat belt yet, and my head hits the steering wheel, and the inside of the car goes black with silver sparks. Then it clears just as I feel the impact again. The clerks from the garden center have run to the door and are standing, staring, mouths open. A woman who was looking for deer repellent when I paid for my plants is cowering behind a shelf of garden ornaments. Her face appears from between a stone squirrel and an angel as I feel the impact for a third time. This time I am braced with both arms.

I look in the rearview mirror and through the glare of her windshield I see Deborah behind the wheel. From what I can tell, she has damaged her car more than she has damaged mine. She looks deranged, her front teeth holding her bottom lip as though she will bite right through it. Her hair is very short, almost a version of the buzz cuts the basketball coach demands, so her eyes look dilated, as though she is seeing visions, or is blind. Her mouth is moving. I hope her windows are closed, so the people watching can't hear what she is saying or screaming.

I want so badly to get out of my car, to walk over to hers and say something. But I can't imagine what that would be. I think she would run me down without a thought.

I wonder if she hears voices, snatches of conversation, the commentary that I sometimes hear. That's the difference in how I feel about Kiernan. I never hear his voice, see his shadow in the hallway, think I glimpse his back as he saunters away from the playing fields at the high school. I suppose that's how I punish him now for what he did: Ruby laughs in my ear, Max makes a comment from the backseat, Glen offers a suggestion from the pillow next to mine. But Kiernan is dead in the garage. He's gone. He's gone forever. Ruby told me I had to take sides. And I have.

I put my head down on the steering wheel and wait, but nothing happens. There's a cloud of smoke in my rearview now, and when it clears there's nothing but the stench of burned rubber and the sound of a car limping down the highway, something damaged in its chassis. I get out, and the young man who runs the garden center cries, "Should I call 911?"

I look at the back of my car. The hatch will need to be replaced. The sundial is split in two.

"No," I say wearily. "Don't do that."

"She hit you on purpose," calls the woman behind the shelf. "I'll tell the police she hit you on purpose."

"Thanks," I say. "It's all right."

I stop at the auto-body shop for an estimate. I tell the mechanic that I left the car parked in the supermarket lot and it was like this when I came out. "Oh, man, people these days," he says.

When I get home, I call Alice and tell her what happened. "Am I crazy?" I say. "I just couldn't do it. I just couldn't throw her to the wolves that way." Or maybe I was worried about what she might say about me. I want people not to look at me anymore, to look right through me the way people used to do. But that wasn't all. I understand why she did what she did. I know how it feels to be mad with grief—to want to blame, to hit, to scream. Maybe in her place I would do exactly what she did. Maybe I would do something worse.

"You're lucky it was just the car," says Alice.

"So you would have called the police?"

Alice is silent for a long time. Finally she speaks in a hushed voice, the same voice she used to use when she lay next to me freshman year while I sobbed with homesickness. She fed me Hershey bars then until the pillowcase was beyond laundering.

"No. I would have done just what you did." I know she's thinking of Liam.

"She's got nothing. Nothing," I say, and my voice breaks.

"And you have Alex."

Glen hadn't wanted to let him go skiing. "We don't even really know these people," he'd said. "We don't know what kind of parents they are."

"They sound nice," I said.

He shook his head. I remember, he shook his head.

"And I have Alex," I say.

I empty the back hatch of the plants and cart the sundial down to the barn. It will become one of those artifacts I encounter from time to time, that I will never use but will probably never throw away. A spider has built a web in one corner of the doorway, and I walk right into it; it closes over my face like a mask, a shroud, and I claw at it, shivering, until my fingers are clotted with lumps of sticky silk. One of them has a small insect inside, still struggling, and I recoil and throw it to the ground.

And then, unthinking, I run back to the house. I pick up the phone, and from somewhere, somewhere where I sense half-remembered birth dates and addresses—467 Wallingford, I suddenly recall, that was the house where I grew up—I retrieve a phone number that I haven't called in years.

"Hello?" says a flat and lifeless voice, and for just a moment I think I've remembered the number wrong. "Hello?" and now I recognize it, and I breathe in, feeling some web still stuck to my bottom lip, and say, "Deborah? Don't ever come near me again." And then I hang up.

You can't plan them, although I suppose those people who meditate and practice yoga think you can, but there are those moments when we experience physical happiness despite ourselves, before our minds remind us of the reasons we shouldn't. A slight breeze, a warming sun, a little bird music: Your senses say something before your good sense says something different. If only we could be creatures of the body more often.

I am at a soccer game. Alex has just scored a goal, and after being pummeled joyously by his teammates he has taken the time to throw up a hand in my direction. Just like televised football: Hi, Mom. I jump up and down. I smile. I feel what I feel, and shove my thoughts to the back, behind the feelings. I will allow myself this moment.

Some days Alex is all right; some days he's not. Some dinners are full of conversation, others silent. A photographer from the local paper takes his picture from the sidelines. It's a warm October afternoon, more summer than fall, and Alex's face is slick with perspiration. He holds the ball. If the photographer is any good, it will be a great picture.

I'm wearing a loose dress and a long cardigan. ("You're wearing that?" Ruby asks. "Shut up," says Max.) My hair needs cutting. That's how I will fill Thursday. I will get a haircut.

"That was some goal," says a voice behind me. It's Nancy. She kisses me lightly on the cheek. This is how it will be. When Alice and I had a falling-out, she would always end it with what she called a powwow. She would attack, I would parry, I would cry, she would cry, each of us would admit fault even if we didn't believe it, we would wrap our arms around each other. Things would be as before. Nancy won't do this. She will talk to me in public, then call, then invite me to dinner. We'll become friends again, in some fashion. There will always be Sarah to bring us together. But there will always be a wire fence between us, crisscross shadows across everything we say and do.

Fred is with her, home from college for the weekend, and he hugs me. From inside his jacket he pulls out a letter. It's from José, who has spent the summer picking tomatoes in New Jersey and wants him to let me know that he has been praying for me and for Alex, and that his elder daughter made the honor roll.

"That's so nice," I say quietly, reaching out a hand. "Can I read it?"

"It's in Spanish," Fred says.

"So you finally told them you speak Spanish?"

"I think they always knew. Maybe they read my face when they said certain things, you know, and could figure out that I knew what was going on."

"What does he say?" I ask.

Fred turns the letter over. "He says his wife is getting a job in Pennsylvania. They're leaving the girls with their grandmother, in Mexico."

"That's sad."

"I think a lot of them do that. The price they pay and all that. He says the little girl had—I don't know this word, she had something taken away from her? Her throat maybe? That can't be right."

"Tonsils. She had her tonsils out."

"Maybe," Fred says. "I don't know this word."

Elizabeth and Allison wander over with the slightly shy demeanor girls have when they approach the mothers of boys, especially boys they like. Ruby never had it, but then she had known Kiernan's mother almost her whole life. And very little made Ruby tentative. "He scored a goal!" I say. "Oh, darn it," Elizabeth says. I like her old-fashioned expressions. She says "golly," too. "We had a Free Tibet meeting," Allison says. "Oh," I say, and then I add, "Ruby was in Free Tibet." Elizabeth watches Alex. He's too busy running downfield to notice her. "Tell him it was a great play," I say. "He'll never know you didn't really see it." She looks shocked. She's probably still young enough to believe honesty is the best policy. Perhaps she thinks my suggestion is dubious. It seems that everyone in the sophomore class is now dubious about everything.

The girls melt away. Nancy is talking to the mother of her youngest son's best friend. A good-looking young man in sunglasses and a blue shirt approaches me. He grins. "I thought I'd run into you here," he says companionably. He looks out at the game, and then I realize that it's Dr. Vagelos.

"Do you usually attend your patient's sporting events?" I ask.

"Only if they're really good," he says.

The other team gets possession, scores a goal. Alex kicks a divot of grass, and the coach says something to him. He looks over at me, and his face brightens, and he nods enthusiastically. "Cool," I can almost hear him say, and then I realize that he's looking at the man beside me.

"Did he invite you?" I ask.

"Would I be here otherwise?"

We watch in silence for several minutes, until he looks at his watch. Nancy stares, looks away when I look back at her. I wonder if she knows who he is.

"I have to go," he says. "I'll tell him how good he looked when I see him tomorrow. We have a session tomorrow at six-thirty. Could you come?"

"Me?"

He nods. The glasses are very dark, a kind of disguise, and I can't see his eyes. "Alex and I agreed that it might be good for us to have a session together, all three of us. I think there are some things he needs to talk about that he wants to talk about with you there." He looks at me and moves closer. "I know it's unexpected. Maybe even unwelcome, I don't know. But I really think it will be helpful. It doesn't have to be tomorrow if you're busy then. We could wait a week or two."

"I'm not busy. I'm never busy."

"That's great," he says, and shakes my hand, then waves at Alex, who waves back.

"I'll see you tonight at six-thirty," I say to Alex when he leaves for school in the morning, and he nods.

The office looks the same. The photograph of Dr. Vagelos and his brother is in the same place on the bookshelves. I arrive first. The two chairs that faced the desk are now facing each other. I take one.

"He's a great soccer player, isn't he?" the doctor says, and almost immediately there's a buzzing sound, and I realize that's how he knows when someone is in the waiting room. He opens the door for Alex. My son smells as though he hasn't showered after practice. Probably there isn't enough time, and Dr. Vagelos has sat here week after week mired in the ripe smell of teenage boy.

"I was just saying you're a great soccer player," he repeats, and Alex reddens. "I had an okay day yesterday," he says. The newspaper will make him player of the week again soon. My heart thumps when I think of Max bringing that clipping here. I try to feel him in the room, then try to put him away so that I can concentrate on Alex. Already I'm losing ground. The doctor is saying that Alex has some things he wants to tell me, and in my reverie I have missed half of what he's said. I love you, I love you, I think to myself, to force myself to pay attention.

Alex and I are knee to knee. He looks tired. The skin beneath his eyes looks bruised. He seems to spend hours in his room doing homework.

"Why don't you just go for it?" Dr. Vagelos says.

"It's my fault," Alex blurts out. It has the feel of a sentence that has been said many times, rehearsed in front of the mirror, written over and over in longhand: It's my fault it's my fault it's my fault.

"What do you mean, honey?"

"What happened. It's my fault. I knew Kiernan was living in the garage. I was out one night and I walked home and I went around to the back of the garage, to—to take a piss, is the truth. And he was back there in the doorway—you know, that doorway that went into the back, that we never used?"

I nod. He needs a moment to catch his breath. I look at the doctor, but he's expressionless. He must have heard all this before.

"I was like, Dude, what's up? And he said he'd come over to see Max and bring him some book or something, but I knew it wasn't true because it was a school night, and Ruby was home, I could see her in her room, you know? And I said, wow, it's really late, or something stupid, and he said he was going home, but then when I went in the kitchen I looked out the window and saw him going back in the garage. And I said to Max, 'Dude, is Kiernan hanging out in the garage?' And he was just like, Be cool. So I didn't say anything."

"So Max knew, too?"

Alex nods. "And if we had told you, you would have made him leave, and then, you know, I don't know, everything, everything—"

His hands are up in the air, held up, cupped, the way they are when he's waiting for someone to throw him the basketball. He has lost his breath again.

"Oh, honey," I say softly. "It probably wouldn't have made any difference. He could have come to our house from wherever he was living. It wasn't your fault. It wasn't anybody's fault."

"You really think that?"

I nod. I want him to feel better. I want him to feel nothing.

"That's bullshit, Mom!" he yells. "It was Kiernan's fault. It was his fault. How could he do that to us? He stayed at our house, he ate dinner with us. We were all so nice to him. How could he do that?"

"I don't know. I don't know. I can't imagine it."

"See, that's bad, too. I imagine it so bad, so terrible, like a horror movie. And that's 'cause I wasn't here. I was skiing, and then I was watching some stupid movie with Colin. You know how people say twins know when the other twin is in trouble? I was watching some stupid movie on TV with Colin just at the time. Or, at least, I think it was the time. I tried to work out the time difference, and I'm pretty sure it was the same time."

"You were away, honey."

"That makes it worse. I didn't see anything, so maybe I make it worse than it was."

"I know."

"But you were there. So at least you do know."

"I wasn't there, Alex. I was asleep." I turn to Dr. Vagelos, and he meets my eyes full-on with his own, and they are so full of understanding and sorrow that I can't hold them, and I can't look at Alex, either. "I went back to sleep after your father went downstairs. I didn't hear anything."

"You didn't?" Alex says.

"I didn't. I didn't see anything. I didn't see any more than you. I didn't know what happened until I was in the hospital. Then they told me. Even then it was almost like it was happening to someone else."

"Is that why you never cry?"

"What?"

"You never cry," Alex says, and his voice is savage. None of my children have ever used that tone with me before. "I've never seen you cry," he says. "Not one time. It looked like you were going to cry at camp, and I didn't know why. But then you didn't." His voice is harsh. It is an accusation.

"I didn't want to upset you," I say, and when I see his face I know it is exactly the wrong thing to say. He roars at me, "How can you even say that? How can I not be upset? Upset—that's a stupid word. Upset?" He thumps his fist hard on his chest, so hard I wonder if there will be a bruise there. "Do you know what I feel like?"

"I don't want you to feel like that," I whisper.

"You can't control how I feel. You can't control how terrible I feel."

I nod.

"I understand," I say.

"How come you don't ever cry? That's what I want to know. You act like nothing happened. We'll get a new house and new furniture and then we'll act like everything's fine. Do you think about them at all? Do you even miss them? You never even say their names."

I must look like a mad person, breathing through my mouth, shaking. And suddenly I break and start to wail, my head down on my knees. I feel Alex pull back, pull his legs back, recoil. I'm gasping for air, and I raise my head and then put it back again, afraid I'm going to faint. I can't stop and I cry for a long time, perhaps long enough to cover all the times when I refused to let him see it, when I got into the car and drove or shut the door to my room so I could cry and not have Alex see me do it. After a few minutes, I put out a mute hand and feel a tissue pressed into it. Finally I shudder, and blow my nose, and raise my head.

"Alex, does that feel like what you wanted?" Dr. Vagelos says softly.

Both of us look at Alex. He is horrified. Tears are silently running down his face. He pushes them away with the flat of his hand.

"I think what's happened," Dr. Vagelos says, "is that you've been trying to be strong for Alex's sake. And Alex has been trying to be strong for your sake. And, because of that, both of you have underestimated how powerfully you've been grieving. And you haven't grieved together."

"We haven't talked about any of this," I say. "I thought I would wait for the right time and place. But there wasn't really a right time and place."

"And a lot of this is what Alex needs to talk about."

"I talk to Max," Alex says suddenly, as though this is another sentence he's been rehearsing. "I put the covers over my head so you won't hear me, and I talk to him at night."

"Oh, honey," I say, starting to cry again, trying to stop by holding my hand tightly over my mouth. "I do it, too. I talk to them all the time."

"I mean, I don't talk about anything big. I go, like, 'Dude, that girl you liked? She really got cute over the summer.' Or, like, 'Man, you should have seen how I schooled this kid in my math class who thinks he's, like, a math genius.' Or, like sometimes, 'Dude, I am in so much trouble with Mom; I was way out of line the other night.' "

"Just ordinary stuff."

"Just ordinary stuff. Sometimes, I'm like, Wow, this is nuts, I'm totally nuts. But I told Elizabeth, and she said she thought it was completely normal and it's what she'd do."

"It's completely normal," I say. "Really, I do it all the time."

"You do?"

I nod.

"Does Max talk back?" Alex says.

"They all do," I say. "They all talk to me."

"That's so cool," Alex says sadly, and I wonder if it's because Max doesn't talk back to him, or Ruby doesn't, or his father.

The doctor smiles slightly. "Alex, I told you I'd like to have some time alone with your mom. Do you want to wait outside? And should we do this again?"

I nod. Alex nods. He rubs at his face. "Can I walk over to Elizabeth's?" he asks me, and he writes the address on my forearm, and his fingers feel strong and warm, and without thinking about it I take his hand in mine, press a kiss into the palm, and wrap his fingers around it. I want to tell him he has saved my life, that he has given me a reason to survive, but I know that's too much for a boy to carry. So, instead, I say, "I love you from the bottom of my heart."

He leans over and kisses the top of my head. "I love you, too," he says.

When he leaves, I cry for a few more minutes. I can feel Dr. Vagelos waiting. This must be what he does a lot—just waits.

"I was wrong about everything," I finally say. "He thought I didn't care."

"No, I don't think that's true. He knows how much you love

him, and how much you loved his father, and his brother and sister. But he needed permission to take his feelings to the next level. He needs to be able to feel rage and grief. Your mother told him he had to be strong and take care of you. His grandfather told him that he was the man of the house. That was a heavy weight. He doesn't sleep because he worries that someone will break into the house and he needs to make sure nothing happens to you."

"Oh, my God. My father-in-law keeps insisting I should get a security system."

"I don't think a security system is going to help with that. We're working through it, through his fear and his tendency to blame himself. But he needs to be able to have more open, emotional expressions of grief. And he needs to share them with you, and have you share yours with him. Not all of them, of course, but some."

"He's never been a particularly emotional kid."

"And have you been comfortable with that?"

"I thought I was. It made things easier."

"Easier for who?"

I shake my head. I am a stranger to myself. "Do you have children?" I ask.

"Explain to me why that's important."

"Sometimes we—sometimes you—there are children who need more. Or not more, but different. I'm sorry, I'm not being articulate."

"There are children to whom parents give more."

"I wouldn't put it like that."

He smiles. Once again, there is something at once sad and sympathetic about his face, or maybe I'm just imagining that. "Let me rephrase," he says. "Sometimes children can get more attention because they seem to be in more need of attention. And then there are children who seem so self-possessed and competent that they seem to need less."

I nod. "Are you speaking from personal experience?" And then I remember his brother, and I shake my head. "I'm so sorry. I meant in terms of your own kids."

"It's fine. The whole point of this is that you can say things here that you might not say anywhere else."

"My children used to talk about which was the favorite."

"What did they conclude?"

"That it was my daughter. Ruby. That it was Ruby."

"Were they right?"

"What difference does it make?"

"I don't know. You brought it up."

"I thought Alex was doing all right."

"Alex is doing all right, considering. But you couldn't really believe he wouldn't have significant issues, given what's happened."

"No. I just wanted to believe it. I wanted someone to come out of this alive. I wanted someone to come out unscathed. I guess that was magical thinking. He couldn't be unscathed. Some days he seems angry. Some days he scarcely speaks. He came in drunk one night."

"All that sounds like fifteen to me."

"Do you think he's depressed? Do you think he'll start to take drugs, and drink all the time, and act out? God, I hate that term. Ruby's shrink used to use it all the time. I'm sorry—do you hate the term 'shrink'?"

He smiles, and I think he seems too young to have children of his own. I wonder if he takes care of his brother, if his parents are older, perhaps even if they're dead. We sit with people, and we tell them things, and we make up their lives in our heads, and we really know nothing about them.

"I'm agnostic about the term 'shrink.' I think 'acting out' is a catchphrase that doesn't mean much, and I don't know what will happen to Alex in a year, or two, or twenty. And neither do you. But I know, and you know, that this will be with him forever."

"I know," I say. "That's all I know. I wish I knew what would happen next."

"Do we ever know that?"

I look up suddenly. "No. But I thought I did. That's what I was most wrong about. I used to worry about them all the time—in utero, when they were babies, toddlers. Light sockets, swimming pools, bee stings. I worried about everything. But you know what I know now? I didn't really believe in the worry. It was a hobby, or a mind game, like a crossword puzzle. I never thought anything really bad would happen. It was all the good things that seemed real to me—where they'd go to college and where they'd live and what my grandchildren would call me."

"What did you decide?"

"About what?"

"What your grandchildren would call you?"

"Why?"

"Because it's still important."

I close my eyes and think, I don't care, I don't care—Granny, Nana, Grandmom. I picture trying to hug a squirmy little boy, imagine having him pull away, saying, "Stop, Grandmom." And at the thought I feel a stab of something inside—something like life, like what I had felt when I was pregnant. I always felt so empty in those first few sleepless months afterward, my hands pressed to my slack belly, as though having something alive beneath my skin was my natural state.

"You know what I think?" I cry. "I think every fear you ever have, every one—thunder or spiders or roller coasters—they're all fear of dying. Every last one."

Dr. Vagelos turns to his desk, takes a card, gives it to me. I look at the woman's name on the front. "She's good," he says. "She does a lot of grief counseling. That might be the next step for you. You said you wanted someone to come out of this alive. It's not going to be enough if it's only Alex."

I put the card in my pocket and shake my head. "I don't know if I can live like this. Do you think it's possible, to live like this?"

"I've never had a patient in your situation before, so I suppose the honest answer is that I don't know."

"But what's your opinion?"

"I think you have no choice. You have a son. You love him deeply. He needs a life. Not only that, he needs a good life, a full life."

"How is that even possible?"

"What's the alternative?"

"What about me?" I ask.

"What do you mean?"

"I don't even know."

"That's a start," he says.

It's Saturday. Alex and Elizabeth are in the kitchen making oatmeal cookies. Allison was here, but she had to go home to see her sister, who is returning from college for the Thanksgiving break. Alex is due at soccer practice in three hours. I will drive him, and drop Elizabeth at her house. She lives in one of those narrow clapboard houses in town, with a square of yard in front and another behind. The first time I went there to pick Alex up, the night when the two of us first met with Dr. Vagelos, her mother opened the door wide, and I saw at once that she was one of the nurses who had cared for me in the hospital. "I've heard so much about you," she said.

She and Elizabeth are coming here for Thanksgiving. They have no one else. Elizabeth's father lives in Phoenix. She has no brothers and sisters. I think they'll like having Thanksgiving at our house. Glen's father and his brothers and their families are coming. They will all stay in Olivia's guesthouse, sleeping bags on every floor. Alice and Liam are coming, too, with Nate, and my mother and Stan. They will stay here, upstairs. There will be twenty people. Rickie and John brought over some sawhorses. There will be ten at the dining-room table and ten on an old door set atop the sawhorses, a tablecloth masking the makeshift. It will be tight, but we'll do it. Sometimes Alex and I are distracted by the prospect and planning for all the guests, and sometimes we're distracted by the soccer playoffs, and sometimes we're not distracted at all. Sometimes we both make an effort to talk about things we don't want to discuss—about Kiernan, about what happened in the house on New Year's Eve, about how much Alex misses his father, his sister, his brother, and how much I miss them, too. Yesterday we hiked through the woods, and we talked about Max and how he was last year.

"I should have been, like, so much cooler about the whole thing he was going through," Alex said sadly. "I was really harsh. I should have been nicer, talked to him more about how down he was, you know?"

"It was hard, the way your brother was last year," I said. "Your dad had a really hard time dealing with it, too."

"I think he would have gotten better."

"Your dad or Max?"

"Both, right? Don't you think Dr. Vagelos would have gotten Max better? Max told me the doc was really cool. That's why I went to see him. At first I just wanted to tell him that, and then I wanted to make sure that Max was really getting better. But then I decided to talk to him myself. I just didn't think it would take so long—you know, like, I'd have to talk to him so many times. Like, maybe years."

"Do you feel better after Dr. Vagelos?" Bless that man—if there's one thing he taught me, it is to ask questions.

"A lot of times I do. Or, at least, I feel like I get things. Like I didn't understand things before and now I do."

"That's how he made me feel."

"You always did, though. We were always, like, isn't it scary how Mom gets what we're thinking while we're thinking it? Or before we're thinking it?"

"I just pretended," I said. "No, that's a lie. A lot of times I did know. I worked really hard at it."

"I know," Alex said then, and I cried a little, and wiped my eyes, and made a face.

"Every time I cry now, I think you think I'm doing it because of what you said," I told him.

"I do sometimes, but that's cool."

I put another log on the fire. In the kitchen I hear Elizabeth say, "We need three eggs." I hear her murmur something else more softly, then hear Alex laugh. The fireplace in the living room is a marvel. It warms the entire first floor of the house so thoroughly that sometimes we have to crack the windows. Then it even heats a small area of the porch. I pull up my old rocking chair and swaddle myself in the throw from the couch and listen as the wood pops. The cat sits on my lap and kneads the throw.

The cat came out of the woods right after the Halloween party was through, when everyone had driven down the drive and we were cleaning cake off the floors. Alex had insisted that we have the party, even if it was a much smaller, more modest version. "In memory of Max," he said. Alex and Elizabeth were picking up piñata candy in the backyard when they saw the cat approach like a tardy guest, his yellow eyes narrowed and skeptical. They decided to call him Jack-o'-Lantern, Jack for short. We're all afraid someone will come and claim him, but so far he is ours. He hisses at Ginger when she comes too close, but when she's sleeping he settles himself nearby, his paws tucked under him so that he is foursquare, a black-and-white brick of fur and sinew.

Rickie and John came over and used a log splitter on some storm-felled trees, so we have plenty of firewood. They stacked some of it at the side of the house—a wall of wood, elm and poplar and lots of oak. They put the rest in the barn. I went up into the loft and looked at the boxes. Near the front is one that says HOME MOVIES. I wonder when I can open that, whether I can ever watch the three of them walk across the den, pet the dog, smile out at me, even if it is only on a television screen.

Somewhere there are the boxes of ashes. I suspect that my mother put them far in the back, so that I won't find them for a long, long time.

A car pulls into the drive, and Sarah and Rachel get out. I throw open the front door and they run to me, one on each side, hugging hard, so hard that I feel as though I might fall, except that the two of them are holding me up, lifting me as though I am the child.

"I love this place!" Rachel squeals.

Inside, Sarah reaches her hands out to the fire, and Rachel gives me two jars of homemade cranberry relish that they bought at the farmers' market. She's still thin, and different somehow—less tentative, secondary. I think Ruby would be pleased to see her like this. Maybe with only the two of them in the charmed circle there is more space for Rachel.

"You seem great," I say.

"I love school," she replies.

Rachel has discovered art history; Sarah is suddenly interested in economics. Sarah is not sure the swimming is worth it—"We're up at six o'clock, and we always wind up hanging out with other swimmers"—and Rachel says her roommate has issues, although she won't be more specific. Sarah is wearing jeans and a peasant blouse, and her hair now falls below her shoulders. She is dressed less like Sarah and more like Ruby. "How's Eric?" I ask, and she says, "Fine, I guess." It seems I was wrong about all those assumptions I'd once made about Sarah's set-in-stone future. But then I was wrong about most of the future, when I dreamed it so long ago, a year ago.

"Where's Alex?" Sarah asks, and then the two of them run into the kitchen, and there are screams punctuated by the rumble of Alex's voice.

"My ears hurt," I hear Max say, the way he did so many times before at the high, piercing girl-shrieks.

"My ears hurt," Alex says with a grin as I go into the kitchen.

"Too bad. These are my girls." That's what Ruby always said. I say it now, and the two of them look at me and blink hard. Then they shake it off and stick their fingers into the batter, and Alex raps Sarah across the hand with a wooden spoon as Elizabeth stands aside and smiles shyly.

"We are so sorry," Rachel says to her intently, and Elizabeth's eyes widen, and she says, "Why?"

"Because you got stuck with this loser!" And she and Sarah repeat the word a few times and make their thumbs and forefingers into a capital *L* and try to put it on Alex's forehead.

"You two are, like, totally dubious," he says.

We all sit in the living room, and Rachel rubs the arm of the chair, and I know she's remembering it from the den. They've both come from the high school, where the swimmers broke off practice to make a fuss over Sarah. "Except for that bitch Amanda," Rachel says.

"Uh, ladies, language, please," I say.

"I can't wait to go to college so I can curse all day," Alex says, and I shiver in the hot house, thinking of it empty.

Soon they're all hungry, and we go back into the kitchen and make grilled-cheese sandwiches. The girls finger their friendship bracelets unconsciously and tell Elizabeth how much she'll like college. They cluster around me at the stove as I press the bread down with a spatula. Alex wants bacon on his, Sarah and Elizabeth tomato. Rachel and I—and Ruby—like ours plain, just cheese and bread. Everyone wants sweet pickles. Sarah looks up at me as she opens the jar, smiling, and then her face changes in an instant to a look of such suffering that I almost cry out. She turns to the sink, hiding her secret self.

I know that there will always be ghosts with these girls. I will buy them graduation gifts and attend their weddings and send baby presents and perhaps even eat at their homes. And there will always be not the ghost of Ruby that was but the ghost of Ruby who might have been. I don't know that person, and yet I miss her. I miss the Max who might have been, too. I miss the Glen who was.

"I'm having Thanksgiving dinner here," Elizabeth says softly.

"Everybody in the world is eating here," Alex says.

"Not me," says Rachel.

"You're invited," I say quickly. "So is your mom."

"No, that's okay, we have plans. I bet you have better plans, though. Also better food." Sandy is said to be dating the pro at the golf club. I know they serve Thanksgiving dinner—"Who the heck has Thanksgiving dinner at a golf club?" Glen always said—and I wonder if they are going to eat there.

We're spending Christmas here, too. Alex says we should decorate the concolor tree, although I've told him it would take a bucket truck and hundreds of lights. The day after Christmas, we leave town for a week. That night after the meeting with Dr. Vagelos, neither of us knowing what to say in the car, both of us afraid of saying too much, or of sinking back into silence, I had suddenly blurted out, "If you could take a trip anywhere, where would you want to go?"

"With you?"

I nodded. His eyes were shiny, picked out in the dark by the dash lights. He suddenly looked like someone I didn't know. I can scarcely see the young Alex in him anymore. There's a suggestion of the young Glen in his jaw and eyes. Or, at least, that's what I tell myself.

"I really want to go to Cooperstown, to the Baseball Hall of Fame, but I don't think you'd like that so much, so maybe not with you."

I waited. I could hear him breathing. "New York," he finally said.

"New York?"

"Yeah. I mean, there are a lot of other places I want to go—like Africa, maybe, someday. Or China. China would be cool. But Nate said there's this whole exhibit of armor at the art museum that we never got to see. And Ellis Island. I told him I was thinking I might like to be a history guy, and he said I had to go to Ellis Island."

"You want to be a historian? I didn't see that one coming." I didn't add, "And neither did your history teacher, judging from your last report card." But, as though he'd heard my thoughts, Alex said, "Mr. Betts is a lame teacher. Like, his idea of history is, Memorize a hundred dates and then I'll give you a test. I was once, like, 'Mr. Betts, did you know that millions of people died in Europe in 1920 when they got the flu?' And he goes, 'Yes, Alex, I did, but that's European history, and the curriculum this year is American history.' Like you can even separate them."

"I didn't know that, about the flu."

"It was really bad. I saw this thing about it on the History Channel."

"With your father."

"Yeah."

We will be going to Ellis Island together, although Alice insists that all of us will freeze on the ferry ride over. We will go to the museum, although I may let Alex look at the armor by himself while I stare at the Impressionist paintings. On New Year's Eve at midnight, there is a four-mile run through Central Park, and Nate and Alex are registered to run it together. Apparently, there are fireworks and noisemakers and champagne and costumes and big, jolly anonymous crowds of people. "Happy New Year," I will say to strangers. Somewhere along the route, I will watch as my son streaks by in the silvery night, the streetlights keeping the dark at bay. Someday Alex will say, "Remember that midnight run in Central Park?" And I will nod, and maybe even smile.

Alex jumps up from the table, afraid he'll be late for practice. Rachel and Sarah are going into town anyway; they will take him. He runs upstairs for his gear. "My dad says he'll be all-state junior year," Sarah says. "He's a great soccer player," says Elizabeth, who goes back to the screened porch for her jacket.

"Has either of you seen Kiernan's mom?" I ask.

"My mom saw her a couple of weeks ago, delivering a cake," Rachel says. "My mom says she's totally crazy. She says she's moving someplace. Maybe California? Or Canada? But really, really crazy."

"Don't say that, honey," I say as I put my arms around her.

Sarah hugs me, too. "My mom really misses you," she whispers.

A sharp voice says, "She knows where I live." I'm going to ignore that voice. Instead I say, "Tell her I miss her, too. Tell her I miss her a lot. Will both of you come over Friday for turkey sandwiches? My friend Alice will be here with her little boy and her boyfriend."

"Is he cute?" Rachel says.

"The little boy or the boyfriend?"

"You always get me with stuff like that."

"They're both very cute," I say.

"I'm going to be late!" yells Alex as he clatters down the stairs. "The coach is going to kill me!"

I can hear the noise inside the car as they pull away, which makes the silence afterward seem deeper. I go into the backyard and sit in an old Adirondack chair that I found in the back of the barn. There's only one, which is odd. I think the other one must have broken. These things always come in pairs.

The cat has followed me outside, and now he sits at the edge of the woods, the tip of his tail threshing the air. Ginger scampers toward him. For a moment, all four paws lifted from the dull autumn grass, she's a young dog again. I have to start cooking side dishes for dinner Thursday. I can make the sweet potatoes and the creamed onions. My father-in-law likes those. My mother is going to make some biscuits at Olivia's and bring them that morning, although she really doesn't bake so well. Olivia and Ted and the boys are coming over after their own dinner, with pies for dessert. She says they're going to hike through the woods together. "I don't doubt that you'll hear us before you see us," she told me.

My mother thinks going to New York is a mistake. "You can't run away from things forever," she said. "It's not forever," I replied. I wanted to add, "Nothing is forever." But I know my mother knows that. In my top bureau drawer is the card Dr. Vagelos gave me, the grief therapist's card. Maybe I will call her in January. I don't plan ahead much anymore.

In the barn is a box marked "Xmas Ornaments." For some reason, the thought of them won't let me be. I can see them all in my mind: The china cherub wreathed in holly that I got as a shower gift when Ruby was born. The candy canes made out of dough that the twins made in first grade. The tiny tawny papier-mâché dog that Ruby bought on a class trip to New York. Max's ceramic dinosaur. Alex's glass soccer ball. I could buy new ones, fresh ones, with no history, no memories. But what sort of tree would that be? It would be like those color-coordinated trees I criticized all those years, the ones I was hired to put up and decorate. I don't want one of those trees. But I'm afraid to open that box.

"Don't be afraid, Mom," I hear Max say. But it's a different Max, a wiser Max, a Max who knows now that most of our fears are petty and small, and that only our love is monumental.

"It's me," I hear Ruby say, the way she did when she came into the house after school. "Who's me?" Glen would say if he was home.

He will be young forever, my Maxie, always shaggy-haired and splayfooted and long-limbed. And Ruby, too, with her incandescent eyes and her dancing hands. And Glen will never get any older, but I will. Maybe someday I will be an old woman with a young husband, a young husband struggling to belt his pants, his mouth set as he goes down to put a stop to that ruckus. Maybe someday I will be an old woman with a grown son, saying to his wife, "That house is just too damn big for my mother. I wish we could get her to move someplace smaller." And his wife—please, please, make her nice, make her like me, make her a good mother herself—his wife will say, "She has a lot of memories in that house."

Ginger snorts and turns onto her side and sighs. And then, because I want to, because there is no one there to think it strange, I call their names, one by one, into the silence. The silence is as big as the sky, and as I call to each of them it is as though the name is a bird, flying out over the trees and into the lowering afternoon. Ginger's ears twitch at the familiar sounds. Maybe *crazy* is just the word we use for feelings that will not be contained.

"How are you holding up?" my mother said the other day when she called to tell me about their Thanksgiving travel plans.

"I'm trying," I replied.

"That's good," she said. "That's all anyone can ask."

I am. Every day, I am trying.

I am trying for Alex.

I am trying for Ruby.

I am trying for Max.

I am trying for Glen.

It's all I know how to do now. This is my life. I am trying.

ABOUT THE AUTHOR

ANNA QUINDLEN is the author of five bestselling novels, *Object Lessons, One True Thing, Black and Blue, Blessings,* and *Rise and Shine.* Her *New York Times* column, "Public and Private," won a Pulitzer Prize in 1992, and a selection of those columns was published as *Thinking Out Loud.* She is also the author of a collection of her "Life in the 30's" columns, *Living Out Loud;* a book for the Library of Contemporary Thought, *How Reading Changed My Life;* and the bestselling *A Short Guide to a Happy Life* and *Being Perfect.* From 2000 to 2009, she wrote the "Last Word" column for *Newsweek.*

ABOUT THE TYPE

This book was set in Bembo, a typeface based on an old-style Roman face that was used for Cardinal Bembo's tract *De Aetna* in 1495. Bembo was cut by Francisco Griffo in the early sixteenth century. The Lanston Monotype Company of Philadelphia brought the well-proportioned letterforms of Bembo to the United States in the 1930s.